Willia

Just—William
a facsimile of the first (1922) edition

The William Companion
by Mary Cadogan

Just William's World – a pictorial map
by Gillian Clements and Kenneth Waller

* A hardback edition of this title is available from Firecrest Publishing Ltd, Bath, Avon

William—The Bad

RICHMAL CROMPTON

Illustrated by Thomas Henry

MACMILLAN CHILDREN'S BOOKS

TO
MY LATEST NIECE,
RICHMAL,
WITH LOVE

First published 1930

ISBN: 0 333 38490 3

First published in this edition 1984 by
MACMILLAN CHILDREN'S BOOKS
A division of Macmillan Publishers Limited
London and Basingstoke
Associated companies throughout the world

7 9 8 6

Phototypeset by Wyvern Typesetting Ltd, Bristol
Printed in Great Britain by
Cox & Wyman Ltd, Reading, Berkshire

Contents

William invites you!

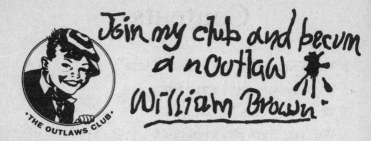

Join my club and becum a nOutlaw

William Brown

You can join the new Outlaws Club!

You will receive

✳ a special Outlaws wallet containing

the new Outlaws badge

the club rules and membership card

a pad for secret messages

a club pencil

and

a letter from William giving you the secret password

To join the club send a letter with your name and address,
written in block capitals, telling us you want to join the Outlaws and
£2.50 (£2 if you are already a member of the club
and write to us, with the Secret Password,
before 31 December 1993) to:

The Outlaws Club
Children's Marketing Department
18–21 Cavaye Place
London SW10 9PG

You must live in the United Kingdom or the Republic of Ireland
in order to join.

Chapter 1

The Knights of the Square Table

It was Ginger's aunt who gave him as a birthday present a book called "King Arthur and the Knights of the Round Table," and it was a spell of continuous wet weather that reduced the Outlaws to such a point of inactivity that they had been driven to read the book for want of anything else to do. They had assembled in the shelter of the old barn (whose roof leaked so badly that the actual shelter it afforded was negligible), and Ginger, stumblingly and with many mispronunciations, had read the book aloud to them. At first they had listened solely in order to exult over Ginger when he got more than usually tied up in the long words, but by degrees the story gripped them, and even William began to listen to it.

"I think that'd be almost as much fun as bein' a burglar or a detective," he said, as Ginger closed the book after the last story, "an' I bet it would be more fun in lots of ways than bein' an engine-driver."

"What would?" demanded Douglas.

"Bein' knights an' goin' out rightin' wrongs."

"But we haven't got armour or horses or anythin'," objected Henry.

"I don't think they're a bit necess'ry," said William.

"I bet I can fight jus' as well without armour as with it. I should think it'd only get in your way. I once tried wearin' it—trays and saucepans an' such-like—an' I found it jolly hard to fight in them."

"There aren't any wrongs to right either nowadays," said Henry.

"I bet there are. You jus' don't hear of 'em, that's all. I bet if we set up rightin' wrongs, people'd begin to come to us from all over the place."

"My father's got a lot of wrongs to start with," said Ginger. "Rates an' income-tax an' that sort of thing."

"We're not going to start rightin' those," said William firmly, "it'd take us *months* to right those. They're not really wrongs, either. They're only things grown-ups go on about at breakfast. They'd go on about somethin' else if we got those righted. They aren't what *I* call wrongs. Not like bein' put in dungeons an' havin' your lands ravidged by giants and your castle stole off you by false knights."

"Those things don't happen to anyone now," said Henry.

"How do you know they don't jus' 'cause you've never heard of 'em?" challenged William. "I bet there's a good many things in the world what you've never heard of. It's no proof that there isn't a thing just 'cause you've never heard of it. Nachurally, if people are shut up in dungeons right underneath the earth you don't hear of 'em 'cause they never get out to tell anyone."

Henry was about to dispute this view when Ginger interposed pacifically:

"Well, the best thing to do would be to set up as knights an' then see what sort of wrongs people come to us with."

So this they decided to do.

*   *   *

The next morning was fine and seemed a good omen for the beginning of their knightly careers. There was in the barn an old packing-case that figured in most of their activities, and had done duty at various times as a stage, a horse, a ship, a desert island and a besieged castle. Today it was to be the round table.

"We'd better call it the square table," said Henry. (Henry possessed a literal mind.) "It seems sort of silly to call it round when it isn't. 'Sides, it's best to give things a little different name from the old ones then people won't muddle us up with them."

"All right," said William, "The Knights of the Square Table, then. An'," hastily, "I'll be the most important one same as King Arthur. I'll be King William. An' the rest of you can just be knights."

"Weren't there any other important ones?" said Ginger, who had been so wholly occupied in trying to pronounce the words that he hadn't taken in much of the story.

"There was that magician one—the one they called Merl something."

"Bags, me be him, then," said Ginger hastily. "Bags, me be Merl."

"All right," said William, "and we'd better have a treasurer an' secret'ry," he went on, with vague memories of a meeting of the village football club which he had attended with his elder brother the week before. "Douglas 'd better be the sec'ry 'cause he spells best and Henry the treas'rer."

"All right," said Henry, and added, "How much did they get paid for rightin' wrongs?"

"It din't say in the book," said William.

"I should say sixpence for a little one an' a shilling for a big one," said Ginger.

"No one'll pay more'n' a penny an' I bet most of them

won't pay that," said Douglas gloomily. "There aren't many people—not that I know of, anyway—with more than fourpence."

"Well, we'll say sixpence, and a shilling on the notice," said William, "but if they won't give it we'll take less."

"What does the sec'ry do?" said Douglas.

"Write out the notice to put on the barn door, an' then write down about all the wrongs we right so's people can read about 'em in books in days to come same as they do about the old ones."

"All right," said Douglas importantly, "I'll go'n' get my Arithmetic exercise-book. I've jus' got a new one. It'll do nicely."

*   *   *

Douglas's reputation for superior spelling was based on the simple fact that, whereas the other Outlaws spelt all words exactly as they were pronounced, Douglas didn't. He realised that some words are not spelt as they are pronounced and, though he had little knowledge of any rules governing these mysterious aberrations, he varied his spelling so effectively that the Outlaws were always intensely proud of any composition from his hand. The notice which he produced to hang up on the barn door pleased them especially.

Gnites of the square tabel,
Rongs Wrighted   6d and 1/-.
Pleese gnock.

They hung it up, closed the door and took their seats in silence around the packing-case.

*   *   *

It was quite four minutes before anyone knocked—so long, in fact, that King William was just ordering Merlin to go and see if anyone was coming and to hurry them up when the knock came. There was a whispered consultation as to whose duty it was to open it—a consultation so prolonged that the applicant finally opened the door himself. His appearance nipped in the bud a promising scuffle between the treasurer and secretary, both of whom were claiming the privilege of opening the door. The new-comer was a tall youth, bare-headed, and with a blunt-featured, humorous face. He stood for a minute in the doorway looking at them, then he grinned and said:

"Good afternoon."

"Good afternoon," said William in a stern tone. "Have you any wrongs?"

"Any what?"

"I said have you got any wrongs?" said William again irritably. William always disliked having to repeat himself.

"Oh," said the young man in a surprised tone, "I thought it was the headquarters of the Spelling Reform League."

"No," said William vaguely, "I don' know anythin' about that. No, we're The Knights of the Square Table."

"The Knights——?"

"The Knights of the Square Table. We right wrongs. Big ones a shilling. Little ones sixpence."

The young man went out and studied the notice again.

"I see," he said, "splendid! And which of you is which?"

"I'm King William," said William. "Same as King Arthur but a different name. And he," pointing to Ginger, "he's Merl."

"Merl?"

"Yes. Merl the magician. And he," pointing to

Henry, "he's the treasurer. He collects the money from the ones we've righted the wrongs of, and he," pointing with pride to Douglas, "he wrote the notice. He's the sec'ry."

"I should like to shake hands with him," said the young man respectfully.

Douglas, much gratified, shook hands with him.

"It may not be spelt *quite* right, of course," he said modestly, "but I bet it mostly is."

"I think it's great," said the young man enthusiastically.

"Well, d'you want to be made a knight?" said William, assuming his most businesslike expression, "or have you got a wrong?"

The young man's smile faded.

"I didn't come in to talk about it, but I *have* got a wrong. I came in because I wanted to meet the author of the notice, but when you begin to talk about wrongs—well, I've got one that'd make your hearts bleed if you've got hearts to bleed."

"We're not goin' to do anything about rates or the income-tax," said William very firmly. "It'd take too long, and we're not going in for that sort of thing at all."

"Quite," said the young man, "I think you're wise on the whole. They're soul-destroying things. You can't touch pitch and not be defiled."

"I don't know that we can do anything about pitch, either," said William doubtfully. "I've never found anything to make it come off myself. Water only seems to stick it on harder."

"No, it isn't pitch," said the young man.

"What is it, then?"

"It's a lady."

"A damosel?" said William in a superior manner.

"Yes, a damosel," said the young man. "It's this

way," he went on, sitting on the packing-case. "This damosel——"

William interrupted him.

"They don't sit on it," he said coldly.

The young man jumped off.

"I suppose not," he said, "where—where *did* they sit?"

"On the ground same as the knights," said William.

The young man took his seat with them on the ground and began again.

"Well, it's this way," he said, "this damosel and I were getting on very nicely, very nicely indeed. We'd clicked on sight and got on like hounds in full cry ever since. Till yester e'en. And yester e'en we had a row. Heaven knows what it was about, I don't. But we each said words of high disdain and that sort of thing, you know. She in particular. She fairly wiped the floor with me."

"You mean she did you much despite?" said William, interested.

"Yes. By Jove. That's the word all right. Despite . . . well, I thought that she'd have slept it off this morning. I had. But had she? Oh, no. Walked past me with her head in the air as if she didn't see me. And where is she now? She's gone off with a fat-headed chump of the name of Montmorency Perrivale, and they're sitting on the river bank together now, and are going to have tea there. He's such a chump that I remember when they took him to the Zoo in his tender boyhood he wouldn't go into the Reptile House because he was afraid of the snakes. And that—*that* is the thing this damosel is preferring to me."

"And you want us," said William still in his most businesslike manner, "to right the wrong for you?"

"Well, if you'll be good enough to undertake it," said

the young man, "I'd be very grateful. Is it at all in your line?"

"AND YOU WANT US," SAID WILLIAM, "TO RIGHT THE
WRONG FOR YOU?"

"Well, we'd rather have someone in dungeons or with giants ravidging their land," admitted William, "but till something like that turns up, we don't mind."

"Thank you a thousand times," said the young man. "Somehow the very sight of your notice cheered me and I felt that fate had led me to it. After all, I said to myself when I saw it, it's a jolly sort of world in spite of all the

GNITES OF THE
ZQUARE TABLE
RONGS
WRIGHTED
6ᴰ ᴬⁿᴰ
0/-

"WELL, IF YOU'D BE GOOD ENOUGH TO UNDERTAKE IT," SAID
THE YOUNG MAN, "I'D BE VERY GRATEFUL."

damosels in it. . . . Still—if you can get this damosel from
the——"

"From the false knight?" said William, again with the
modest air of one who speaks fluently some difficult
foreign language.

"I was going to say from the fat-headed chump," said
the young man, "but yours sounds better. Yes, save yon

damosel from yon false knight and I will e'en richly reward ye."

"All right," said William, "it'll depend on how hard it turns out to be whether we charge you sixpence or a shilling. Me an' Merl will go. The treas'rer an' sec'ry 'd better stay case someone else comes with a wrong."

The young man, with Ginger on one side of him and William on the other, walked briskly along the road till they reached a spot from which a wooded slope led down to the river. And there, upon a fallen tree trunk beneath an oak tree, sat the damosel with the false knight.

"There they are," whispered the young man, "now would you think that a peach like her would fall for a fat-headed chump like that?"

But William did not wish to waste time moralising over the situation. "You go down the road and wait," he said shortly, "an' me an' Merl'll think out a plan an' we'll call you when we want you."

"All right," said the young man. He sauntered slowly down the road and William and Ginger conferred in quick business-like whispers beneath a bush.

* * *

The couple on the bank were unaware of onlookers. Montmorency, dazzled by the sudden kindness of one who had hitherto treated him with lofty scorn, was wasting no time in pressing his suit, his only trouble being the suspicion that it must be rather damp on the log under the tree, for Montmorency was passionately thoughtful for his health.

"I simply can't tell you what you've meant to me," he was saying, "but I never seemed to get a chance to get near you because that other chap was always knocking around."

"Oh, *him!*" said the vision with the utmost scorn.

"Whenever I saw you I used to think how—how beautiful you were. You—you reminded me of——"

Just then a small boy ambled up, his hands in his pockets, his eyes on the ground, and stood just near them. The young man pursed his lips, waiting for this unwelcome visitor to depart. But he didn't. He continued gazing about the grass as if he hadn't seen them.

"Looking for something?" said Montmorency pointedly.

The boy looked up as if surprised to see them there, and answered simply:

"Yes, I'm looking for a snake."

"Don't be silly," said the damosel severely, "there *aren't* any snakes about nowadays."

"No, I don't think there are really," agreed the boy, "but they're sayin' further up the bank that they saw one."

"*Where?*" gasped Montmorency.

"On the bank. Goin' along this way. Then they said they lost sight of it. I said I'd come an' look to see if I could see it anywhere. They said it was one of those big snakes like what you see in the reptile house in the Zoo."

"Are you sure it was coming *this* way?" said Montmorency through chattering teeth.

"What *rubbish!*" said the damosel spiritedly, "I don't believe a word of it."

"I don't either," said the boy, "but I thought I'd just come along and look."

"Well, you've looked," said the damsel, "and you haven't found it, have you? So you might as well go back where you came from."

"Yes, all right, I will," said the boy with disarming humility, and added, "they said it might have got up a tree, but I don't think it could possibly have done that.

They couldn't climb trees—great big snakes like that."

With that he vanished up the river bank.

"How perfectly ridiculous," said the damosel—then to Montmorency, "what were we talking about? I've quite forgotten."

But Montmorency was gazing about him distractedly.

"They *can* climb trees—those big snakes," he said, "I've seen them in pictures. Coiled round tree trunks. Great big ones."

"Don't be so absurd. . . . Well, anyway, you've only to look at these tree trunks to see that there aren't any snakes coiled round them, haven't you?"

"Yes, but of course when they're pictured as coiled round trees it means that they're in the act of climbing them. Th—this one may actually have c-climbed. It m-may actually be in the b-branches ab-b-bove our heads."

"What rubbish! What *were* we talking about when that awful boy came? I've forgotten."

"Then they d-dart down through the branches you know and—and—and bite you. And there's n-n-n-n-no cure."

"I do wish you'd stop gibbering. There *aren't* any snakes like that in England."

"There are. In Zoos and shows and things. And they escape and r-roam the countryside."

"All right. Would you like to go home?"

"Would you?"

"No."

"I—then, of course, I wouldn't," he said unhappily. "I—I'll stay with you."

"I remember what we were talking about. You were saying that you always wanted to get to know me. You were saying that I reminded you of something."

Montmorency forgot the snake and threw her a soulful glance.

"Of course you did—you do. You remind me of—of——"

He stopped—the soulful look died away from his face and his teeth began to chatter again. A slight rustling came from the tree above.

"D-did you hear that?" he chattered.

"What?" said the damosel sharply.

"A—a sort of r-rustling noise in the tree."

"Of course. Birds rustle in trees. I do wish you'd stop making stupid interruptions like that. You were just going to tell me what I reminded you of. . . ."

"Oh yes, of course. You may think it silly and poetical, but I can't help it. I *am* poetical. Well, whenever I saw you it flashed into my mind that you were just like——"

At a given signal from William, who was concealed in the tree, Ginger, who was concealed in the undergrowth, shot out a hand, nipped Montmorency's ankle very neatly between two sharp nails, and withdrew as swiftly into the undergrowth.

Montmorency uttered a piercing scream.

"A *snake!*" he yelled.

"A snake?" said the damosel angrily, "in what way, pray, do I resemble a snake?"

"I mean I'm bitten by a snake," screamed Montmorency who was struggling wildly with the suspender that suspended his multi-coloured sock. "I distinctly felt the fangs penetrate the skin." He uttered a hollow moan. "I'm dying."

"You don't look much like it," said the damosel unsympathetically.

Montmorency had torn down his multi-coloured sock and now disclosed the faint red impress of Ginger's nail.

MONTMORENCY POINTED TO THE MARK WITH A SCREAM
OF HORROR. "LOOK!" HE SHRIEKED. "ITS FANG! THE MARK
OF ITS FANG!"

He pointed to it with another scream of horror.

"Look! Its *fang!* The mark of its *fang!*"

The damosel looked at it without much interest.

"Doesn't seem to have gone through the skin anyway,
whatever it is," she said coldly.

"B-but it d-did," he chattered. "I f-felt it, I f-felt it most distinctly. And—and in any case the—the most d-deadly ones p-poison without going through the skin."

He began to tie himself up into knots, rolling over and over in striking acrobatic postures on the grass.

"What on earth are you doing?" said the damosel.

"I'm t-trying to g-get to it to s-suck the p-poison out," panted Montmorency.

"Well, you can't," said the damosel. "It stands to reason that you can't. No one can suck the backs of their ankles. It's impossible. It makes you look so silly too. I wish you'd stop."

"Can't you do *anything?*" wailed Montmorency sitting up to take breath. "I thought you'd done a V.A.D. course."

"Well, snakes didn't come into it, or if they did I wasn't there that night. What are you doing *now?*"

Montmorency, still panting, was tearing up handfuls of grass and rubbing his ankle with them.

"They say there's healing in n-natural herbs," he chattered. "They say——" then he uttered another scream of terror.

"What on *earth*——?"

"It's getting worse. The poison's beginning to work. It's—it's *agony!*"

"Well, I should think so. You've just rubbed a handful of nettles into it."

"My whole leg's swelling. Can't you see it?"

"No, it looks to me just the same size as it always was."

Montmorency lay down upon the grass full length and spoke in a faint voice.

"I'm dying," he said, "I'm dying from the feet up. I can feel the poison creeping up to my heart. It—it's nearly there now. . . ."

William in the bushes began to feel rather nonplussed.

The scene wasn't working out as he'd meant it to work out. He'd meant Montmorency to leap to his feet in mortal terror at the snake bite and rush wildly away, leaving the field clear for his client. And he wasn't doing. Moreover the damosel wasn't really angry. She was only amused. William hastily began to lay his plans afresh. William possessed an elder sister who was both beautiful and temperamental, and he had made an exhaustive study of feminine psychology as exemplified by Ethel. He knew that whereas she would be as likely as not to extend her favour to a murderer or a robber or a forger or an anarchist if she met one, she would never as long as the world lasted forgive anyone who had ever put her into a humiliating or ridiculous position. And so William lightly descended from his tree, crept quietly away for a few yards, and then reappeared, sauntering along the bank whistling. He stopped by Montmorency's prostrate form and said innocently:

"What's the matter with him?"

Montmorency opened his eyes to explain.

"I've been bitten," he said, "by that snake you told me about."

"Have you?" said William. "That's funny. They were talking about what you ought to do for snake bites."

"Who were?"

"The men what were saying about a snake being on the bank."

"What did they say?" said Montmorency faintly.

"Oh, they didn't really know, of course," said William vaguely, "but one was saying that when he lived in the countries where snakes live the natives used to have a way that sounds funny, but he said that the queer thing was that none of the natives that did it when they'd been bit ever died of it."

Montmorency sat up and removed some dead leaves from his hair.

"You'd better tell me quickly," he said, "because it's a matter of minutes now. It's about an inch off my heart. I'm not sure that it isn't too late. . . ."

"Well," said William, "it sounds so silly but it's what this man I'm telling you about said they did. It's all because of the circulation. It sends the blood round circulating in a special sort of way and that sort of kills the poison."

"What does?" said Montmorency.

"Hopping," said William. "They hop. They hop for about a mile without stopping. And that sort of sends the blood round circulating in a special sort of way."

Montmorency leapt to his feet.

"I'll try it," he said, "I'll try it quickly before it's too late."

"But there's jus' one other thing," said William, "they have to have their heads covered right up so as to keep their brains warm. Otherwise the poison sort of goes into their brains."

Montmorency stared about him wildly. He was bare-headed and William was bare-headed, but the damosel's hat lay on the bank beside her. It was a pretty hat with a pompom at one side. Frenziedly Montmorency seized it, pulled it upon his head and scrambling up the river bank began to hop down the road to the village. By chance he wore the hat quite correctly, pulled closely down over his eyes, the pompom projecting over one ear.

The story of how Montmorency Perrivale hopped through the village, his face set and staring under a lady's fashionable hat, followed by a gaping crowd, has now grown into a local legend. The children who formed the gaping crowd will probably describe the sight to their

**FRENZIEDLY, MONTMORENCY PULLED THE HAT UPON HIS HEAD,
AND BEGAN TO HOP DOWN THE ROAD.**

great-great-grandchildren, though no description could
really do it justice.

The damosel, bewildered and annoyed, followed for a
short distance, then, as the applause of the spectators
grew louder, retreated to the river bank.

"OH!" EXCLAIMED THE GIRL. "OH, THE FOOL!"

It was then that William approached the young man
and said:

"He's gone now. You'd better go'n' talk to her."

William only stayed for a few minutes to make sure of
the success of his scheme. The damosel was sobbing.

"And it's a practically new one, and it cost two guineas, and I'll *never* be able to wear it again, and, anyway, everyone knows it's mine, and they'll *never* stop teasing me about it, and it wasn't a snake bite at all—I saw it and I'm *sure* it wasn't. I couldn't see anything. He rubbed nettles into it and, of course, it hurt and I'd like to *kill* that boy and I'll never speak to *him* again, and people'll tease me about it for the rest of my life because I'd shown nearly everyone that hat and they all know it's mine. I wish I'd never been born and . . ."

"He's a fat-headed chump," said the young man gathering her into his arms.

"Yes, he is," sobbed the damosel, allowing herself to be gathered. "I *hate* him, and I'm so sorry I said all those hateful things to you yesterday. . . . I didn't mean any of them. . . ."

At this point William and Ginger, satisfied, crept away.

* * *

They found the barn empty and the treasurer and secretary engaged in a rough-and-tumble scuffle in the next field. They explained that as no one had brought any other wrongs to be righted, they'd thought that they'd better keep in practice by having a few jousts.

"Well, we've got to write it up," said William, assuming his air of authority, "we've got to write it up before we forget. 'S no good rightin' wrongs if it isn't put into a book. Come on Douglas. I'll tell you what to put an' you put it."

The knights returned to the barn and resumed their seats about the square table. Douglas took out his book and waited. William cleared his throat and began to dictate.

"Well, this knight came complainin' of his damosel

being took off him by a false knight, so King William and
Merl set off to get her back for him. It was a shilling
wrong. Well, the false knight was scared of snakes so
Merl the magician turned himself into a snake and——"

"If you think," said the secretary coldly, "that I c'n
write as fast as people talk you're jolly well mistaken.
There's no one in the world can do that, let me tell you.
If you want someone that'll write as fast as people talk
s'pose you get your ole Merl the magician. . . . I s'pose
he'll start turnin' into pen nibs an'——"

Merlin was preparing to avenge personally the slight-
ing tone of this reference when the village clock was
heard to strike. The knights listened and counted in
silence . . . Five. Then:

"Tea-time," they said joyfully, "come on. Let's go
home to tea. We can go on rightin' wrongs afterwards."

Chapter 2

William and the Little Girl

"I think," said William, "that when I grow up I'm prob'ly goin' to turn into one of those people that talk."

"You're one of them now," said Ginger dispassionately.

"But I don't get paid for it," objected William. "Grown-ups get paid for it."

"I *bet* they don't," said Ginger indignantly. "Why, my father talks all day nearly, an' no one pays him. I bet they'd pay him to stop if it would be any good."

"Well, that's jus' 'cause he doesn't do it in the right way," protested William. "If he did it in the right way he'd get paid for it. You're gotter be on a platform in a big room an' then folks come an' sit in rows an' pay money to listen to you talk. They don' interrupt or argue or anythin' like that. They jus' sit an' listen to you. *An'* pay money."

"Oh, leckcherers," said Henry, who was generally agreed to be the best informed of the Outlaws.

"Yes, them," said William, "I'm goin' to be one of them. I bet I can talk as well as anyone."

"They've gotter go on for *hours*," said Henry.

"Well, I bet I could go on for hours," said William. "I've never had a chance. People always start int'ruptin' me or arguin' with me or tellin' me to shut up as soon as I begin. I bet I could go on as long as anyone if they'd let me. If they started carryin' on like that with a real leckcherer they'd get chucked out. They always have a policeman there to chuck people out that start arguin' before the leckcherer's finished, I bet it would be more fun bein' a leckcherer than a robber or a chimney-sweep after all."

There was a slight regret in William's voice as he thus relinquished two of his favourite careers. Then his voice hardened again into determination as he said, "Yes, it would be more fun. *Lots* more fun. Rows an' rows of 'em all *havin'* to listen to you for hours an' gettin' chucked out if they started arguin'." Again his resolution seemed to waver. "I don' know that it wouldn't be better fun bein' the policeman that chucks 'em out, though. But still," his determination returned, "it'd be jolly dull bein' the policeman if no one started arguin'. An' I 'speck that you could come an' help a bit if you were the leckcherer. I bet I could chuck people that started arguin' out an' go on talkin' at the same time. I bet I won't have a policeman at all in my leckchers. I'll talk *an'* chuck 'em out. Yes. That's what I'm goin' to be. I'm goin' to be a leckcherer."

The Outlaws were accustomed to the frequent changes of William's future career, but they took each one quite seriously.

"How d'you start?" said Ginger. "D'you have to pass examinations or anythin' for it?"

"No," said William, "you jus' start talkin' an' shuttin' up everyone that starts arguin' with you an' then after a few years you find that you've turned into a leckcherer an' folks pay money to come an' listen to you talkin' an' watch other folks get chucked out."

"When do you start?" said Douglas, with rising

interest. "You can't start before you leave school, can you?"

"You can start practisin'," said William, "you can start talkin' an' shuttin' up people that int'rupt. That's how they all start. You can start 's young as you like. You've only gotter have a strong voice. I've gotter *jolly* strong voice. An' you've gotter be able to shut up folks that keep int'ruptin'. That depends on how big they are, of course. You've gotter be careful who you start practisin' on. When you've grown up, of course, it's all right. An', anyway, there's the policeman to help. I bet mine's about the worst family anyone could have what's goin' to be a leckcherer. I bet that not many leckcherers had families like mine when they were young. They never even let me finish a sentence hardly. They start shuttin' me up before I've started to speak. But I bet I'll turn out a better leckcherer with havin' had to work so hard to get started. I bet by the time I've finished, I'll have a voice you can hear miles off (you can hear it a good way off now), and I'll be able to shut anyone that starts arguin' up without any policeman at all."

William was so carried away by his own eloquence that he saw himself standing on a platform, filling a crowded hall with his stentorian voice, desisting only to indulge in occasional hand-to-hand struggles with inter- rupters. Ginger broke into this pleasant picture by saying:

"What'll you talk *about*? You've gotter have somethin' to talk *about*, haven't you?"

"You can talk about *anythin'*," said William, rather irritably, for William always disliked being brought down to earth, "it doesn't matter *what* you talk about so long as you keep on talkin' an' chuckin' people that start arguin' out. I know 'cause I went to one once with an aunt. There wasn't a single word in it that anyone could understand, but nobody seemed to mind. No one even started arguin' or int'ruptin'. An' they *all* paid money to listen. Well, it seems to me a jolly easy way of gettin' money."

"Why doesn't everyone get money that way, then?" said Henry.

"'Cause everyone can't *talk*," said William firmly. "It's a sort of *gift*, same as bein' able to do sums an' Latin an' such-like. Everyone's not got it. Some people can do one thing an' other people can do other things. I can't do sums an' Latin an' such-like, but I can talk. I expect that the ones who can do sums an' Latin can't talk, so they'd be the ones that'd pay to come and listen."

"But you must talk about *somethin'*," persisted Ginger. "If you talk at all you've gotter talk about *somethin'*. You can't help it."

"You talk about *anythin'*," said William. "*Anythin'* at all. I *can* talk about anythin'. That's why I'd make such a good leckcherer. You give me somethin' to talk about an' see if I can't go on talkin' about it for hours and hours."

The Outlaws were on their way home from school and Henry, struck by a sudden idea, stopped and slung his school satchel from his shoulders.

"I've got my diction'ry here," he said. "I'll open it jus' anywhere an' give you the first word I see to talk about."

"Well, and I jolly well bet I'll be able to talk about it too," said William challengingly, "unless it's in a foreign langwidge."

Henry opened his dictionary and read out slowly and doubtfully: "Epitome."

"That's a foreign langwidge," said William very firmly and without hesitation.

"What's it doin' in an English diction'ry, then?" said Henry.

"There's lots of foreign words in the English diction'ry," said William; "they get put in by mistake."

"I bet it's English," said Henry.

"What does it say it means, then?" said William.

"Compendium . . . abridgment . . . summary," read out Henry stumblingly.

"There!" said William, triumphantly. "I told you so. They're all foreign words! They're French. Or else Latin."

Henry, convinced, shut the book and opened it again at random.

"Civilisation," he read slowly.

"I know what *that* means," said William. "It means bein' different from savidges."

"Well, can you *talk* about it?"

"Yes, I can. It's all wrong——"

"What is?"

"Civ—— what you said. Being diff'rent from savidges. It's all wrong."

"Why's it wrong?"

"That's what I'm jus' goin' to tell you. It *is* wrong. School an' lessons an' such-like. Savidges didn't have them."

"How d'you know they didn't?"

"'Cause there wasn't anythin' for them to learn. Euclid and Algebra hadn't been born in those days."

"Well, they had to learn to tell the time by the sun an' to scout each other."

"I wish you'd shut up int'ruptin'. They were *born* knowin' those 'cause their fathers knew them."

"Well, my father knew Latin an' I wasn't born knowin' it."

"If it was a real leckcher you'd 've been chucked out by this time."

"All right. Come on. Chuck me out."

They met joyously in the middle of the road with Ginger and Douglas as seconds.

William claimed that he had succeeded in ejecting the interrupter because at the end of the struggle Henry was in the ditch, but, as the effort of precipitating Henry into the ditch had precipitated William into it as well, the result was considered by the majority to be indecisive. But the battle had invigorated them and they continued scuffling in and out of the ditch purely in a spirit of goodwill till they came to William's house—quite forgetting William's incipient lecture.

But William remembered it as soon as he entered his bedroom to perform his toilet before lunch. There he placed a glass of water upon his chair, and took up his position behind it. Then, flourishing his hair-brush in one hand the better to emphasise his points, he began with vehement facial contortions and wild gestures of both arms to lecture in dumb show. No words issued from his eloquently moving lips, but occasionally he stopped and raised the glass to them, then, reassuming his expressive grimaces and gestures, he continued his silent lecture. He moved his eyes about the room as he spoke, addressing now the towel-rail, now the window curtains, now the wardrobe, and finally his eyes rested upon his reflection in the dressing-table looking-glass. An interrupter. William addressed it sternly. It replied defiantly. William pointed a finger at it accusingly. It replied insolently by pointing a finger at William. With terrible determination written on his brow, William advanced upon it. A fierce battle took place in which it was evident from William's actions that he first wrestled with his adversary, then got him on to the ground, then pummelled him mercilessly, and finally took him by the ear and led him unresisting from the room. He held the imaginary ear at first about the level of his own, and then suddenly reconstructing the scene, held up his hand as high as it would go, clearly indicating that his vanquished enemy was six feet or more in height. He flung him ruthlessly upon the landing, closed the door, returned to the space behind his chair that represented the platform, took a draught of water, and, after bowing acknowledgements to the applause with a deprecating smile, continued the lecture till again he caught sight of that aggressive interrupter in the dressing-table looking-glass, and stepped forth sternly to deal with him. Before the battle was half-way through, however, the lunch-bell rang and William, abandoning his rôle as lecturer, brushed his hair and washed his hands with perfunctory haste, and descended to the hall by way of the balusters. His elder brother greeted him as he entered the dining-room.

"What on earth have you been doing upstairs? I thought you were coming through the ceiling."

"Me?" said William blankly. "I've not been doin' nothin' but washin' and brushin' my hair."

"Well, you made enough noise about it, and not much to show for it, I must say."

William contented himself with a mental vision of himself lecturing in a large hall and descending from the platform to eject Robert from the front row for interrupting.

On his way to afternoon school he met the other Outlaws as usual at the end of the road and they enlivened the journey by continuing the morning's game. Henry opened his dictionary at random and gave William a subject to discourse upon. William, never at a loss (except in the case where he rejected words as foreign), discoursed and the others challenged his views till they were attacked by William as interrupters, and a series of lively scuffles ensued. It was an exciting and enjoyable game and might have continued indefinitely if, at the corner of the road that led to school, they hadn't met—the little girl. She was a stranger to the neighbourhood. None of the Outlaws had ever seen her before. She was small and dainty, with dark eyes and a round, dimpled face. She was rather like Joan, the little girl next door, to whom William's proud spirit had unbent as far as to enrol her as the only female member of the Outlaws, but who had now gone to boarding-school. William was not, on the whole, susceptible to feminine charm. Passing this little girl, he was conscious only of an overwhelming desire to talk to her. He wanted to talk to her about civilisation, and pianos and ostriches and sacks (a few of the subjects that Henry had found for him). He wanted to begin to talk to her now and to go on talking to her all afternoon. But she passed him with a look of cold disdain (his recent scuffles and frequent descents into the ditch had added nothing to his personal attractions), and at the same time Henry (the only one of the Outlaws who possessed a watch) informed them that they'd be late if they didn't hurry, and they all began to run down the road to the school, trying to push each other into the ditch as they ran. But William's thoughts were elsewhere, though he pushed and was pushed into the ditch with the others automatically as he ran. They were elsewhere all afternoon while he did sums about hours, days and weeks, and gave in the answers (wrong in any case) in pounds, shillings and pence. They were with the little girl. He wanted to talk to her about civilisation and pianos and ostriches and sacks) that the others hadn't let him say. He wanted to talk to her for hours and hours and hours. The memory of that look of cold disdain intrigued him. It was to William incredible and monstrous that anyone at all, much more SHE, should look on him like that. He longed to perform some striking deed of valour before her. In imagination he slew dragons for her, leapt from aeroplanes to trains for her, fought whole battalions of villains for her, climbed church steeples, and dived into shark-infested waters for her, while in reality he morosely added up six and four and three and two and made it come to forty-five. . . .

*   *   *

He was still thinking of the little girl when he reached home, after having been kept in to finish his sums.

Before he performed his inadequate toilet preparatory to descending to the dining-room for tea, he again stood upon his imaginary platform behind his glass of water and addressed a hall full of people who listened to him spellbound. The little girl was in the front row. Interrupters as large as mountains rose to defy him. He wrestled with them and flung them out one after the other like ninepins. The whole room rose to applaud him. The little girl gazed up at him in rapt admiration. He bowed his acknowledgments, took a deep draught of water, and proceeded with the lecture till the tea-bell rang. Again his elder brother greeted him disapprovingly as he entered the dining-room.

"Good Lord! What on earth have you been doing upstairs again? You've brought a great lump of plaster down from the ceiling. Are you keeping an elephant up there, or what?"

William gave him a dark look as in imagination he ejected him again from his lecture, sending him flying through the door and half-way down the flight of stairs that was just outside the lecture-room. Having thus disposed of Robert, he turned to his mother, prepared aggressively to defend at great length the state of his hair, face, hands, suit and boots. But instead of attacking these very assailable points his mother said:

"I've had an invitation to tea for you to-morrow, William."

"Where?" said William without enthusiasm.

"Mrs. Stacey. She's got a little niece staying with her."

William's heart leapt. He was sure that it was the little girl. But without relaxing an atom of the severity of his expression he said:

"I don' want to go to tea with a *girl*."

"Oh, she's got a little boy staying with her too, the son of an old school-friend, who's convalescing after measles. He's just about your age, I believe."

"Huh," said William shortly. The monosyllable expressed equal contempt for the boy, the girl, the tea-party, measles, and the world in general. Dreamily, mechanically, he stretched out for a bun. Dreamily, mechanically, he took a Gargantuan bite. In reality he was alone with the little girl. They were walking along a country lane. He was talking to her on every subject from beginning to end of Henry's dictionary. She listened enraptured.

* * *

But when he went to tea with her it was quite different. The boy was such a boy as William had never even imagined. He was tall and languorous. He spoke with an exaggeratedly refined accent and he talked of his travels in Italy and Switzerland and the South of France, of the theatres he had visited lately and the latest dances. And the little girl admired him. There was no doubt at all that the little girl admired him. She listened to him as in William's dreams she had listened to William. In reality she ignored William completely after one disdainful glance that took in his shock of wiry hair, his unprepossessing features, and his stocky, unkempt-looking (even after an hour of Mrs. Brown's ministrations) figure. William wasn't used to being ignored and set to work at once to dispel any impression of nonentity that his appearance might have given her. He realised, of course, that physical means of asserting his supremacy would defeat their own purpose. He could have felled the languid youth to the ground with one stroke, but he was sufficiently versed in feminine psychology to realise that this would only have concentrated the little girl's affection and concern still further upon the languid youth. He must attract her attention by other and more subtle means. If only she could hear him lecture. . . .

"Civilisation's all wrong," he began firmly, "savidges didn't go to school or learn Latin an' they——"

But she wasn't listening to him. She was listening to Claude who was talking about Nice.

"There's topping bathing there," he was saying languidly, "and some jolly drives over the hills behind the town. Plenty going on in the town itself too."

She was gazing at him open-mouthed with admiration.

William, warming to his theme, continued.

"They din't wear collars neither, nor have to keep themselves clean, nor go to church on Sundays. They did jus' what they liked on Sundays. They din't even have Sunday School. An' they could go jus' where they wanted without people chasin' 'em out of woods and fields an' such-like. An' they could fight each other whenever they wanted to an' it din't matter if they got their clothes all messed up 'cause they din't wear any an' "——

But she wasn't listening. His famous lecture on civilisation was falling on deaf ears.

"The Charleston's not a bit difficult," the languorous youth was saying, "but it's getting a bit old-fashioned now."

And still the little girl was gazing at him with adoring eyes and listening to him enraptured.

William was silent for a minute. It was quite evident that his lecture on civilisation was not striking enough to arrest her attention. He must lead up to it with more care. He must arrest her attention by some more dramatic means and then when he was sure of it, introduce his lecture on civilisation. He was certain that no one who heard his lecture on civilisation could fail to be impressed by it.

"I never cared for the Blues," the languorous youth was saying.

"I'm a leckcherer," announced William with startling abruptness, "I give leckchers to people. Roomfuls of 'em. Chuck 'em out when they start arguin'."

But neither of them paid the slightest attention to him.

"They say," the languorous youth was saying, "that the polka's coming back. I hope not. Ghastly affair."

William summoned his faculties again with an effort. There was evidently need for some yet more startling conversational opening.

"I killed a lion once," he said in a loud voice.

They took no notice of him.

"Shot it straight through the heart jus' as it was going to spring."

"The waltz," said the languorous youth, "is the only one of those old dances that's any use and even it's jolly rotten the way they used to dance it."

"Shot a whole crowd of elephants with one bullet once," went on William. "They were standing in a row an' the bullet went straight through 'em one after the other an' they all fell down on the top of each other."

William, determined to be heard, had raised his voice and the little girl became aware, apparently for the first time, that he was speaking. She turned to him and the look of adoration with which she had regarded the languorous youth changed to one of distaste.

"I wish," she said distantly, "that you wouldn't *shout* so."

So amazed was William at this treatment that he hardly spoke again till it was time to go home. Yet, so perverse is human nature, the plainly evinced dislike of the little girl had only increased her desirability in his eyes. He felt that his soul would know no rest till the little girl had looked at him as she now looked at the languorous youth and till he had expounded to her at full length the lecture on civilisation that was the star of his repertoire.

As William was going home Mrs. Stacey asked him if he would come the next afternoon (a half-holiday), and take her two little visitors for a walk as he knew the country and they didn't. William, with a show of reluctance that was merely formal, agreed and departed, leaving the languorous youth teaching the little girl a new and complicated step that he had lately learnt at his London dancing class.

Most people would have regarded the situation as hopeless, but not William. William was of the stuff that never regards anything as hopeless.

He was very thoughtful that evening and the next morning sought out Ginger. A long and confidential conversation took place between them. Ginger was at first too amazed and indignant for words. When he found words they were in the nature of firm and unqualified rejections of William's plan.

"I should jolly well think I *won't*."

"No, I should *jolly* well think not."

"If you want someone to do that you can jolly well get someone else, not *me*."

It was only after a ball, a lump of putty, a set of cigarette cards and a treasured whistle had passed from William's possession to Ginger's that Ginger began to waver.

"It'll get me into an *awful* mess an' I'll get into an awful row as well," he still protested.

"Well that whistle's worth a *shillin'*," said William, "it's the finest whistle I've ever had, I can jolly well tell you, and I wouldn't give it to you 'cept for this."

Ginger considered the situation for a moment in silence. He had certainly coveted that whistle for a long time. He realised that the situation had its possibilities. With the air of one who comes to a momentous decision, he said:

"All right. If you'll give me your glass marble—the big one—and your catapult too—I will."

After a brief inward struggle, William agreed.

The bargain was sealed.

The next afternoon William called for the little girl and Claude to conduct them over the neighbouring countryside. The conversation followed pretty much the lines it had followed the day before except that Claude was now discussing the latest jazz music and that it was to his feats in life-saving that William vainly essayed to attract their attention.

"I've got a saxophone," said Claude carelessly. "They cost a lot of money."

"Have you *really?*" said the little girl admiringly.

"I've saved ever so many people's lives," said William.

"Some of the jazz bands one hears on the wireless are rotten."

"Drownin' mostly. Jus' plunge in an' drag 'em out."

"They have one person doing too many instruments. It makes it slow."

"I simply couldn't count the people I've saved from drownin'."

"I've played in a jazz band myself."

"Oh, Claude, have you *really?*"

"Plunged in an' dragged 'em out."

But it was useless. They refused to take any notice of him. Raising his voice still higher, he said:

"There's a very deep pond jus' round this corner. It's quite shallow round the edges but in the middle it'd drown *hundreds* of people all standing on the top of each other."

They turned the corner and at once came upon a very shallow pond in the middle of which lay Ginger, reposing at full length, his head emerging at an uncomfortable angle from the surface of the water.

"Why," said William as if surprised, "there's a boy drownin' in it now!"

With a heroic gesture he flung off his coat and plunged into the pond, descending upon his hands and knees and making much play of battling against waves as he neared the middle where Ginger was reclining. Having reached Ginger, he began with much realism to rescue him. There was in fact more realism than Ginger liked.

"Here! Shut up pulling my ears about like that," said Ginger indignantly.

"That's the way you have to rescue people," panted William. "You stay still an' let me rescue you. I din't give you that marble and catapult an' all those other things to carry on like this."

"Well, you stop pullin' my hair."

"I've *gotter* pull your hair. You're supposed to be drownin'."

"Leave me *alone*. You're drownin' me."

"I'm not. I'm savin' you. If you'd only keep still, I'd——"

But clawing the air and spluttering wildly, Ginger arose to his full height (showing that the water came well below his knees) and hurled himself furiously upon his rescuer. His rescuer, equally wet and furious, joined battle and for a few minutes they wrestled in the middle of the pond forgetful of onlookers. It was William who remembered the onlookers first. The swaying fortunes of the battle had brought them to the water's edge and William, remembering suddenly the business in which he was supposed to be engaged, disentangled himself from Ginger and splashed, dripping, out of the pond and up to the two startled watchers.

There he sputtered for a few minutes, rubbed the water out of his eyes, stroked it out of his hair and, still sputtering though less violently, said:

"Saw me rescue him, din't you?"

They stared at him in an amazement which had little of admiration in it.

"Looked as if we were standin' up in the water, din't it?" went on William with a careless, though still rather water-logged laugh. "I got him onto a narrer bridge that runs across the water jus' under where you can see an' then he started to struggle same as drownin' people always do. It was jolly hard to keep him on that narrer bridge. I bet most people 'd've let him go an' then he'd've been drowned."

"You look *awful*," said the little girl dispassionately.

She had been so much engrossed in Claude's conversation that she had seen nothing till she suddenly noticed the terrible boy who was supposed to be taking them for

WILLIAM SPLASHED OUT OF THE POND AND FACED THE
TWO STARTLED WATCHERS. "SAW ME RESCUE HIM, DIN'T
YOU?" HE ASKED.

a walk fighting with another boy as terrible as himself in
the middle of the pond.

"He looks the limit," agreed Claude.

"Well, I'm *certainly* not going anywhere with him
now," said the little girl. "He looks too *awful* for words.
Let's go home, Claude. He ought to go home too and
change his clothes. He's got himself into an *awful* mess. I

THEY STARED AT HIM IN AMAZEMENT. "YOU LOOK *AWFUL*,"
SAID THE LITTLE GIRL.

expect his mother will be *very* cross with him. I should be
if I was his mother. I'm not going home the way he goes
home, either. I wouldn't be seen with him *anywhere*."

Her glance of scorn only increased William's admiration for her, made him long all the more to talk to her
about civilisation and pianos, and ostriches, and sacks.
He opened his mouth passionately to defend himself,

but a fit of choking came over him (he'd swallowed several quarts of pond water), and by the time he'd recovered from it Claude and the little girl had disappeared.

William wandered dejectedly homewards in the wake of the dripping Ginger.

In his heart was a furious hatred of all mankind, except the little girl, and a fierce regret at having given Ginger the glass marble and the catapult.

He was still without a plan when his mother announced that Mrs. Stacey had asked him to tea again.

"It's little Cynthia's last day with her," she said, "and so she wants to have someone to tea and she said that you behaved so nicely the last time you went that she thought she'd like to have you again. I want you to go, too, because at least if you're there to tea I shall know that you aren't wandering over the countryside falling into ponds."

William groaned. But he was secretly much elated by the invitation. He felt that Fate was giving him another opportunity of cutting out the obnoxious Claude and winning the admiration of the little girl. He saw himself walking alone with her along a country road talking. He still wanted to talk to her. . . .

*   *   *

He was told the exciting news by a friend who passed him as he was on his way to Mrs. Stacey's. A lunatic had escaped from the asylum just beyond Croombe Woods. The keepers were out searching the woods for him. William hastened to announce this thrilling piece of information to his hostess and her household. The result fulfilled his highest expectations. The little girl lost all interest in the attractions of Nice and the composition of a jazz band. Her only interest—and that a consuming one—was the escaped lunatic. She could talk of nothing but the escaped lunatic. She insisted on going to the edge of the wood in order to peer fearfully through the railings.

"They murder people," she said impressively. "All escaped lunatics murder people."

"They're very cunning too," said Claude, "it's very hard to catch them when once they've escaped."

Claude spoke as one having a long and exhaustive familiarity with escaped lunatics.

William as bringer of the news had achieved a distinct but very passing fame. It had been quickly eclipsed by Claude's assumption of knowledge of the subject in all its branches. There was evidently nothing about escaped lunatics that Claude did not know. Every time that William tried to speak, Claude interrupted him. The little girl hung on to Claude's words. The whole situation was suddenly more than William could bear. He took out his penknife with a flourish and examined it ostentatiously. They stared at him. Casually he remarked:

"Seems sharp enough. I may not need it anyway. He may come quiet once I catch him."

With that cryptic remark he leapt over the railing and swaggered off through the trees into the wood.

The little girl called out, "*William!* Come back. He'll *kill* you."

There was fear and pleading in her voice.

It was balm to William's soul.

When, however, he had advanced so far into the wood as to be no longer visible to them, something of the ardour with which he had set out upon his quest faded. He was alone in a wood with a dangerous lunatic. There might, of course, be a few keepers about too, but they'd probably be at the other end of the wood when he met the lunatic. His heart began to fail him. It is one thing to set out upon a daredevil exploit before admiring eyes, and quite another to pursue it unencouraged and alone, as many people besides William have discovered. But after a brief inward struggle he resisted the temptation to creep back to another part of the road by a devious route. After all, he played the part of Chief of a Thousand Braves almost daily. Almost daily in that character he put to flight scores of hostile tribes, and slew in a series of mighty single combats the ferocious fauna that infested the district near his camp. Was he to be turned back by one lunatic? No, he informed himself with a scornful "Huh," and strode forward into the wood, still with an indescribable swagger in his walk. He was, however, more than a little discomfited on turning a bend in the tiny track among the trees to run into a tall red-haired bare-headed man wearing leggings and carrying a stick. For a minute his heart quailed, and he was on the point of turning to flee when the man said:

"Hello, you've not seen anyone about here have you?"

"No," said William, and added with relief, "you're lookin' for the lunatic?"

"Yes," said the man, "I'm one of the attendants from up there."

"I—I'll stay with you an' help look," offered William readily.

He felt unspeakably grateful for the protection that the presence of this large red-headed man would afford if they met the lunatic.

"I've got a penknife," he added, "for if he starts carryin' on any way."

He was eager to prove himself a valuable ally.

The red-headed man inspected the weapon carefully.

"*That* wouldn't be much good," he said.

"But it'd scare him if he saw it," protested William

eagerly. "Look. Here's a thing for taking stones out of a horse's hoof. I bet that'd scare him."

"I bet it wouldn't," said the red-headed man.

"What's he like?" said William, "is he dangerous?"

"I should just think he is," said the red-headed man; "he'd make mincemeat of *you* soon as look at you."

William scornfully ejaculated "Huh!" and added, "It'd take more'n *him* to make mincemeat of *me*"; then after a slight pause: "Are there many of you looking for him?"

"There's one or two more but he likes me. He thinks I'm his aunt. I can do what I like with him."

They were walking down the path looking among the bushes as they went.

"He's not a bad chap," went on the red-headed man, "not as bad as some of them. He's closely related to the Emperor of China."

"Is he?" said William, impressed.

"Yes. It makes him difficult to deal with sometimes. He has to have birds' nests and bamboo to eat."

"*Crumbs!*" said William, deeply impressed, "but why?"

"They eat those things in China. Didn't you know?"

"No. Do they really?"

"Yes. You should see him in spring and summer sitting in trees in the grounds holding a bird's nest in his hand and taking great mouthfuls out of it same as you would a bun."

"*Crumbs!*" said William again, his eyes and mouth wide open.

"Yes, and as for bamboo! The first night he came we put him in a room with a bamboo suite in it, and, believe me, in the morning there wasn't a stick of furniture left in the room. Dressing-table, wardrobe, washstand, chairs—he'd eaten 'em all up in the night."

"*Golly!*" said William faintly, feeling the inadequacy of that and every other ejaculation at his command.

"Yes," said the man calmly, "it's all along of him being related to the Emperor of China."

Suddenly he stopped and pointed through the trees.

"*There* he is," he whispered, "look at him. He's got hungry an' he's looking for birds' nests."

William peered through the wood in the direction of the man's finger. Another man could be seen some distance away stooping down and looking among the bushes.

"That's him," whispered the red-headed man, and repeated, "he's got hungry an' he's looking for birds' nests."

"You goin' to catch him now?" whispered William excitedly.

The man shook his head.

"We've got to go very careful," he said, "he's a bad-tempered man, an' he'll be mad at havin' found no birds' nests. Sometimes he thinks he's found a bamboo tree, and of course, it isn't 'cause bamboo trees don't grow here. Then he eats other sorts of trees and they don't agree with him. He ate a young beech tree once, and he was in bed for a week after it."

"How're you going to get him?" said William, breathless with excitement. He was drawing out from his penknife the thing to get stones from a horse's hoof so as to be ready for any emergency.

"We've got to use cunning," said the red-headed man. "It's no use attacking him straight off. He's got the strength of ten men, especially when he's not been over-eating on birds' nests and bamboo. Tell you what. I've got a plan." He sank his voice and William bent to listen. "You see he knows me and he doesn't know you. Now he's the sort of man what believes everything you tell him. If you go up to him and say that he's a keeper he'll believe he *is* a keeper, and you can tell him that *I'm* the one what escaped an' you've found me and he'll come over here to catch me, an' then I'll catch *him*. See?"

The idea appealed to William. He chuckled and set off to the man who could just be seen through the trees.

As he approached the man straightened himself.

"Hello," he said to William, "what are *you* doing here?"

"You're the attendant at the asylum lookin' for the lunatic, aren't you?" said William persuasively.

"I am," said the man, "have you seen him?"

The simple success of this deep-laid plot delighted William so much that he could hardly keep his face straight.

"Yes," he said, "I've got him. He's just over there."

The man followed William to where his new friend stood waiting. He laid a hand on William's new friend's shoulder, and blew a whistle.

"Now come on, Charlie," he said kindly to the red-headed man, "come along back with me. You know it's far nicer at home than out here. It's cold out here and it's going to rain in a minute."

"Did you find any birds' nests to eat?" said the red-headed man with interest.

"Yes, lots," said the other man, "you come back with me and I'll tell you all about it."

William looked from one to the other, and for the first time a doubt came to him. There was something terribly sane-looking about the man who had just come up.

"No, I'm not coming," said the red-headed man. "I'm looking for escaped lunatics. They're all over the wood. All eatin' birds' nests," he turned and cocked a careless thumb at William. "*He's* one of them."

Other keepers were coming up in answer to the whistle. One of them approached the red-headed man, and said:

"I say, Charlie, the Emperor of China's giving a party. He wants to know if you're coming to it."

"Are there birds' nests to eat?" said the red-headed man majestically.

"Hundreds of them," said the keeper.

The red-headed man considered for a moment, and finally bowed graciously and said:

"I'll come. Lead the way."

The keeper prepared to lead the way when the red-headed man wheeled suddenly round and pointed at William.

"He's my page," he said, "but I dismiss him. He's utterly incompetent. Utt-er-ly."

Then he swung round to the keeper. "Lead me to his majesty," he said.

They went off arm in arm. The red-headed man seemed quite friendly with the keeper. He was pointing up into the trees as they went and talking about birds' nests.

The other keepers were surrounding William and congratulating him. Someone gave him five shillings.

William having got over the first shock of surprise was carrying the situation off rather well.

"Oh, I jus' thought I'd have a shot at tryin' to find him," he said carelessly. "I found him almost at once, and then I jus' walked on with him, hum'ring him till we met a keeper. I knew that we'd be meetin' a keeper soon, so I jus' walked on with him, hum'ring him till we saw one. Then I left him for a minute while I went to tell the keeper that I'd found him, I jus' kept on hum'ring him. I *knew* he was a lunatic all right."

One of them escorted him back to the road and to

Mrs. Stacey's, and handed him over to his hostess with an account of his exploit.

They found the little girl sobbing. It appeared that she had been sobbing ever since William had gone into the wood. She had refused all comfort.

"I wasn't a b-bit n-nice to him," she had sobbed. "I was h-horrid to him. And now he's g-gone and got k-killed. I know he's g-got k-killed. He's g-got k-killed by a l-lunatic."

She listened open-mouthed and open-eyed to the story of William's capture. All through tea she gazed at him in mute admiration. William, in the intervals of making a very adequate meal, enlarged upon his adventure.

"The minute I saw him I *knew* he was a lunatic, of course," he said, speaking indistinctly through a mouthful of currant bun. "He'd got red hair and he—he sort of *looked* like a lunatic. They've gotter sort of *look*, lunatics have. You can tell 'em at once. Well, I told this one at once. I *saw* he was a lunatic from the *look* of him, the minute I saw him, so I got my penknife out. It's got a sort of thing that's meant for taking things out of a horse's hoof, but it'd go right into a man's head if you stuck it in hard enough. I let him see I'd got it so's he wouldn't start struggling or anythin', and then I started hum'ring him. Yes, I'll have another bun, thank you. . . . Well," still more indistinctly, "I started hum'ring this lunatic. I *knew* he was a lunatic all right. It's quite easy hum'ring lunatics. You talk to 'em about birds' nests and bamboo an' things like that. Well, I kept walkin' with him an' hum'ring him talkin' about birds' nests and bamboo and things like that same as you do to lunatics —thanks, yes, the sort with sugar on, over there— thanks—till we came to where we saw a keeper. Of course, I knew that if we went on walkin' long enough we'd meet a keeper, 'cause they were out in the wood lookin' for him, so as soon as we met this keeper, I thought of a very cunning plan—yes, thanks very much. I'd like a piece of that currant cake, thank you very much—I thought of a very cunnin' plan. I sort of made him think that he was the keeper and the other the lunatic. I daresay he wun't've believed it if *anyone'd* told him so, but I'm good at hum'ring lunatics so he believed it an' so I sort of got 'em together an' the real keeper got him. They gave me," he added modestly, "a lot of money for it. They thought it was a jolly clever thing to do. But it din't seem very clever to me. . . . Yes, thank you very much, I'll have one of those biscuits. . . . I mean there doesn't seem much in jus' catchin' a lunatic to me."

"Oh, *William*," sighed the little girl, "I think you're *wonderful!*"

"I remember when we were staying in Nice," began Claude in his languorous high-pitched drawl, but the little girl said impatiently, without even looking at him:

"Oh, Claude, *do* be quiet,"—then sinking her voice to tenderness again—"do tell us all about it again, William."

And William, nothing loth, stretched out his hand for a jam tart and told them all about it again.

*   *   *

When William set off at the appointed hour to go home it appeared that the little girl had decided to accompany him. She wanted a last glimpse of William's home and family and person, all of which were now invested with a dazzling glamour in her eyes. Claude, who had not been allowed to finish a sentence since William had returned from his heroic exploit, did not

"OH, *WILLIAM*," SIGHED THE LITTLE GIRL, "I THINK YOU'RE
WONDERFUL!"

even offer to accompany them, but retired sulkily to
listen to the wireless.

William and the little girl set off together down the
road.

"I'm so sorry I'm going home to-morrow, William,"
said the little girl regretfully.

"Uh-huh," said William distantly as from immeasur-
able heights of heroism.

"I shall miss you *awfully*."

"Uh-huh," said William again.

He was alone with the little girl. There was a whole mile of country road before them. He could talk to his heart's content about civilisation, pianos, ostriches, sacks—anything. She'd listen with awe and reverence. She wouldn't interrupt. And quite suddenly all his desire to talk to her had faded. He realised that without interruption it wouldn't be any fun at all. He looked down at the little girl's face. It was raised to his, alight with adoration. And quite suddenly he discovered that her charm for him had completely vanished. It was her disdain of him that had made her so desirable in his eyes.

His hand closed over the two half-crowns in his pocket. They at any rate were real and desirable enough. They were just passing Mr. Moss's sweet shop. With a murmured excuse he disappeared inside to reappear a few minutes later with a paper bag.

"Bulls eyes," he explained tersely. "Big 'uns. They last for miles." He handed her one. It was gigantic. He took one himself. Their lips could not quite close over them. Conversation for some minutes at any rate was quite impossible. William walked on in enforced, but quite enjoyable silence. A rosy haze of content was upon his spirit. He'd soon be at home. Ginger would be waiting for him. They'd have time for a game before bed-time. He was already forgetting the past except as food for the future. Lunatics and keepers . . . it would make a jolly fine game. It held endless possibilities. A change from Red Indians and smugglers and the other games.

The little girl spoke with an effort through her bulls eye.

"What are you going to be when you grow up, William?"

William considered the question in silence for a

minute. He didn't want to be a lecturer after all. He was tired of it already. He wasn't really sure that he wanted to be a robber or a chimney sweep either. It was a jolly good bulls eye, the best he'd ever tasted. Bottles and bottles of bulls eyes all your own. He made up his mind suddenly.

"Keep a sweet shop," he said indistinctly.

Chapter 3

William, Prime Minister

"What's this gen'ral election they keep talkin' about?" said Ginger. He directed the question at Henry because Henry had a reputation for universal knowledge, but he wasn't really interested. The general election was just a grown-up topic of conversation like the weather and the price of petrol, and so he took for granted that it must be as dull as any other grown-up topic of conversation. Still, it had been mentioned so often lately that he felt an idle curiosity as to its meaning.

"It's somethin' to do with makin' a tunnel under the sea," answered William who never liked to own himself at a loss.

"No, it isn't," said Henry earnestly, "it isn't anythin' to do with that. That's somethin' quite diff'rent. The general election means choosin' people to rule the country."

"I thought the King ruled the country," said William.

"Well, he sort of does and he sort of doesn't," said Henry, still with his air of deep wisdom.

"Oh, shut up," said William impatiently, "if he does, he can't doesn't as well, can he? Stands to reason."

"No, but what I mean is," said Henry still more earnestly, "that there's a sort of man under him called the Prime Min'ster that sorts of help him govern an' he's chosen out of a general election."

"Like the man they have in It'ly called the duck?" said Douglas anxious to air his knowledge.

"You're thinking of the dog," said Ginger scornfully, "the man we had in history what ruled a place called Venice an' was called a dog."

"I'd have called myself somethin' better than a dog or a duck if I was goin' to be a ruler," said William. "I'd be called a lion or an eagle or somethin' like that."

"Do shut up int'ruptin'," said Henry, "I'm tryin' to tell you 'bout this gen'ral election. There's four sorts of people tryin' to get to be rulers. They all want to make things better, but they want to make 'em better in different ways. There's Conservatives an' they want to make things better by keepin' 'em jus' like what they are now. An' there's Lib'rals an' they want to make things better by alterin' them jus' a bit, but not so's anyone'd notice, an' there's Socialists, an' they want to make things better by taking everyone's money off 'em an' there's Communists an' they want to make things better by killin' everyone but themselves."

"I'm goin' to be one of them," said Ginger promptly, "they sound more excitin' than the others."

"Well, they get everyone they can to vote for them," went on Henry patiently, "and the ones that gets the most votes win and their head man's called Prime Min'ster an' tells the King what to do."

"I'd smack his head if I was the King an' he started tellin' me what to do," said William with spirit.

"I *say*," said Ginger excitedly, "there's just four of us. Let's be them an' have one. How do they make people vote for them?"

"They get 'em together an' make speeches to 'em," said Henry, "an' then they give 'em little pieces of paper to vote on an' they count 'em up an' the one that gets the most's won."

"I'm jolly good at making speeches," said William complacently, "there's not many things I can't make speeches about. I once thought of bein' a leckcherer but it'd be a bit dull when you got used to it."

"Well, who'll be which?" said Ginger. "I've bagged bein' the one that wants to kill everyone."

At this moment the church clock struck five and expressions of the four Outlaws changed.

"Tea-time," said William eagerly. "Let's come back after tea an' fix up what we'll be. There's goin' to be doughnuts for tea an' I don't want to be late. Robert's going to be in for tea an' he likes them too."

Despite his haste, William was late for tea and found that Robert had eaten all the doughnuts but two. He decided that in view of Robert's eight years' seniority it would be waste of time to enter upon hostilities on these grounds so he merely fixed Robert with a cold stare and said:

"Which are you votin' for, Robert?"

"What do you mean?" said Robert, stretching out his hand for the last doughnut, but being artfully foiled by William who neatly abstracted it from the plate when it seemed that Robert's hand was actually closing over it.

"I mean are you Conservative or what?" said William, keeping one hand closed over his rescued doughnut till he should have finished the one he was eating.

"You ought to be in the Zoo," said Robert dispassionately. "Anyone'd think you were starving."

"I wish I was in the Zoo," said William, "they have a jolly sight better time than I have. An' I jolly well *am* starving. I've had nothin' to eat since lunch. Are you a Conservative?"

"No," said Robert shortly, "I'm a Liberal."

"Well then I'm jolly well goin' to be one of the others," said William crushingly.

"I don't care what you are," said Robert, rising from his seat and brushing a few doughnut crumbs from his trousers to the carpet with an air of great fastidiousness.

"I bet you do," said William darkly.

Robert went out, leaving William alone at the table eating the last of the doughnuts. William's mind went over the political careers still open to him. He couldn't be a Communist because Ginger had bagged it and he couldn't be a Liberal because Robert was a Liberal, and Robert had eaten nearly all the doughnuts. Socialism and Conservative were still open to him. Socialism sounded rather fun. Then suddenly he remembered a friend of his father's who'd stayed a week-end with them last month—a tall bronzed spare man who'd just returned from a shooting trip in the African Veldt where he'd shot elephants, buffaloes and numerous other animals, and had once met a lion face to face on a jungle path when he was totally unarmed and had walked past it showing no more concern than if it had been a hen. This man had, of course, become William's hero, replacing Robin Hood, Hereward the Wake, Buffalo Bill and Sexton Blake, who had successively held that position. William had decided to go out big game shooting as soon as he'd left school, to meet a lion unarmed and to stroll past it with no more concern than if it had been a hen. He felt that life could have no real savour for him till he'd done that.

His mother came in and sat down by the fire knitting socks. Mrs. Brown had a husband and two sons, and so she was always knitting socks.

"Enjoying the doughnuts, dear?" she said to William.

"I only had two," said William.

"I think two's quite enough," said his mother.

William uttered a sound expressive of mingled amusement, incredulity, sarcasm, bitterness, cynicism and resignation, and after a short silence said:

"Mother, you remember that Mr. Martin what stayed here last month?"

"Yes, dear."

"Well, what was he?"

"He was a friend of your father's, dear."

"I mean, was he a Communist?"

If Mr. Martin were a Communist, William had decided to fight Ginger for the post of head of the Communist party.

"Of *course* not, dear," said Mrs. Brown, deeply shocked, "he was a Conservative."

"Then I'm one too," said William importantly.

"Are you, dear?" said his mother vaguely, and added, glancing with a worried frown at his legs, "Haven't you any garters, William?"

"No, I lost 'em," said William shamelessly.

Every day his mother made him a new pair of garters to keep his stockings up, and every day he took them off and used them as catapults.

"Well, you mustn't go out like that," said his mother, "it looks so untidy. Wait a minute and I'll make you another pair. I can't think what happens to all the garters I make you."

"Make 'em of good strong stuff, won't you?" said William.

"Yes, I will, dear," said Mrs. Brown, pleased that William should be beginning at last to take an interest in his appearance and should want his stockings to look neat.

* * *

When he returned to the old barn the other three were waiting for him.

"Let's get it settled," he said importantly. "I'm bein' the Conservative, an' Ginger the Communist. Then there's the Socialist that wants to take other people's money off them——"

"I'll be that," put in Henry hastily.

"You'll have to be the Lib'ral, then," said William to Douglas.

"I don't care," said Douglas gloomily. "I don't care what I am. I don't think it's goin' to be half such fun as Red Indians."

"Well, what do we do now?" demanded Ginger; "how do we start?"

They looked at William. William turned to the encyclopædical Henry.

"What do they do now?" he said, with the air of a potentate asking advice of his head tribesman.

"They get meetin's together," said Henry, "an' they make speeches, an' then they give 'em papers an' pencils to vote, an' the one that gets the most votes wins."

"Well, let's do that, then," said William cheerfully. "We'll tell 'em about it at school to-morrow an' have the meetin' here after school. We can think out what we'll say in our speech in school to-morrow morning."

They followed him out of the old barn into the sunshine.

He picked up a small stone from the ground and pointed.

"See that tree over there? I bet I can hit it."

He slipped off one of his new garters and took careful aim.

*   *   *

The gathering in the old barn the next evening was larger than even the Outlaws had expected. It was not that the juvenile population of the village was interested in politics. It was merely that any function of any sort got up by William and his Outlaws was apt to be exciting and no one wanted to be out of it.

The audience sat on the floor facing the Outlaws who sat on upturned packing-cases at one end.

William—garterless once more—stepped forward to explain the situation.

"Ladies an' Gent'men," he began in his best platform manner, "we're goin' to have a gen'ral election jus' the same as what grown-ups have. We're goin' to make speeches an' when we've finished you've all got to vote for us an' I hope you've all brought pencils and pieces of paper same as what we told you to. We're all goin' to make speeches tellin' you about what we are an' askin' you to be the same, so you've got to choose between us after hearin' us make speeches, same as what grown-ups do. Douglas is a Lib'ral an' Henry's a Socialist an' Ginger's a Communist an' I'm a Conservative. Now we're all goin' to make speeches, startin' with Douglas."

William, who possessed a pretty sound knowledge of psychology, had decided to be the last speaker. He pulled Douglas up by his collar and said: "Ladies an' Gent'men, this is Douglas what's goin' to speak to you about bein' Lib'rals."

Douglas stepped forward amid faint applause.

"Ladies an' Gentlemen," said Douglas, "I'm makin' this speech to ask you all to be Lib'rals same as what I am. Nearly all of you came to my birthday-party las' month an' if you don't vote Lib'rals I won't ask you again next year. My aunt's gotter parrot that talks, an' I'll let you come an' listen to it through the window when

she's not there if you'll vote Lib'rals. I can't let you
listen when she's there 'cause she doesn't like boys. I'll
let you look at my rabbits too, an' I'll give you all a suck
of rock if my aunt sends me a stick when she goes to
Brighton same as she did last year."

He sat down breathless.

There were certainly the makings of a politician in
Douglas. He didn't care what he promised. William
stood up.

"Now you ask him questions," he said. "Go on! Ask
him questions! Tell him anythin' you didn't like in his
speech. That what's they do when they've finished
speakin'. It's called hecklin'."

"It was a rotten party," said a small boy in the front
row bitterly, "I gotter whistle out of a cracker an' it
wouldn't whistle."

"Well, that wasn't my fault," said Douglas indignantly. "I didn't make the crackers."

"They must 've been rotten crackers," said the small
boy.

"All right, you jolly well needn't come next year,"
said Douglas heatedly, forgetting the spirit of propitia-
tion that the occasion demanded. "It was a jolly sight
better than your party, anyway. Did you have a
conjurer?"

"No, but we had a Punch and Judy."

"Yes, an' a jolly mess-up it was too. Your aunt's
baby started crying an' we couldn't hear a word they
said."

"All right, you jolly well needn't come next year."

"No, I won't, an' you needn't come to mine."

"No, I'm not goin' to. An' I'm not goin' to vote for
you, either."

"I don't want you to. I'd soon not win than have
people like you votin' for me."

William had listened to this spirited interchange with pride and interest. He now rose to his feet and said:

"That's jolly good hecklin'. Anyone got anythin' else to say?"

Someone had. A boy with red hair in the back row said:

"What does your aunt's parrot say?"

"It says, 'God Save the King' and 'Polly put the kettle on.' "

"That's nothing. I know someone that's got a parrot that says 'Go to hell.' "

"And your rabbits aren't any different from other people's rabbits," said a little girl with freckles and a snub nose. "I don't want to see 'em."

"Well, I never asked you to," said Douglas.

"Oo, you *story-teller*," said the little girl. "Oo, you did." She appealed to the room. "Didn't he?"

"I didn't," said Douglas.

"You did."

"I didn't."

"You *did*."

"I shun't *want* my rabbits to see you. I don't want 'em killed, do I?"

"It would take a lot to kill 'em if they've lived seein' you every day," returned the spirited damsel.

"Who cried when she fell in at the deep end?" said Douglas, turning to more direct personalities.

"And who stayed up in a tree all day because he couldn't get down?" retorted the damsel.

"That's enough hecklin' about Liberalism," said William in his character of master of the ceremonies. "If you go on hecklin' all day about that we won't have any time to listen to the others. Now it's Henry's turn to talk about Socialism. Socialism means takin' other people's money off 'em. Henry's goin' to talk about it." He turned to introduce the speaker. "This is Henry, goin' to make a speech to you about Socialism."

Henry stepped forward and performed the bow that he had learnt at the dancing-class (Henry was the only one of the Outlaws who attended a dancing-class). This was greeted with enthusiastic applause.

"Ladies and Gentlemen," began Henry, much encouraged by his reception, "I'm goin' to make a speech to you about Socialism 'cause I want you all to vote for Socialism. Socialism means takin' other people's money off 'em. Well, think how much richer we'd be if we'd got other people's money as well as our own."

"It's wrong to steal," said a small but earnest boy who had won the Sunday School Junior prize last quarter.

"Yes, but it's not stealin' when you do it by lor," said Henry, "we'd do it by lor."

"You'd get put in prison," said the Sunday School prodigy; "that's what happens to people who take other people's money. They get put in prison. And serve 'em jolly well right too."

"You shut up," said Henry. "I keep tellin' you that it doesn't count if you do it by lor. We're goin' to do it by lor."

"Whose money are you goin' to take?" said another member of the audience, emboldened by the success of the hecklers so far.

"Everyone's money that isn't a Socialist."

"An' s'pose everyone turns Socialist so's to get other people's money, what're you goin' to do then?"

"They couldn't."

"Why couldn't they?"

" 'Cause there's *gotter* be four sorts of people same as what we are. Well, there couldn't be four sorts of people if everyone was a Socialist, could there? Stands to reason. If you'd got any sense you'd see there couldn't."

"I've got a jolly sight more sense than what you have."

"Oh, you have, have you?"

"Yes, I have."

"All right. Come on, then——"

But William hastily interposed.

"They don't fight," he said, "they only talk same as you've been talkin'. It's called hecklin', like what I told you. They don't start fightin'." He pushed the still recalcitrant Henry into the seat and addressed the audience.

"Now you've heard all about Socialism from Henry. Now you c'n hear about Communism from Ginger." He turned and pointed out Ginger to the audience. "This is Ginger, goin' to make a speech to you about Communism."

Ginger rose and cleared his throat importantly.

"Ladies an' Gentlemen," he began. "Communism means havin' a war against all the people that aren't Communists an' conquerin' 'em an' killin' 'em."

"Killin' people's wrong," interposed the hope of the Sunday School. "People who kill people get hung. And serve them jolly well right too."

"Not if it's in a *war*," said Ginger, "this is goin' to be a war. Jus' like what we read about in history books, with battles an' camps an' noble deeds an' such-like. Well, when we've won the war——"

"S'pose you don't win it," said the boy with red hair.

"What?" said Ginger irritably.

"I say, s'pose you don't win it."

"*Course* we're goin' to win it."

"Oh, you'll win it all right if you run away as fast as

you do when Farmer Jenks is after you. Oh! yes! you'll
win it then all right."

"Well, so do you run away when he's after you."

"Yes, but I don't say I'm goin' to conquer the world.
If you're afraid of Farmer Jenks——"

"I'm *not* afraid of Farmer Jenks. I'm not afraid of
anybody."

"Oo, aren't you?"

"No, I'm *not* . So there!"

"All right, then. Jus' you——"

"That's enough hecklin' about Communists," interrupted William. "Now I'm goin' to make a speech
about Conservatism to try'n' get you all to vote
Conservative."

He stood up and looked around him. Silence fell.

They gazed at William expectantly.

"Ladies an' Gentlemen," said William, "There was a
man stayin' with my father last month. He only stayed
two days but p'raps some of you saw him."

"I did," said a small child excitedly from the back of
the barn.

"Well, that proves I'm not makin' it up," said William. "Well, this man had been in Africa. He'd been
shootin' there—jus' livin' in a sort of forest they call the
felt an' pitchin' his camp in it by night an' shootin' by
day. An' he shot lions an' elephants and about twenty
other sorts of wild animals. An' once he went into a sort
of tunnel that a buffalo makes in the bushes an' this
buffalo came chargin' out at him down the tunnel an' he
shot it there in the dark tunnel. Shot it dead. Didn't turn
to run away or anythin' same as you or me would have
done. An' another time he met a lion an' he hadn't got a
gun an' he jus' walked past this lion without runnin'
away or anythin' an' it wasn't hungry so it didn't eat him
but it'd've eat him if he'd run away, because they do.

You an' me would have run away without stoppin' to think, but this man I'm tellin' you about, this friend of my father's, didn't. An' one of them elephants he killed was comin' chargin' down at him too. It hadn't any tusks an' they're always speshully savidge when they haven't any tusks. But he never got scared. He jus' shot it clean dead. An' when he'd put up his tent an' lit his fire at night, he used to hear the lions roarin' in the darkness an' hippopotamusses used to come out of the river to sniff round it an' once he heard somethin' sniffin' about an' in the mornin' he saw a leopard's foot marks round his tent an' it had come just inside the open doorway to look at him. But this man I'm tellin' you about, this friend of my father's, wasn't any more scared than if it had been a mouse." He stopped for a minute. His audience was listening in breathless silence. Slowly he brought out his climax. "An' this man is a Conservative. He votes Conservatism at gen'ral elections."

The audience heaved a deep sigh, waking slowly from its dreams of camp fires, roaring lions and buffalo tunnels.

"Anyone want to do any hecklin' about Conservatism?" said William, surveying his audience.

"Yes I do," said a boy in the second row, "how do you tell whether a lion's hungry?"

"Only by whether it eats you or not," said William, "if it isn't hungry it doesn't eat you an' if it is it does. That's the only way you can tell."

"Oh," said the boy in an awestruck voice. "Well, I bet I'd run away every time to be on the safe side."

"Then he'd eat you every time," said William. "Any more hecklin'?"

The hope of the Sunday School, feeling that he had been hiding his light under a bushel too long, said:

"I think it's cruel killin' wild animals."

"Oh, do you?" said William. "I s'pose you'd rather they killed you?"

"Yes, I would," said the young humanitarian unctuously.

He was attacked by his neighbours on either side and subsided temporarily, rubbing his bruises, his face wearing an expression of smug satisfaction as of one who has suffered for his faith.

"Well, if there's no more hecklin' about Conservatism," said William, "we'll have the votin'. Have you all brought pencils and paper." It turned out that no one had, so William proceeded.

"All right, then, hands up those who want to vote Lib'ral." The audience remained motionless. "Hands up those who want to vote Socialist." The audience remained motionless. "Hands up those who want to vote Communist." The audience remained motionless. "Hands up those who want to vote Conservative." Every member of the audience immediately raised a hand.

"That's me," said William complacently. "I'm Prime Min'ster now. I'm same as the ones they call the duck an' the dog. I'm goin' to rule the country."

"What are you goin' to do for us first?" said the boy with red hair.

"Do for you?" repeated William indignantly. "I'm not goin' to do anythin' for you. I'm goin' to *rule*."

"But that means *doin'* things for us," persisted the boy with red hair. "I know it does. We learnt it at school. It's somethin' called civics. An' I vote you get back the tadpole pond for us."

The tadpole pond was a small pond that till lately had stood by the roadside just outside the garden of a Miss Felicia Dalrymple. It had been the favourite resort of the juvenile population of the village in the tadpole season.

"HANDS UP THOSE WHO WANT TO VOTE CONSERVATIVE,"
SAID WILLIAM, AND EVERY MEMBER OF THE AUDIENCE
RAISED A HAND.

But a month or two ago Miss Felicia Dalrymple had
discovered that the pond had originally formed part of
her garden and had reclaimed it, putting a hurdle fence
around it and keeping a gardener near the spot to inflict
punishment on any youthful invaders. Feeling on the
subject ran high among those who had previously spent
all their leisure moments at the pond, and the suggestion
of the red-headed boy was greeted by a deafening cheer.

"THAT'S ME," SAID WILLIAM. "I'M PRIME MINISTER NOW. I'M
GOING TO RULE THE COUNTRY."

William was for a moment too taken aback to reply,
then he repeated:

"I'm jolly well not goin' to do anythin' for you. I'm
Prime Minister. I'm one of them like the duck an' the
dog. I'm jus' goin' to *rule*."

But the red-headed boy was not to be put off in this
way.

"Well, I've learnt it in history. It's in the chapter

called civics, an' we did it last week, an' I know 'cause I
was kept in to learn it again. It says that the Prime
Min'ster an' such like's the servants of the people an'
does things for them."

"Well, I'm jolly well not goin' to be that sort," said
William with spirit. "I'm goin' to *rule* . . . same as the
ones they call the duck an' the dog."

"You're afraid of ole Miss Dallypots."

"I'm not. I'm not afraid of anyone."

"You are. You're afraid of ole Miss Dallypots."

"I'm *not*. You say that again an' I'll——"

"All right, then. Prove you're not afraid. Get our
pond back off her again."

"I'm jolly well not goin' to."

"'Cause you couldn't."

"I could."

"You couldn't."

"I could."

"All right, do it, then."

"All right, I will."

At this hasty unthinking announcement deafening
cheering broke out again. William was torn between
gratification at the reception of his rash promise and
apprehension at the magnitude of the task he had
undertaken. He struck a careless attitude of aloof
omnipotence.

"I'll do that for you," he said. "It seemed such a little
thing to do that it didn't hardly seem worth while at first,
but if you really want it——"

From the cheering it appeared that they really did
want it.

"All right," said William casually, "I'll try'n' get it
for you by Saturday afternoon."

*   *   *

It seemed best to begin operations by approaching Miss Felicia Dalrymple direct. He had not high hopes of this, but it seemed the obvious first step. He refused the help of Ginger, Douglas and Henry. He had by inquiries at home been extending his political knowledge.

"No," he said, "you're the other side. You're against everything I do. You ought to try'n' stop me gettin' back the pond."

"But we *want* the pond," objected Ginger.

"That doesn't matter," said William. "You're the other side, so you oughter try'n' stop me doin' it even if you want it. They do in pol'tics. You've gotter be against me. It's one of the rules."

"Where's the *sense* in it?" demanded Douglas.

"Oh, it jus' makes it more fun," said William vaguely. "Anyway, I'm goin' off to Miss Dalrymple now to ask her. I'm goin' to plead with her."

"Well, if you need us, you'll let us help?" said Ginger anxiously. They didn't like being debarred from participation in William's adventures.

"Oh yes," said William, "if I'm in any deadly peril I'll give the deadly peril whistle an' you come an' help."

They had to be satisfied with that.

* * *

With a certain amount of misgiving at his heart, William raised the brass knocker of Miss Dalrymple's green-painted door and let it fall again heavily. It was rather a fascinating knocker. It represented a lion's head with its tongue out. When you raised the knocker the tongue went in, and when you dropped it, it came out again. When you went on knocking, the lion put its tongue in and out continually. William, deeply absorbed in this phenomenon, went on knocking. An indignant housemaid opened the door.

"What on earth's the matter?" she said.

William reluctantly dragged his attention from the lion's tongue.

"I want to see Miss Dalrymple," he said.

"Well, you needn't knock the house down for that," said the housemaid angrily.

"I wasn't knocking the house down," said William in his most distant manner.

"Come in then," she said sharply, "and wipe your boots."

"Does it ever get stuck?" asked William.

"What?"

"The tongue."

"None of your impudence," said the housemaid, as she showed him into the morning-room.

William, who was used to hostility from housemaids, and accepted it as part of the natural order of things, entered the morning-room dreamily, wishing that he lived in a house with a knocker like that. So absorbed was he in dreams of himself making the tongue go in and out, in and out, all day long, that when Miss Dalrymple entered, it took him a few moments to remember what he'd come for.

Miss Dalrymple was a lady of about fifty with an earnest expression and a dignified manner.

"Yes, my boy," she said to William, "what is it you wish to see me about?"

William tore his mind from the knocker.

"It's about our pond," he said.

"Your pond?"

"Yes. Our pond what you've put fences round."

"But, my dear boy, it's *my* pond. Until comparatively recently it was part of this garden, and now it's going to be part of this garden again. It *belongs* to me."

"Well, we want it for tadpoles an' things," said

"WELL, WE WANT THE POND FOR TADPOLES AN' THINGS,"
SAID WILLIAM.

William, remembering that he was a Prime Minister and
trying to speak firmly.

"I can't help that, my dear boy," said the lady,
smiling condescendingly. "The fact remains that it's my
pond. I can *prove* that it's my pond. I have a map of the
garden as it was in my grandfather's time and various
letters to prove it."

"P'raps the government bought it off your grandfather after that map and letters was wrote," suggested William. She smiled again.

"Nonsense, my dear boy."

"But if anyone could prove that they had, you'd let us have it again?"

"Naturally, my dear boy, naturally." William still sat there, gazing stolidly into space. Something of the lady's geniality began to wane.

"I'm rather busy this morning, my boy, so I'm afraid I must ask you to go now."

"All right," said William, rising slowly.

The lady saw him to the door, and closed it on him firmly. He stood looking at it dreamily. The tongue was out now, it would go in and come out again when you lifted the knocker and dropped it. He lifted the knocker and dropped it several times. It was a fascinating spectacle. Then he set off to the gate.

The housemaid had rushed to the door again, and the lady had hurried breathlessly into the hall.

"What on *earth* is it?" she said.

"It's that *boy* again," said the housemaid.

William was just closing the gate. He was quite unaware that he had roused the entire household.

*   *   *

That night William sat up in his bedroom laboriously drawing a map of Miss Dalrymple's garden that did not include the pond. As a map it was not particularly successful, but there was no doubt at all as to the position of the pond. William had drawn a fence as large as the house, and by the side of the pond he had put a cross and the words: "This pond is rite outsid the garden." He had then, after innumerable attempts, drafted a letter supposed to be written to Miss Dalrymple's father by the government. It ran as follows:

Dear Mister Dalrimpul,

      Thank you very much for selling us the pond at the end of your garden. We want it to be rite outsid your garden so that the boys can studdy tadpols and things in it. We want it to be a fre pond for everyone who liks to go and fish in. Thank you for putting the fens on the other sid of the pond so as to make it a fre pond and rite outsid your garden.

   We hop that your dorter Miss Felisher Dalrimpul is quit wel,

Yours cinserely,
The Government.

Having finished this letter William regarded it with deep satisfaction.

It seemed to him a masterly and Machiavelli-like achievement, proving irrefutably that even if the pond had belonged to Miss Dalrymple's grandfather, her father had since sold it to the government, and so it belonged to her no longer. The subtle touch of the introduction of Miss Felicia Dalrymple's name caused him many chuckles.

"I bet not many people would've thought of that," he said complacently.

The next thing to decide was how to bring the map and letter to Miss Dalrymple's notice. To take them to her in person of course would be to invite suspicion that they were forgeries. She must come upon them as if by accident just as people did in books. But how could he put them anywhere where she would come upon them by accident? Dearly as he would have liked to return to her house and knock at her fascinating knocker, he knew that he would not be a welcome visitor, and in all probability would not even be admitted this time. Even if he were, how could he put the papers in a place where they might be supposed to have lain unnoticed ever since the time of Miss Dalrymple's father? Then—quite suddenly—the inspiration came to him, The Pond! Miss Dalrymple was going to have the pond drained and lined with concrete in order to make a water garden of it. When they drained the pond they should find a bottle with the letter and the map inside.

* * *

The next night at an hour when the gardener might be supposed to have gone home after his day's work William cautiously approached the disputed territory. In his pocket was a ginger beer bottle emptied of ginger beer, but containing the map and letter tightly screwed up. This he was going to drop into the middle of the pond. To enter the garden and throw it boldly into the pond would be to court detection and risk the failure of his deeply laid plot. So he had evolved a cunning plan. He was going to climb a tree that grew on the roadway outside the fence, creep along a branch shielded by its leafage till he was just over the middle of the pond and then drop the bottle into its depths.

Fortunately the road was empty. William swarmed lightly up the tree and began to crawl along the branch that stretched to the middle of the pond. Then he looked down. The familiar pond lay beneath him covered by a thick green slime. It had always been covered by a thick green slime ever since William remembered it. It was one of its charms. Miss Dalrymple was going to spoil it completely by taking off its covering of thick green slime. He lifted the bottle out of his pocket and held it poised over the centre of the pond. Then—he never knew exactly how it happened. It might have been the wind or it might have been the effort of pulling the bottle out of his pocket or it might just have been pure bad luck but, whichever it was, he overbalanced and fell into the very centre of the green slime.

He crawled out as best he could, having had the presence of mind to leave his bottle behind, and made his dripping and ignominious way homeward.

* * *

The next morning he cautiously approached the scene of his adventure. The pond stood by the roadside as it had always stood till a week ago. The hurdle fence had been moved back to the farther side. The pond was in Miss Dalrymple's garden no longer. He shut his eyes and opened them quickly. It was still there. They couldn't surely have found the bottle in this short time. Still —there it was. He hurried back to the old barn where his supporters were waiting for him.

"I've done it," he announced carelessly. "I've made her give it us back an' move her ole fence."

They gazed at him incredulously.

"Go on! You've not!"

"All right," said William, "come an' see for yourselves."

They followed him to the spot and gazed in amazement at their beloved pond standing once more by the road side.

* * *

Inside the house, Miss Dalrymple was having breakfast with a cousin who was staying with her.

"No, no toast, thank you," she was saying. "I'm not feeling at all well this morning. I've had a most terrible experience last night. A most shattering experience."

She paused, and so the cousin said obligingly:

"What was it, dear?"

"Well," said Miss Dalrymple, absentmindedly taking

a piece of toast, "it was so terrible that at first I thought I'd never be able to tell anyone about it."

She paused again and the cousin, who had a genius for saying what she was expected to say, said:

"I think that perhaps you'd feel better if you told me about it, dear."

"I don't know that I *can*, said Miss Dalrymple with a shudder; "it's—it's about that pond."

"The pond that you're going to turn into a water garden?"

Miss Dalrymple shuddered again, and closing her eyes held out a hand as if to ward something off.

"Not now," she said, "*never* now. Look out of the window."

The cousin looked out of the window.

"Gracious!" she said. "It's gone."

"I've had it fenced off again," said Miss Dalrymple. "I gave the order as soon as I got up this morning. I insisted on its being done at once. I shouldn't have slept another night under this roof if it hadn't been done."

"Why, dear?" said the cousin mildly.

"I'll try to tell you . . . though it was such a terrible, such a *shattering* experience that it's not easy to talk about it. You remember that there was a story that our grandfather had the pond fenced off from his garden because someone committed suicide in it and the servants used to say it was haunted?"

"I remember something like that vaguely."

"Well, I never gave the story a minute's thought till last evening, and last evening—my dear, it was such a terrible experience that even now I tremble when I think of it. Last evening—I'd gone to bed early with a head-ache—you remember, and I—I happened to look out of the window and—my dear, I simply can't describe what I saw—a slimy green THING crawling out of the pond."

"Oh my *dear!*" screamed the cousin, "was it a human being?"

"All I can tell you," said Miss Dalrymple in a low sepulchral voice, "is that it was a THING in human shape covered with green slime *crawling* out of the pond as if to come straight up to the house. I need hardly tell you that I fainted. As soon as I came to myself, I looked out of the window again, but the figure had vanished. First thing this morning however I ordered the fence to be put back. I dread to think what might have happened to us all had I not acted promptly. One night it would have reached the house. . . ."

The cousin screamed again in horror, and Miss Dalrymple, feeling slightly fortified by the effect of her story, took another piece of toast.

* * *

"But how did you get her to do it?" said William's supporters, crowding round him eagerly.

William stood in the middle, his hands in his pockets.

"I jus' went to her," he said carelessly, "an' I said that I was Prime Min'ster an' she'd *gotter* give us back our pond. I said that if she didn't I'd go to lor about it. So she said she would an' told them to change the fence again."

His supporters cheered loudly and the red-headed boy spoke.

"Well, I think it was jolly good," he said, approvingly, "an' the next thing we want you to do for us——"

"I'm not doin' anythin' else," interposed William hastily, "I'm sick of bein' Prime Min'ster. I'm sick of pol'tics altogether. There isn't any *sense* in 'em. I'd sooner be a Red Indian any day. I'll give up bein' Prime Min'ster to you an' *you* c'n start doin' things."

And he went off with his Outlaws to play Red Indians.

Chapter 4

William Gets His Own Back

As William said, they were always worst to you when you'd been trying to do something for them. He'd been trying to help Robert. He told them all that he'd been trying to help Robert. Robert ought to be grateful to him instead of going on at him like that. Well, he thought Robert *wanted* to marry her. He was always acting as if he did, anyway, and he'd been trying to help him. Well, no one would marry anyone—would they?—unless they asked them. And *he'd* never heard of anyone being in love without writing poems to the person. He'd been trying to help Robert. . . . It was silly of Robert to go on like that saying he'd nearly ruined his life when he'd been *helping* him. You couldn't ruin a person's life by *helping* them, could you? It was ridic'lous.

What had happened was this. Robert had evinced a sudden interest in a very pretty girl who lived in the next village. There was nothing, of course, exceptional in this. Robert was continually evincing sudden interest in pretty girls who lived in the villages around. (He had exhausted his own village long ago.) Each one in succession was the most beautiful girl in the world and in the case of each he was convinced that his life would be an arid desert unless he married her. It was not Robert's fault that fresh suns were continually rising upon his horizon and that his inamoratas, too, were continually finding fresh and (for the moment) more attractive swains. Each affair was quite sincere while it lasted. William had watched these affairs with little emotion except a deep and all-consuming pity and contempt. Not thus would he, William, waste the golden hour of manhood when it arrived. He'd be too busy sailing the seas as a pirate or terrorising the countryside as a bandit or, at the very least, driving an engine. Certainly he wouldn't be going on the river with soppy girls or writing long letters to them. No, all he'd be writing would be sinister warnings to his enemies (he meant to have innumerable bloodthirsty enemies whom he would continually foil), signed by his name in blood and a skull and crossbones. He'd practised the skull and crossbones and signing his name in blood till he was an expert at it.

So, though he had a healthy respect for Robert's right arm, he hadn't much opinion of his intelligence. It wasn't till Ginger's grown-up brother got married that William began to see possibilities in that part of Robert's character that before he had looked upon with unmixed contempt. For Ginger's brother left home and went to live at least ten miles away from home. Ginger saw him only once a week and then on the terms of distant politeness that the presence of the new sister-in-law demanded. No longer did he claim to exercise elder brother tyranny over him. Moreover, upon marriage, he had presented Ginger with his old push bike, watch and a wireless set, all of which had been replaced by wedding presents. Ginger's life seemed now to William to be one of vast possessions and untrammelled liberty and William had decided to leave no stone unturned to get Robert married as quickly as possible before his bicycle, watch and wireless should be completely worn out.

It was this resolve that made him turn his whole attention to Robert's love affairs. He hadn't been taking much notice of them lately, and so, naturally, the girl he thought Robert was in love with was already two or three back. It wasn't Dolly Clavis, the girl with red hair, or even Molly Cotton, the girl with the arpeggio laugh or even Betty Donber, the girl with the turned-up nose. Those all belonged to the past. It was Peggy Barlow, who lived five or six miles away, and whom William had never even seen. It was evidently quite an intense affair, but then Robert's affairs were always intense affairs. He met her or wrote to her every day. Having discovered this, William, who never let the grass grow under his feet, determined to ascertain tactfully whether there were any prospects of Robert's immediate departure from home. He happened to discover it on a day when there was every reason for going carefully with Robert. Robert had promised William a shilling to clean his bicycle. William had cleaned it, and the shilling was to be paid before the afternoon. There was a fair in a field outside the meadow, and the Outlaws had arranged to visit this and spend the afternoon there upon Robert's shilling, which was their sole capital. William therefore decided to go very carefully.

He found Robert in the morning-room reading a novel called "The Corpse in the Thicket." William sat down on the empty chair opposite him, and looked at him in silence for a few minutes, considering his tactics. At last he said in a tone of casual interest:

"How old are you, Robert?"

Robert, who had just got to the point where the corpse was found in the thicket, was so deeply absorbed that he did not hear this question till it had been repeated three times. Then he said curtly: "Nineteen," and added still more curtly: "and shut up."

"Nineteen!" repeated William with a note of surprise and concern in his voice.

As Robert went on reading without taking any notice of this, William had to repeat it also several times, deepening the surprise and concern in his voice till it raised Robert's curiosity despite himself. Leaving the corpse in the middle of the road where the police inspector had laid it, he returned to William.

"What's the matter?" he said curtly. "Why shouldn't I be nineteen?"

"I didn't sort of think you were *quite* as old as that," said William. "Seems to me most people are married by the time they get to nineteen."

"Oh, it does, does it?" said Robert, returning to the corpse which had proved to be that of a notorious international criminal; "well, you can jolly well shut up."

"Seems to me," went on William, undeterred by this permission, "seems to me that if anyone's goin' to get married they oughter be thinking about it when they get to nineteen. I mean, you don't want to wait till you're *old* before you get married, do you? Old people mus' look jolly silly gettin' married. An' if you keep on waitin' like this till you're old there won't be any girls left for you to marry. Look how they're all marryin' off. Look at Gladys Brewster. She's got married last year. An' Ann Sikes, she's gettin' married next month. It's *you* I'm thinkin' of, 'cause I think it would be *nice* for you to be married, an' I'm afraid that if you wait much longer you won't find anyone to marry you. I mean, girls don' like marryin' *old* people. Nineteen an' not married! Gosh! Somehow I hadn't thought you was as old as that."

"*Shut* up," said Robert, who, in the character of the hero, had just received a threatening note from the murderer forbidding him to continue his investigations into the murdered man's death.

"Peggy Barlow's a nice girl, isn't she?" said William casually after a pause.

Robert was hot foot in pursuit of the murderer, but the name of the beloved arrested him. He flushed and said with an unsuccessful attempt at nonchalance: "D'you know her?"

"I've never spoke to her," said William, "but I've seen her. She's jolly pretty, isn't she? I mean, if I were grown up—say nineteen—I'd want to marry her before I got so old she wouldn't have me."

"Oh, you would, would you?" said Robert. "Well, you won't get anyone to marry *you* ever, let me tell you, unless you look and behave a jolly sight different from what you do now."

"Oh, won't I?" said William, stung by the reflection upon his manners and appearance. "Well, that's all *you* know about it. Well, let *me* tell *you* that there won't be a girl in the world that won't be *proud* to marry me when I'm grown up. I bet I'll be famous all over the world by the time I'm your age."

"Yes, famous for your dirty collars, perhaps," said Robert crushingly.

"Well, it was clean on this morning," said William. "Nothing's touched it but the air. I can't help air being dirty, can I?"

But Robert was again lost to the world around him. He was confronting the murderer in a dingy underground cellar lit only by a candle in a bottle.

After another short silence William said casually: "Have you asked this Peggy Barlow to marry you, Robert?"

The name of the beloved again drew Robert out of his underground cellar. He fixed a dreamy sentimental gaze on William, and then, realising that it *was* William and not the beloved, glared at him fiercely and said: "You mind your own business and shut up." From this William rightly concluded that he had not yet proposed to her.

Robert returned to the underground cellar and William to his meditations. Finally, William said:

"Have you wrote any poems to this Peggy Barlow, Robert?"

Robert, who was holding a pistol to the murderer's head, dropped it on hearing the beloved's name and returned to the morning-room.

"What d'you say?" he demanded curtly.

"I say have you written any poems to Peggy Barlow?" repeated William.

"*No*," said Robert fiercely, "and you can jolly well get out."

Robert here made quite a convincing movement as of one about to arise from his chair, and William got out with alacrity while Robert returned to the underground cellar.

* * *

William walked slowly down the garden path. Evidently the affair wasn't getting on as quickly as he had hoped. Robert hadn't proposed to her or even written a poem to her. William knew, of course, that every serious love affair included the writing of poems to the beloved. And it was certainly high time that Robert proposed to her. He'd been going about with her for nearly a week. A sudden misgiving came to William. Suppose this affair fizzled out as so many of Robert's affairs fizzled out, and that to-morrow or the day after Robert had almost forgotten her and was taking some other girl on the river while Peggy Barlow's blue eyes were smiling upon another swain. It had happened so often. . . . William had a further horrible vision of Robert's staying at home for years and years and years, still engaged in his swiftly-changing kaleidoscopic love affairs with the neighbouring damsels, till the bicycle, watch and wireless set were completely worn out. Something must be settled, and the sooner the better. There was no doubt at all that Robert was in love with Peggy Barlow, and someone must strike while the iron was hot. It was absurd that Robert hadn't written a poem to her yet. William returned to the house, found pencil and paper, and went upstairs to his bedroom.

There for over an hour he wrestled in the throes of creation, stopping at intervals to refresh himself from a bottle of liquorice water that he carried in his pocket. William was not a born poet and (unlike many people who are not born poets) he didn't enjoy writing poetry. He was upheld, however, in his laborious task by a pleasant vision of a house empty of Robert and by the thought of Robert's bicycle, watch and wireless set. And, of course, as he frequently told himself when he stopped for refreshment, he was helping Robert. He'd be jolly grateful to anyone that helped him like he was helping Robert. The result of his labours, though not perhaps in the highest traditions of poetry, was, at any rate, clear enough in its meaning, which is more than can always be said of the highest traditions of poetry. It ran as follows:

To Peggy Barlow.
    Your hair is gold,
    Your eyes are a sort of blue.
    Some people might not think you butiful,
    But I do.

> Your teeth are wite,
> Your eyes are blue and round.
> I should like to marry you,
>   Your loving Robert Brown.

William gazed at the finished production with whole-hearted satisfaction. He considered that he had very neatly combined an eulogy of the lady's personal charms with an unmistakable proposal of marriage. He'd spent a long time trying to find a word to rhyme with Robert Brown. Robert ought to be jolly grateful to him. . . .

He put it in an envelope, addressed it to Miss Peggy Barlow (he knew the address because Robert's envelope addressed to her lay every day in the letter basket), and went to his mother's writing-table to get a stamp. Having stamped it, he was just taking it to the front door, meaning to waste no time before he posted it, when Robert emerged suddenly from the morning-room and they collided violently in the hall. Both William and Robert were in a hurry. Robert, while engaged in a hand-to-hand struggle with the murderer upon the highest peak of the Alps in Switzerland, had suddenly remembered that he had promised to call for the beloved and take her out that afternoon, and that if he meant to be in time he'd better hurry. If he weren't in time, of course, he knew that it was the last appointment the beloved would make with him, for she was a damsel of spirit who wouldn't brook being kept waiting. So he leapt to his feet, flung himself out of the room and into William, who also felt that his present business was urgent and was hurrying accordingly. When they raised themselves from the sitting postures into which the impact had driven them, the envelope that William had been carrying lay on the floor between them, address side up. Robert gazed at it wildly, seized it and tore it

open. Then all was chaos. Robert raved and stormed
and executed immediate personal retribution upon William. He accused William of deliberately trying to ruin
his life. He said that no girl would look at him again after
receiving a thing like that and what on earth would
she have thought, and that there would have been
nothing left for him, Robert, to do but drown himself,
but that he'd have jolly well drowned him, William,
first.

Mrs. Brown, roused from her midday slumbers by the
uproar, came down to see what it was all about. Robert
had to go through it all again. He said that William had
nearly ruined his life and that no girl would have looked
at him again after getting a thing like that, and that there
would have been nothing left for him, Robert, to do but
drown himself, but that he'd jolly well have drowned
him, William, first. He demanded wildly of his mother
why William had not been strangled at birth, but had
been allowed instead to grow up to ruin people's lives for
them like this. He added with considerable bathos that
William jolly well wouldn't get that shilling now. Mrs.
Brown found her spectacles and read the offending
poem.

"How naughty of you, William!" she said at last.

"But I was trying to *help* him," protested William.
"He *wants* to marry her, doesn't he? He carries on as if
he did, anyway."

"Shut up," said Robert fiercely.

"Well, it'll be a long time before I try to help anyone
again," said William.

"If you want to help someone, William," said his
mother, "you can go and weed the rose-beds."

"Will you give me a shilling if I do?" said William.

"Certainly not," said Mrs. Brown.

"Well, I'm no good at weeding," said William. "Why

don't you get some of this weed-killer there's always such a lot about in the papers?"

"I jolly well know who I'd use it on if we had any," said Robert darkly, and added: "Good thing for you it didn't go. Wouldn't have been very nice for you to have to go through life with the knowledge that you'd ruined your brother's only hope of happiness."

"I don't know what you're talking about," said William. "I wasn't ruining your only hope of happiness. I was *helping* you. Well, if you don't want to marry her why do you carry on as if you did and——"

"Shut up," said Robert again.

Then he looked at the clock and discovered again that he'd have to fly if he wasn't going to keep the beloved waiting, which would indeed be the culminating ruin of his life, so he flew, leaving William to face the black void that this afternoon had suddenly become.

"I *earned* that shilling," he said darkly to his mother. "People get put in prison for doing things like that. It'd jolly well serve him right to get put in prison, too."

"It was very naughty of you to write that silly poem," said Mrs. Brown. "I'm sure you didn't mean to send it, but it was naughty of you to pretend you were going to."

"It was a jolly fine poem," said William. "I thought he *wanted* to marry her. I was only trying to help."

"Well, it doesn't help anyone to write silly poems like that," said Mrs. Brown mildly.

William sighed, despairing of the possibility of ever making anyone understand anything, then turned his attention to the black void.

"Well, what'm I goin' to do this afternoon without that shilling?" he demanded.

"What were you going to do?" said his mother.

"I was going to the fair," said William.

"Well, you can still go to the fair, can't you?" demanded Mrs. Brown.

"Go to the fair? With no money?" said William bitterly. "S'no use goin' to a *fair* without *money*."

"Well, dear, you shouldn't have teased Robert like that," said Mrs. Brown. "He's older than you and it's very wrong to make fun of him. Especially about a thing like that."

"I wasn't makin' fun of him," persisted William in a frenzy of despair and exasperation. "I keep *tellin'* you. I was tryin' to *help* him. I thought he *wanted* to marry her. It was a jolly good pome too, an' I took a lot of trouble over it an' if he'd had any sense he'd've been *grateful* to me. Well, he needn't blame *me* if no one'll marry him. I've done my best for him. He doesn't *deserve* anyone to marry him an' I'm sure I'm jolly sorry for anyone who does."

But Mrs. Brown had gone upstairs to continue her interrupted nap and William was left fulminating in the empty hall at a couple of mackintoshes that hung on the stand. He glared at them for a moment in silent scorn, ejaculated a bitter "huh!" at them, then flung out of the house, slamming the door.

The other Outlaws were waiting for him by the old barn. Their faces wore the care-free expectant expressions of those whose afternoon's enjoyment is secured.

"Got the shilling?" they called blithely to William as soon as he appeared. They asked the question not because they had any doubts about his having the shilling, but merely as an expression of their happy confidence.

Then they caught sight of his face and their glow faded.

"I say!" gasped Ginger. "He's not——"

"He *promised* it you," expostulated Henry faintly.

"Yes," said William bitterly. "He promised it me all right, an' then jus' because I tried to help him he took it off me."

"Din' he give you *any* of it," said Ginger.

"No," said William dramatically.

"But why'd he take it off you?" demanded Douglas.

"I've told you, haven't I?" said William impatiently. "'Cause I tried to help him. He wanted to get married to a girl an' I tried to help him. Well, if he'd've let me help him he'd've been almost married by now. Well, an' jus' 'cause I tried to help him get married to this girl he wanted to get married to, takin' a lot of trouble an' Brown's a jolly hard name to find anything that rhymes with, an' I bet a real pote, the sort that's famous and gets paid, couldn't've done it any better—well, jus' 'cause I took a lot of trouble to get him married to the girl he *wanted* to get married to—he got mad at me an' wouldn't give me the shilling."

"Well, I call that jolly mean," said Ginger emphatically.

"I call it more'n mean," said Douglas. "I call it stealin'."

"I call it more'n that," said William. "Well, seems to me anyone that'd do that wouldn't mind *what* they'd do. They'd murder anyone soon as look at 'em."

"Or worse than murder," said Ginger with sinister vagueness.

"It makes one want to go off an' be a robber," continued William whose feelings of bitterness had been deepened and enriched by this hymn of hate. "I've often thought I'd like to do something like that."

"Well, it's not much use goin' to the fair now," said Ginger, "without any money to spend."

"The nex' time Robert wants to marry anyone," said William, "he can jolly well fix it up himself. I'm not

"IT MAKES ONE WANT TO GO OFF AN' BE A ROBBER,"
CONTINUED WILLIAM.

going to help him anyway. If he comes to me nex' time *beggin'* me to help him, I won't. An' no one'll have him without a pome an' bet *he* won't be able to write a pome. It's not so easy as mos' people think it is. 'Specially with a name like Brown."

"I've often thought it would be fun to run away to sea same as people do in books," said Ginger, expressing the general feeling of reckless despair to which the situation had driven them.

"I used to think that," said William, "till I went on the sea. You ever been on the sea?"

Ginger admitted that he hadn't.

"Well, it's not a bit like what you'd think it is from books," said William. "It gives you a sort of feelin' that you don't find anythin' about in books. After I'd been on the sea I made up my mind that if I ran away I'd sooner set up as a robber than go to sea. I bet robbers never have that sort of feeling that sailors mus' have all the time. You only get it when you're on the sea an' I'd jolly well rather stay at home all my life than go away to sea an' have that sort of feelin' all the time same as what sailors mus' have."

"Well, we won't go away to sea then," said Douglas finally, "an' we can't start bein' a robber band an' terrorisin' the country-side till we're grown up so I don't see we can do *anythin'*."

"Well, I don' see why we shun't start bein' robbers an' terrorisin' the country-side now. I know I've had enough of tryin' to *help* people. So I'd jolly well like to have a go at terrorisin' them instead for a change. They're always terrorisin' me anyway an' takin' money off me an' I'd jolly well like to try it on *them*. If we got a place somewhere on the top of a hill where we could roll down stones an' boilin' pitch an' things onto people, I bet no one'd be able to take us. An' other people'll join us—criminals an' fugitives from justice an' such-like. I shun't be surprised if we get to rule the country in the end. That happens in foreign countries an' I don't see why it shun't happen here. Anyway, I'm jolly well sick of livin' an' ordin'ry life an' havin' all my money took off me. Yes," he added darkly, "an' I bet Robert'll wish he'd given me that shilling when I'm a robber chief an' he's on his bended knees to me beggin' for his life."

"All right," said Ginger, simply, "when'll we start?"

William, who hadn't realised that he was committing himself quite so definitely to his new career, was silent for a minute.

Then through the silence came mingled sounds of merriment from the distant fair-ground—the blare of the merry-go-rounds, the shouts of the showmen, the excited screams from the swings and helter-skelters. He thought of the shilling that should have been his and he steeled himself against softer feelings.

"We'll jolly well start this afternoon," he said firmly.

*　　　*　　　*

With unexpected good luck they found an empty house on the top of a hill.

"This'll be our fortress," said William, "an' if anyone comes to try'n' take it we'll pour down boilin' pitch on them'n' drive 'em off."

"Where'll we get boilin' pitch from?" demanded Douglas.

"Oh, do shut up always makin' objections," said William. "How d'you think we'll ever get to be bandits terrorisin' the country-side if you start makin' objections to everythin' anyone says? *Anyone* can get boilin' pitch. They mend the roads with it. It's all over the place. An' we'll roll stones from the house down onto 'em an' throw slates an' hundreds of more people'll join us an' then when we've got enough for an army we'll conquer England an' then——"

"Yes, but what're we goin' to do now?" demanded Douglas. "I mean this afternoon."

William, brought down abruptly again from his flights of fancy, looked about him vaguely. They were sitting outside the empty house that was to be their fortress, gazing down into the valley. The irritating, enchanting sounds of the fair floated across to them from the meadow. Once more it stiffened William's resolve.

"We'll jolly well start at once," he said grimly, "an' in time to come there'll be books wrote about us with pictures an' such-like same as there is about history. The first thing is to get into the house an' fortify it an' then get wood for a fire. An' while you're doin' that I'm goin' to start off as a bandit. I'm goin' down to the village an' I bet I come back with some money. I bet I jolly well scare it out of someone. I'm goin' to get a mask same as they have in books. So that's one of the first things I've gotter do—after gettin' into the house."

Getting into the house proved less difficult than they had thought it would. The windows were sash windows and William slid back the catch with his penknife and opened one easily. The inside of the house proved to be in a fascinating state of disrepair, with traces of rat inhabitants that delighted the explorers. William, however, resisted the temptation to dally in this paradise.

"I'm goin' to start off bein' a bandit," he said. "I'll have a look round for rats an' things afterwards."

Bidding farewell to his gallant band he set off down the hill. Under their eyes he felt himself a superhuman figure, a mighty giant of a bandit endowed with miraculous strength. It was not till he'd reached the road in the valley that he shrunk to human stature. He encountered a farm labourer of sturdy physique, who, in passing, playfully pushed him into the ditch, and the *rencontre* brought William up sharply against the facts of life. Not thus were the bandits of his imagination treated by passers by. Then he consoled himself by the reflection that after all the smallest men were really the most terrible because, as William put it to himself, all their strength went to their brains. And, of course, he'd soon grow as big as anyone—or rather bigger. And after all it was cunning that told in a bandit, not strength, and he was jolly well as cunning as anyone. And, of course, there was the mask. He must get a mask. There was something terrifying about a mask. No one would push you into a ditch if you were wearing a mask. In all the stories he'd ever read a mask inspired terror in the beholder. But he was again brought up against the hard facts of life. He hadn't any money to buy a mask. Then—he looked down suddenly and saw his knees covered with black slime from the involuntary descent into the ditch. It was as good as a mask any day. Without stopping to think further, William leapt again into the ditch and took up a handful of the glutinous mud. Smeared across the top of his face, it would, he decided, make as good a mask as you could buy anywhere. He worked with silent concentration for some moments and the result, as he imagined it, was highly satisfactory. His imagination erred, however, on the side of optimism. He did not look a sinister figure with a cruel mouth and eyes that glared malevolently through a black mask. He looked what he was, a mud-bedaubed schoolboy. The mud had refused to confine itself to the upper part of his face. It had spread itself and splashed itself in joyous abandon over the whole of his head, face and collar. But William was happily unaware of this. He walked with a sinister gait and a threatening expression. He held a small twig in his hand as though it were a revolver.

On the opposite side of the road from the ditch was the bank that sloped down to the river. It was from here that William suddenly heard voices. He stopped to consider the situation. There were obviously two people there at least, and, despite the terrifying picture of himself that he carried in his mind's eye, he thought it rather imprudent to make his first attack upon more than one antagonist. Moreover, though he carried his twig with as great an air as if it had been a revolver of the latest and most dangerous type, and had, in fact, almost persuaded himself that it was, he was aware in his inmost mind that it was only a twig. He stood in the road irresolute for a few minutes considering the situation, a deep frown upon his mud-bedaubed countenance. Then the frown cleared. A tree grew on the roadside whose branches stretched over the bank to the river. He could climb this, make his way along the branches till he was exactly over the owners of the voices, then, hidden in the leafage, accost them in his most terrible voice, telling them that he had ten men up in the tree with him who all held loaded revolvers pointed at them and ordering them to deposit all their valuables upon the ground and go away without looking back. Otherwise they would be dead men. Then when they'd gone he'd slip down and collect the booty. Perhaps the girl (one of the voices was a girl's) would be wearing diamonds or pearls that he'd be able to sell for hundreds of pounds. It would be a jolly good beginning.

He climbed the tree and made his way along the branch till he was just over the speakers and then—a strange chill crept over him. One of the voices was horribly familiar. Cautiously he peeped through the

branches. Below him on the grass on the river bank sat
Robert and a girl.

*   *   *

Robert had been barely in time for the meeting with
the beloved. So barely, in fact, that he arrived to it hot
and panting and for the first five minutes, at any rate,
could not do himself justice. Even when his breath and
normal colour returned, he was distrait and absent in his
manner. He couldn't help thinking about that little
wretch. He kept going hot and cold at the thought of
what might have happened if the note had actually
been sent. She'd never have looked at him again. And
the most beautiful girl in the world. His whole life
would have been completely ruined. The little wretch
. . . the little *wretch*. Someone ought to have wrung his
neck.

"Well, where shall we go?" said the beloved.

"Wherever you like," said Robert. He tried to make
his voice soulful and adoring, but succeeded only in
sounding hoarse.

"Have you got a sore throat?" said the beloved.

"Nothing to speak of," said Robert, who could not
bear to forfeit the note of sympathy in her voice.

"That's all right," said the beloved, dismissing the
note of sympathy from her voice. "I think a sore throat
always makes people sound as if they were drunk, don't
you?"

Robert hastily assumed a treble voice and said that he
hadn't got a sore throat at all. The beloved, losing
interest in the subject, demanded again where they were
going that afternoon.

"Where would you like to go?" said Robert again,
carefully retaining his clear treble voice.

"I do wish you had a few ideas," said the beloved.

"You never seem to have any. I never knew anyone with so few ideas."

Robert searched feverishly in his head for ideas.

"What about going down by the river?" he said at last. "It's always nice by the river. It's never too hot or too cold there, you know."

"Of course it's too hot and too cold there sometimes," said the beloved. "It depends on the weather not the place."

"No, but it ought to be all right there to-day," said Robert meekly.

Robert's home circle, among whom Robert liked to show himself of a proud and haughty spirit, would have been surprised at his meekness when alone with the beloved.

"All right," said the beloved without enthusiasm. "I suppose one might as well go there as anywhere."

They went down to the river bank and settled themselves comfortably on the grass beneath a tree, and there the hauteur of the beloved began to melt as Robert told her not for the first time what a difference her coming into his life had made to it, how the thought of her had roused noble feelings and aspirations to which formerly he had been a stranger. Robert said that to all his lady loves in succession, and sincerely meant it in each case. For Robert, as I have said, was no idle philanderer. Each infatuation was, in its turn, the One True Love of his life. And, as he talked, the stormy feelings aroused by his *rencontre* with William faded from his breast and peace stole into it. Here, at least, he was far enough away from the little wretch. Here, at least, the little wretch couldn't come ruining his life. He glanced up at the tree above him, and became aware of a curious phenomenon. The light and shade on the leaves had at one point taken on a curious and striking likeness to William's face. He

shuddered at the horrible fancy and looked quickly
away, answering rather absently the beloved's question
as to when exactly he'd first begun to feel like that about
her. Then, realising her question, he answered with
enthusiasm. From the first time he met her. The very
first. He remembered the first time he met her. There
was a certain horrible fascination about that curious
effect of light and shade in the tree above. He had to
look to see if it were still there. He raised his head and
threw a quick, half-apprehensive glance. Yes, it was still
there. It seemed to give an exact reproduction of
William's face—only making it black instead of white.
Most curious, most unpleasant. Just when he wanted to
forget the little wretch and how he'd nearly ruined his
life.

"I don't believe you really care for me a bit," the
beloved was saying. "You don't sound as if you do. You
say those things as if you had to say them and didn't
mean them a bit."

"I *do* mean them," protested Robert, casting another
fascinated glance into the tree to see if the phenomenon
were still there. It was.

"Whatever do you keep looking at up in the tree?"
said the beloved, craning her neck, too, to look up into
the branches.

It was at this moment that Robert realised with a
shock of horror beyond mortal power of description that
the face in the tree above him was not a trick of light and
shade but was actually the face of William, smeared with
some black substance, looking down at him. The sight of
the beloved, craning her head in order to see this
monstrous sight, increased his horror to nightmare
proportions.

"Look," he said sharply, pointing across the river.
"Look there!"

The beloved's eyes descended hastily from the tree and followed the direction of his pointing finger.

"Well," she said, "what is it?"

Robert gazed at the spot where he had pointed. There was nothing but the grass-covered bank of the opposite side on the river. He smiled a ghastly smile, and put up a hand as if to loosen his collar.

"I—I thought I saw something," he said. "I—I thought I saw something over there."

"What did you think you saw?" said the beloved.

"I—I don't know," said Robert. "I—I just thought I saw something."

"Well, I wish you wouldn't," said the beloved coldly. "You gave me quite a start shouting out 'Look!' like that, as if someone had fallen in or something." Then her manner softened and she said:

"When was it you said you first began to feel like that about me?"

"The first time I saw you," said Robert, speaking in a low whisper so that the words should not reach the listening William.

"Do speak up, I can't hear what you say. Tell me again, anyway, how did it make you feel?"

Robert swallowed. He felt like a man in the throes of a nightmare. The knowledge of William above listening to every word of the conversation was the culmination of the horror.

"Let's go further up the bank, shall we?" he said. "It's not very nice here, is it?"

"Oh, it's all right," said the beloved, "I can't be fagged to move any more. What's the matter with you this afternoon? You're very restless. Thinking you see things and always wanting to move on. Go on with what you were telling me. You said that after you knew me you felt that your life had been wasted up to then. How did you feel that your life had been wasted?"

Robert opened and closed his mouth like an expiring fish without emitting any sound.

"You said yesterday that it made you feel you wanted to be kind to everyone for the rest of your life. . . ."

Robert coughed loudly to prevent further confidences reaching the listening William. He had had sinister proof of William's retentive memory in such circumstances.

"What an awful cough," said the beloved without much sympathy. "Is that your throat again?"

"Yes," he said faintly, "I think it's a bit damp here. Let's move on a bit, shall we?"

"It's not a bit damp," snapped the beloved. "I can't think what's the matter with you. What on earth do you keep staring up at the tree for? What *is* there——"

She turned her face up again to examine the branches above her.

"*Look!*" said Robert wildly, pointing again to the empty expanse of grass on the opposite bank.

The beloved started and once more followed the direction of his pointing finger.

"Well, I don't see anything," she said. "What on *earth's* the matter with you? Anyone would think you'd gone potty. Why——"

It was at this minute that William, who had completely forgotten that he was a bandit and was trying to conceal himself more thoroughly in the branches in order to hear the rest of this intriguing conversation that seemed likely to supply him with weapons against Robert for many years to come, overbalanced and came crashing down from the tree at the feet of the beloved. There he sat up and rubbed his head. The beloved, speechless with amazement, gazed for some moments at his mud-covered hair and face.

Then she said faintly:

"Good heavens! What an *awful* boy. Who is he?" She looked at the crimson-faced Robert as if for enlightenment.

And then, Robert, acting on the spur of the moment, made his great mistake.

"I've never seen him before," he said faintly.

William continued to rub his head in silence, waiting till the situation should make further demands upon him.

Robert, still crimson-faced, was gazing in front of him with a fixed glassy stare. The silence—of amazement on Miss Barlow's part, of caution on William's, and of sheer horror on Robert's—seemed unending. It was broken at last by Miss Barlow.

"Why were you up that tree?" she said sternly to William.

William considered this question for some time, and finally said:

"Well, I've gotter be somewhere, haven't I?"

Miss Barlow seemed rather impressed by the logic of this retort.

"I know," she said, "but why should you be up a tree? I mean, why can't you be——" she seemed to consider the places where William might be, and finally said, "well, at home?"

William emitted a bitter laugh.

"You wun't ask me that if you knew what sort of a home I've got."

In saying this he glanced at Robert for the first time—a glance devoid of any sort of expression whatsoever.

Miss Barlow's curiosity was roused.

"Why, what sort of a home have you got?" she said. "Aren't they kind to you?"

William again emitted the bitter laugh.

"GOOD HEAVENS! WHAT AN *AWFUL* BOY!" EXCLAIMED MISS
BARLOW. "WHO IS HE?"

"*Kind* to me!" he repeated ironically. "If I told you
how they treat me you'd hardly believe it."

"What a *shame!*" said Miss Barlow indignantly.
"Who is it? Your father?"

"It's my big brother chiefly," said William, with
another expressionless glance at the still purple-faced
Robert. "You'd hardly believe how he treats me."

"Is he—really unkind to you?" said Miss Barlow. "I
mean does he actually ill-treat you?"

"He ill-treats me something dreadful," said William, "knocks me about and take my things off me an'—an' if ever I have any money he takes that off me too."

WILLIAM RUBBED HIS HEAD IN SILENCE TILL THE SITUATION SHOULD MAKE FURTHER DEMANDS ON HIM.

"Why?"

"Jus' for spite. Las' week someone gave me a mouth organ an' I was learning some nice tunes on it—some nice quiet tunes—an' jus' for spite 'cause he was jealous of me bein' able to play nice tunes on it when he couldn't he took it off me an' threw it away."

"He sounds *horrid*, I think," said Miss Barlow sympathetically. Then she turned to Robert, and said, "don't you?"

Robert again opened and closed his mouth soundlessly like an expiring fish.

"An' not long ago," went on William, "I'd got a lovely Indian head thing with feathers an' he took it from me an' threw it into the fire."

Here Robert found his voice.

"Perhaps you'd put a tin-tack on his chair for him to sit on," he suggested hoarsely.

"*Me?*" said William, and Miss Barlow said coldly:

"I'm sure he'd never do a thing like that. To me he looks terribly neglected. Look at his face and hair and clothes. He looks as if no one had ever troubled to wash him since he was born."

"He was perfectly clean this morning," said Robert. "He gets like that in about five minutes. It's impossible to keep him clean."

"I thought you'd never seen him before," said Miss Barlow.

"I haven't," said Robert. "I—I mean he *looks* like that sort of a boy to me."

"I think you're very unkind," said Miss Barlow distantly. "The poor boy's neglected and ill-treated. You might, at least, show a little sympathy. Tell me more about your home, dear," she said to William. "are your father and mother unkind to you too?"

"No, it's mostly this brother," said William. "He's awful to me. Never leaves me alone. Always on at me."

"What a shame," said Miss Barlow again.

Robert unable to restrain himself broke in furiously. "Who completely spoilt my razor last week fooling about with it so that it's never been any use since?" he said sternly.

"How on earth should *he* know who spoilt your razor?" said Miss Barlow coldly.

"I—I thought perhaps he might," said Robert, lamely.

"Why should he?" said Miss Barlow.

"I don't know," said Robert.

She turned to William again.

"Do you live near here?"

"Only about three miles off," said William.

"Who are your people?" said Miss Barlow.

Robert had a sudden fit of coughing that bordered on apoplexy, during which he threw at William a glance that hovered between menace and appeal.

William met it with his blankest stare.

"I think you must be tubercular," said Miss Barlow to Robert. "I hope I haven't caught it from you."

"I'm not," Robert assured her earnestly. "I'm most healthy. I always have been most healthy."

"This brother I was tellin' you about," said William, "once he thought he'd drunk poison because there was poison on the bottle and he said he'd got most awful pains and was dying till he found that it was only liquorice water and someone'd forgot to wash the label off."

"That was years ago," said the unhappy Robert, and added hastily, "at least, I should imagine so."

"Why? Do you know his brother?" said Miss Barlow.

"Er-no, no, of course I don't," said Robert.

"Because, if you do, you ought to have protected the poor little chap," went on Miss Barlow, "and stopped him being so ill-treated."

"No, of course I don't know him," sputtered Robert.

"Well, I hope if you did you'd have protected the poor little chap," went on Miss Barlow compassionately. Robert made an inarticulate sound that might have meant either that he would have protected the poor little chap or that he'd have murdered the poor little chap, and William continued: "This brother I told you about," he said casually, "he's always goin' about with girls!"

"Girls?" said Miss Barlow. "Do you mean with different girls?"

"Yes," said William. "He never likes one for long. Las' month he was going about with a girl called Dolly Clavis."

"I know her," said Miss Barlow. "A very plain girl with red hair."

"He said she was the mos' beautiful girl he'd ever met in all his life," said William. "He said that he'd never call any girl really beautiful again what hadn't red hair. He said she made all girls with fair hair look washed out."

Miss Barlow tossed her fair head. "I can't say I think much of his taste," she said coldly.

"No, I don't, either," said William ingratiatingly. I *like* fair-haired girls."

"And he really thinks Dolly Clavis beautiful?" said Miss Barlow.

"Yes. At least, he *did*," said William, "but he's going about with another girl now."

"Who's he going about with now?" said Miss Barlow.

At this point the unhappy Robert had a fit of choking so violent and prolonged that further conversation was for some minutes quite impossible. When at last he had to stop choking from sheer lack of breath, Miss Barlow gazed at him coldly and said: "I think you ought to see a specialist."

"No, I'm perfectly all right," Robert assured her breathlessly, "perfectly all right. Absolutely all right."

"Well, I don't think you are," said Miss Barlow. "I think you've got what they call galloping consumption.

I've heard of it coming on suddenly like this. It seems to have come on since we started out."

"I haven't got it," protested Robert. "I haven't got anything. It was just a—a sort of spasm."

"This brother I'm telling you about," said William, "he's gotter awful temper that comes on suddenly like that."

"The one who's so unkind to you?" said Miss Barlow.

"Yes," said William, "and the one that said that all fair-haired girls looked washed out."

"I think he sounds awful," said Miss Barlow. "I wonder if I've ever met him. What's his name?"

At this point William felt something small and hard and round pushed into his hand by Robert. A sixpence. He pocketed it thoughtfully. The possibilities of the situation were beginning to dawn on him. He had looked upon it solely as a situation that would enable him to get his own back on Robert. Now he saw it as a situation that might retrieve his fallen fortunes.

"Well, I don't know that I ought to tell you," he said. "I don't know that it's quite fair on him. I mean, what I've told you might sort of put you against him so's if you met him you mightn't like him——"

"I certainly shouldn't like him," said Miss Barlow with spirit.

"Well, then it seems sort of mean to tell you his name," said William.

"I don't think so at all," said Miss Barlow earnestly. "I think you ought to. I think that it isn't fair to let a person go about without people knowing what he's really like. I think it isn't fair to people. I mean, people *ought* to know what a person's like. I might meet him and—well, he might seem all right and of course I'd not know that he was the one that was so unkind to you and thinks Dolly Clavis the most beautiful girl in the world."

"I *don't* think Dolly Clavis the most beautiful girl in the world," put in the goaded Robert.

"Who said you did?" said Miss Barlow, "we're talking about the boy's brother. You seem very self-centred this afternoon."

"I—I think *you're* the most beautiful girl in the world," said Robert.

But Miss Barlow's whole interest was centred on William.

"*Do* tell me your brother's name," she said. "I think you really ought to. Is he nice looking?"

"No; *very* ugly," said William emphatically.

Robert choked in impotent fury.

"Well, I think that people *ought* to know what he's really like and, of course, if you just meet a person in the ordinary way you often never find out."

"Y-yes," said William thoughtfully. "Perhaps I ought to."

As he spoke, he moved his hand nearer Robert's, and something passed quickly between them. William fingered it tentatively. A shilling.

"No, I don't think I'd better," he said, slipping it into his pocket; "it doesn't seem fair to him. Seems as if I'd set people against him."

"But if he's so unkind to you——"

"Oh, yes, he's jolly well *that*," said William.

"Well, it might pull him up a bit," said Miss Barlow, "and make him more careful when he found that people knew what he really was like."

"Y-yes," said William, "yes, I see what you mean."

"What I simply *can't* understand," went on Miss Barlow, "is him thinking Dolly Clavis the most beautiful girl in the world."

"I felt quite different after I'd met you," said Robert earnestly.

She looked at him in surprise.

"Quite different from what?" she said.

"Oh-er-different from what I felt before," said Robert lamely.

"I don't know what you're talking about," she said. "You seem to me quite potty to-day."

"Yes, I see what you mean," said William. "I see what you mean about perhaps it doin' him good to tell you his name. Yes, perhaps it *would* be kind to him really. It——"

Something harder and rounder passed into William's hand. A half-crown. William rose. Unlike the ordinary blackmailer, he knew where to stop.

"Well," he said, "I'd better be going home."

"Won't you tell me his name?" said Miss Barlow in a tone of deep disappointment.

"No," said William bluntly, "I don't think I will. Good-bye."

She watched his retreating figure.

"I don't believe there was a word of truth in it from beginning to end," she said at last.

"Neither do I," said Robert. "At least, I bet that if he has got a brother, he's quite a decent sort of chap."

"I dare say he is," said Miss Barlow.

"He looked to me like a real little ruffian," said Robert.

"I dare say he was," sighed Miss Barlow. "I don't know much about boys."

"They're all little wretches," said Robert.

"I dare say they are," said Miss Barlow. "*You* don't think Dolly Clavis beautiful, do you?"

"I think she's hideous," said Robert. "I think *you're* heaps more beautiful than anyone else in the world."

"That's awfully sweet of you," sighed the beloved.

* * *

William found his bandits awaiting him by the empty house. They looked bored and depressed. Ginger's finger was wrapped in a blood-stained, grimy handkerchief, Douglas was limping, and Henry's face was cut.

"You've been a *jolly* long time," said Ginger gloomily.

"Well, you ought to've had plenty to do," said William.

"Well, we hadn't," said Ginger. "The fire wouldn't light. An' we caught a rat an' it bit my finger nearly through, an' Douglas fell through a hole in the floor and nearly got killed, an' Henry tried to get through a place where the window was broken an' it wasn't big enough, an' I bet you've not got anythin'."

"Well, I have," said William, and he proudly brought out his spoils.

They gazed at him with admiration and amazement.

"How d'you get it?" said Ginger.

"Jus' bandittin'," said William casually. "I jus' made folks give up their money to me."

"What'll we do with it?" said Ginger, accepting the explanation quite simply.

Through the air came the glorious strains from the fair-ground.

"Let's go to the fair," said William. "An' then go on livin' ordinary again. I don' think there's *really* much in this bandittin' business."

"Neither do I," said Ginger, sucking his bitten finger.

"Nor me," said Douglas, rubbing his leg.

"Nor me," said Henry, stroking his face.

"All right. Come on," said William. "We'll go'n' spend the money at the fair."

Singing zestfully and untunefully, the Outlaws walked down the hill to the fair-ground.

Chapter 5

William and the Prize Cat

William and Ginger ambled slowly down the lane. Henry and Douglas had succumbed to a local epidemic of mumps and so William and Ginger were the only two representatives of the Outlaws at large. Each carried sticks and slashed at the grass by the roadside as he went along. The action was purely mechanical. Neither felt properly dressed out of doors unless he had a stick to slash at things with.

"Couldn't we get underneath the flap?" Ginger was saying.

"No," said William, "I thought of that. They've got someone there to stop you. Jimmie Barlow says he tried that yesterday, and it wasn't any good."

"You asked your father for money, din't you?" said Ginger.

"Yes," replied William bitterly, "and he said that he'd give me some if ever he noticed me being clean and tidy and quiet for three days together. That's a jolly mean way of sayin' 'no.' 'Sides, if ever I was like that there prob'ly wouldn't be any circus here so it would all be wasted and if there was I bet I wouldn't feel like goin' to it if I'd been clean and tidy and quiet for three days. I bet you wouldn't feel much like doin' anythin' if you'd been clean and tidy and quiet for three days. You asked your father, too, din't you?"

"Yes," said Ginger gloomily, "an' he went on and on and on and on about every window or anythin' that had got broke in our house for—for all my life I should think. He even remembered that time that I fell through the roof and broke the skylight. Well, that's so long ago I'd almost quite forgot that till he said about it. Anyway I hurt myself jolly badly over it an' you'd have thought he'd've been sorry instead of makin' it an excuse not to give me money to go an' see a circus."

"We haven't even anythin' we can sell," said William taking up the antiphonic lament. "I tried to sell my whistle to Frankie Dakers, but it hasn't any whistle in and he wouldn't buy it. He'd been to the circus."

"Jolly fine one, isn't it?" said Ginger wistfully.

"He said it was a rippin' one," said William. They walked on for a moment in silence, frowning and slashing absently at the roadside with their sticks.

Then suddenly round a bend in the roadway, all unprepared and unexpecting, they ran into the Hubert Laneites, their rivals and enemies from time immemorial. Hubert Lane, standing in the centre of his little band, smiled fatly at them. It happened to be a period of armed neutrality between the two bands. Had it been a period of open warfare the Hubert Laneites would have fled on sight of even two of the Outlaws, for the Hubert Laneites, though possessed of deep cunning, lacked courage and strength in open warfare. But as it was, Hubert Lane smiled at them fatly.

"Hello," he said, "been to the circus?"

Hubert Lane had a knack of finding out most things about his enemies, and he was well aware that the Outlaws had not been to the circus, because they had not enough money for their entrance fee.

"Circus?" said William carelessly. "What circus?"

"Why the one over at Little Marleigh?" said Hubert, slightly deflated.

"Oh *that* one," said William smiling, "you mean *that* one. It's not much of a circus, is it?"

Hubert Lane had recourse to heavy sarcasm.

"Oh no," he said. "It takes a much grander circus than *that* to satisfy *you*, I s'pose?"

"Well," said William mysteriously, "I know a jolly sight more about circuses than *most* people."

The Hubert Laneites laughed mockingly.

"*How* do you know more about circuses than most people?" challenged Hubert.

William considered this in silence for a moment, wondering whether to have been born in a circus and worked in it till he was rescued and adopted by his present parents, or to have an uncle who owned all the circuses in England and took him to see one every week. He rejected both claims as being too easy for Hubert to disprove, and contented himself with saying still more mysteriously;

"*Wouldn't* you like to know?"

Hubert eyed him uncertainly. He suspected that William's assurance of manner and deep mysteriousness of tone was bluff, and yet he was half impressed by it.

"All right," he said. "You prove it. I'll believe it when you prove it."

"All right," retorted William. "You jolly well wait and see."

Hubert snorted contemptuously, deciding that this unfounded claim of William's would make a good weapon of offence against him for some time to come, and already framing in his mind simple unvarnished allusions to it as, "Who said he knew all about circuses an' couldn't afford to go to the one at Little Marleigh?"

Such challenges, however, needed to be issued from a safe distance, so for the present he turned to another subject.

"I'm gettin' up a cat show to-morrow," he said innocently. "There's a big box of chocolates for the prize. Would you like to bring your cat along?"

The brazen shamelessness of this for a minute took away William's breath. It was well known that Hubert's mother possessed a cat of gigantic proportions, who had won many prizes at shows. That the Hubert Lane-ites should thus try to win public prestige for themselves, and secure their own box of chocolates by organising a cat show at which their own exhibit was bound to win the prize was a piece of assurance worthy of them.

"Like to enter your cat?" repeated Hubert carelessly.

William thought of the mangy and undersized creature who represented the sole feline staff of his household. Hubert thought of it too.

"I suppose it wouldn't have much chance," said Hubert at last, with nauseating pity in his voice.

"It would. It's a jolly fine cat," said William indignantly.

"Want to enter it then?" said Hubert, satisfied with the cunning that had made William thus court public humiliation. The Brown cat was the worst-looking cat of the village.

"All right," he said, "I'll put you down. Bring it along this afternoon."

William and Ginger walked dejectedly away.

*   *   *

Early that afternoon they set off, William carefully carrying the Brown cat, brushed till it was in a state bordering on madness, and adorned with a blue bow (taken off a boudoir cap of Ethel's) at which it tore furiously in the intervals of scratching William.

"It's got spirit, anyway," said William proudly, "and that ought to count. It's got more spirit than that fat ole thing of Hubert's mother's. I think spirit ought to count."

But Ginger refused to be roused from his dejection.

"It doesn't count," he said. "I mean it doesn't count *for* them—scratchin' the judges an' such like." He inspected their entry more closely and his dejection increased. "Why are there so many places where it hasn't got any fur?"

"It's always like that," said William. "It's quite healthy. It eats a lot. But it never has fur on those places. It's all right. It doesn't mean that there's anything wrong with it. It just means that—that it hasn't got fur on those places."

"And look at its ear. It's all gone funny."

"That's where it had a fight," explained William, "it goes out fighting every night. It's a jolly brave cat. I bet there's not many cats that fight as much as this one does."

As if to corroborate his statement, the cat shot out a paw and gave him a scratch from forehead to chin, then, taking advantage of his suddenly relaxed hold, leapt from his arms and fled down the road still tearing madly at its blue bow.

"There!" said Ginger. "Now you've gone and done it. Now we've got to go without a cat or not go at all, and they'll laugh at us if we go without a cat, and they'll call us funks if we don't go at all."

William considered these alternatives gloomily.

"An' they'll go on and on 'cause they know we can't go to the circus," he added.

"Go after it and try and catch it again," suggested Ginger.

"No, I'm jolly well not going to," said William. "I'm sick of it. I'd rather fight someone."

"Well, what shall we do?" said Ginger. "Go without a cat or just not go?"

"Let's sit down and wait a bit," said William, "an' try'n' think of a plan. We might find a stray cat bigger'n' their's. Let's jus' sit down an' think."

Ginger shook his head at William's optimism.

"I bet there aren't any stray cats nowadays. I never see any. And if there were they wouldn't just come when you wanted them. And if they did they wouldn't be the big fat sort of cat what like the Lane cat is."

They were sitting down on the roadside, their backs to the wood that bordered the road. William turned to look into the wood.

"There's wild cats anyway," he said, "I bet there's still a few wild cats left in England. I bet *they're* bigger than his mother's old cat. I bet that if we could find a wild cat and tame it and take it along it'd get the prize all right. I shun't be a bit surprised if there was some wild cats left in this wood. I'm goin' to have a look anyway."

And he was just going to make his way through the hedge that bordered the wood when the most amazing thing happened. Out of the wood gambolling playfully came a gigantic—was it a cat? It was certainly near enough to a cat to be called a cat. But it was far from wild. It greeted Ginger and William affectionately, rolling over on to its back and offering itself to be stroked and rubbed.

They stared at it in amazement.

"It's a wild cat," said William, "a tame, wild cat. P'raps hunger made it tame, or perhaps now that there aren't any other wild animals to fight wild cats have got

tame. P'raps it's the last wild cat left in England. Puss!
Puss! Puss!"

It leapt upon him affectionately.

"It's a *jolly* fine wild-cat," he said, stroking it, "and
we're jolly lucky to have found a cat like this. Look at it.
It *knows* it belongs to us now. Let's find something for it
to eat."

"We'd better take it to the show first," said Ginger,
"it's nearly time."

So they made a collar for it by tying Ginger's tie
loosely round its neck, and a lead by taking a boot-lace
out of William's boot and attaching it to the tie and set
off towards the Lane's house.

The wild cat ambled along the road with them in
friendly fashion. William walked slowly and ungrace-
fully in the laceless boot, but his heart was overflowing
with pride and affection for his new pet.

"I bet it's the finest wild cat anyone's ever found," he
said.

The show was to be held in the shed at the back of the
Lanes' house. The other competitors were all there,
holding more or less unwilling exhibits, and in the place
of honour was Hubert Lane holding his mother's enor-
mous tabby. But the Lane tabby was a kitten compared
with William's wild cat. The assembled competitors
stared at it speechlessly as William, with a nonchalant
air, took his seat with it amongst them.

"That—that's not a cat," gasped Hubert Lane.

William had with difficulty gathered his exhibit upon
his knee. He challenged them round its head.

"What is it, then?" he said.

They had no answer. It was certainly more like a cat
than anything.

"'Course it's a cat," said William, pursuing his
advantage.

"Well, whose is it then?" said Hubert indignantly. "I bet it's not yours."

"'It *is* mine," said William.

"Well, why've we never seen it before then?" said Hubert.

"D'you think," said William, "that we'd let a valu'ble cat like this run about all over the place? Why, this is one of the most famous cats in all the world. We'd have it stole in no time if we let it run about all over the place like an ordin'ry cat. This isn't an ordin'ry cat, this isn't. Let *me* tell you this is one of the most famous cats in all the world, a speshully famous cat that never comes out except to go to shows, and that's won prizes all over the world. An' we don't tell people about it either for fear of it being stole. Well, I've not got much time and I've got to get our cat back home, so if our cat's bigger'n yours you'd better give me the prize now, 'cause this cat's not used to be kept hangin' about before being give its prize."

The Hubert Laneites stared at William and his burden limply. It was no good. They had not the resilience to withstand this shock. They sagged visibly, eyes and mouth open to their fullest extent, gazing at the monster who sat calmly on William's knees rubbing its face against his neck affectionately.

Hubert Lane at last roused himself with an effort from his paralysis of amazement. He knew when he had met defeat. He took the large box of chocolates on which the Hubert Laneites had meant to feast that afternoon and handed it to William, still gaping at the prize winner. The other exhibitors cheered. They were not at all sorry to see the Hubert Laneites worsted. William put the box of chocolates under his arm and set off, leading his exhibit and shuffling awkwardly in his laceless boot. It was not till they reached the gate leading to the road that the Hubert Laneites recovered from their stupefaction. They recovered all at the same minute and yelled as with one accord.

"Who can't afford to go to the circus? *Yah.*"

William was still drunk with the pride of possession.

"It's a *jolly* fine wild cat," he said again.

"Where'll we keep it?" said Ginger practically.

"In the old barn," said William, "an' we'll not tell anyone about it. They'll only manage to spoil it somehow if they find out. We'll keep it there an' take it out walks in the woods an' bring it food from home to eat. Then I vote we send it in for some real cat shows. I bet it'll win a lot of money. I bet it'll make us millionaires. An' when I'm a millionaire I'm goin' to buy a circus with every sort of animal in the world in it, an' I bet I'll have a jolly fine time."

The mention of the circus rather depressed them and Ginger, to cheer them up, suggested eating the chocolates. They descended into the ditch (fortunately dry), and sat there with the prize cat between them. It seemed that the prize cat, too, liked chocolates and the three shared them equally, eating one each in turn till the box was finished.

"Well, it's had its tea now," said Ginger, "so let's take it straight to the old barn for the night."

"You don't know that it's had enough," said William, "it might want a bit of something else. I bet we get it up to my bedroom without anyone seeing us and give it a bit of something else to eat there. I bet we can easily get it up without anyone seein'."

They had reached William's home now.

He picked the animal up in both arms and concealing it inadequately in his coat entered the side door in a conspiratorial fashion followed by Ginger. As soon as he had reached the foot of the stairs, however, there came the sound of the opening of his mother's bedroom door and her footsteps on the landing. William turned and fled into the drawing-room still followed by the faithful Ginger.

"We'll just wait here till she's gone," he whispered.

Her footsteps descended the stairs and unmistakably began to approach the drawing-room.

"Here! Quick!" gasped William plunging behind a Chesterfield that was placed across a corner of the room. The triangular space thus formed was rather inadequate for the accommodation of William, Ginger and the prize cat, but by squeezing themselves together they just managed to get themselves into it. The prize cat was evidently of a philosophic disposition. It accepted this new situation as calmly as it had accepted all the other situations in which it had found itself that afternoon, licking William and pawing him with playful affection.

The door opened almost as soon as they had reached their hiding place and Mrs. Brown entered.

"I don't expect she'll stay here," whispered William breathlessly, holding his pet in both arms to keep it still.

But Mrs. Brown closed the door and sat down. From her bedroom window she had caught sight of a visitor coming up the drive and she had come down to the drawing-room in order to receive and dispose of her as quickly as possible.

Almost as soon as she had entered the maid announced "Miss Messiter," and a tall lady wearing horn-rimmed spectacles entered and, after greeting her effusively, took her seat on the Chesterfield behind which were William, Ginger and the prize cat.

William was so much occupied in restraining his prize cat as soundlessly as possible that he did not hear what the visitor and his mother were saying till they had been talking for several minutes. Then as his pet seemed to have settled down to sleep on the top of Ginger he turned his attention to what the visitor was saying.

"I *do* hope you'll come," she was saying. "I'm trying to get everyone in the village to promise to come. He's a *marvellous* speaker. In the forefront of the movement."

"Yes?" said Mrs. Brown vaguely. "The movement?"

"I told you, you know," said the visitor earnestly, "the Thought Mastery Movement. It's closely allied to Christian Science, of course, but it's wider. It embraces more spheres, so to speak. It begins with that of pain, of course, teaching that there's no such thing. No such thing at all. I never feel pain. Never. Why? Because my thoughts know that there's no such thing as pain so naturally they don't feel it. Never."

At this moment the prize cat who had made its way under the Chesterfield and discovered one of Miss Messiter's ankles on the other side put out an exploratory paw and touched it with extended claws. Miss Messiter uttered a scream.

"Whatever's the matter?" said Mrs. Brown.

The visitor was clutching her ankle.

"A sudden excruciating pain," she said.

"Neuritis perhaps, or arthritis," suggested Mrs. Brown soothingly. "They do come on suddenly."

"Where had I got to?" said the visitor, still rubbing her ankle.

"About your never feeling pain," said Mrs. Brown.

"Oh yes . . . well the *reason* I don't feel pain is simply that I've trained my thoughts to ignore it. My thoughts mechanically reject the notion of pain. It's all so simple." She withdrew her hand from her ankle to wave it in the air. "All so simple and so beautiful. The lecturer will put it to you in all its beautiful simplicity. You will never

THE PRIZE CAT HAD TOUCHED ONE OF MISS MESSITER'S
ANKLES, AND MISS MESSITER UTTERED A SCREAM.

feel pain again. When people say to me that they are in
pain I say to them: 'Pain? What is pain?' "

At this minute the prize cat put out his paw again in
order to experience a second time the delicious sensation of sinking his claws through Miss Messiter's woollen
stockings into her skin beneath.

"*Whatever's* the matter?" said Mrs. Brown when
Miss Messiter's scream had died away.

"Another of those excruciating pains," said Miss

"WHATEVER'S THE MATTER?" ASKED MRS. BROWN.

Messiter. "I can't explain it. I've never known anything of the sort before. Excruciating."

"Neuritis probably," said Mrs. Brown, showing more interest than she had shown in the Thought Mastery Movement. "I had a cousin who used to have it. It came on just like that."

But Miss Messiter was looking behind her.

"There's a boy behind the sofa," she said excitedly, "and he must have been running pins into my foot."

"I didn't," said William rising, partly to refute this accusation and partly in order to prevent the visitor's discoveries extending to Ginger and the prize cat. "I *never* stuck pins into her foot."

"But whatever are you doing there at all, William?" said his mother in a bewildered fashion.

"I jus'—jus' happened to be there," explained William coming out into the room, "when you came in an' I thought I'd jus'—jus' stay there till you'd gone but I never stuck pins into her foot. I couldn't have even if I'd wanted to 'cause I haven't any pins. And what's more," he continued bitterly, "I haven't any money to buy any pins even if I wanted some. If I'd got money to buy pins to stick into her foot I'd be going to the circus."

"How do you account for the excruciating pain that I felt then?" demanded Miss Messiter of him sternly.

"It must be neuritis," said William's mother. "I'm sure he didn't stick pins into your foot. He's very troublesome and untidy and I can't think *why* he was behind the sofa but I'm *sure* he wouldn't stick pins into your foot. He's never done anything like that."

"Then I must go at once and consult a specialist," said Miss Messiter firmly. "It was an *excruciating* pain. It came on quite suddenly, then went quite suddenly."

"I think that's the best plan," said Mrs. Brown deeply sympathetic. "I know that neuritis can often be cured if you catch it in the early stages."

"And I shall give up the organisation of the Thought Mastery Campaign. I think that it has been too much for me. I'm highly strung."

They drifted out into the hall. William cautiously returned to the corner of the room. Ginger was engaged in a fierce struggle with the prize cat who wanted to return to his investigations under the Chesterfield. He wanted to find the thing into which it was so pleasant to sink one's claws. He was uttering soft little growls as he fought with Ginger.

"Let's get him out quick," said William, "while they're talkin' at the front door."

Ginger, who was suffering agonies from cramp and was pinned helplessly beneath the prize cat, said in a muffled voice:

"A'right. You take him off me an' I'll try to get up."

William bundled his pet under his arm, and followed by the bowed and limping Ginger, went to the open window, scrambled through with a skill born of long practice and made his unobtrusive way through the shrubbery to the hole in the hedge that was the Outlaws' unofficial entrance to William's garden. Ginger was still limping.

"I've got that pain like what she said she'd got," he said. "Cruciating like what she said it was. I bet I've caught it off her. It mus' be something infectious. I shun't be surprise if I die of it."

"I think hers was the cat scratchin' her," said William.

"Was it?" said Ginger with interest. "I couldn't see what it was doin'. It'd got one of its hind feet in my mouth an' I couldn't get it out. It's a wonder I'm not choked."

But his pins and needles were wearing off and the prize cat, gambolling by their side, was so engaging that it gradually ousted every other thought from their minds.

"We'll take it to the old barn," said William, "then you go home an' get some food for it. I'd better not go home jus' now 'cause of that woman sayin' I stuck pins into her foot. My mother'll prob'ly want to go on talkin' about it."

"All right," said Ginger, "what'll I get it?"

"Milk an' a bit of bread an' butter an' a bit of cake," said William.

"Oh yes," said Ginger sarcastically. "Why don't you say a bit of roast turkey as well?"

"A'right," said William, "if you can find a bit of roast turkey, bring it along. I bet it'd eat it."

"I'll bring it what I can find with no one catchin' me," said Ginger. "It'll depend whether the larder window's open. I can't do more'n that, can I?"

"Get it as much as you can anyway," said William.

Ginger departed and William amused himself by playing with his prize cat. It was an excellent playfellow. It made little feints and darts at William. It rolled over on the ground. It ran away and challenged him to catch it. It growled and pretended to fight him. The time passed on wings till Ginger returned. Ginger's arms were full. Evidently the larder window had been open. He was carrying two buns, half an apple pie, and a piece of cheese. And yet, despite this rich haul, his expression was one of deepest melancholy. He placed the things down absently upon a packing-case, and said:

"I met a boy in the road and he'd just met a man and he said that they were looking for a lion cub that had got away from the circus."

William's face dropped. They both gazed thoughtfully at the prize cat.

"I—I sort of thought it was a lion cub all the time," said William.

"So did I," said Ginger hastily.

After a long and pregnant silence, William said in a far-away voice:

"Well—I suppose we've gotter take it back." He spoke as one whose world has crashed about him. In his mind had been roseate dreams of a future in which every day the lion cub gambolled round his feet, played hide and seek with him and attacked him with growls of mock ferocity. Life without the lion cub stretched grey and dark before him, hardly worth living.

"I s'pose we've gotter," said Ginger. "I s'pose it's stealin' if we don't, now that we know."

They placed the food before the cub and watched it with melancholy tenderness.

It ate the buns, sat on the apple pie and played football with the piece of cheese.

Then they took up the end of William's boot-lace again and set off sorrowfully with it to Little Marleigh.

*   *   *

The proprietor of the circus received the truant with relief, and complimented the rescuers on its prompt return. They gazed at it sadly, Ginger replacing his tie and William his boot-lace.

"He's a cute little piece, isn't he?" said the proprietor. "Don't appear yet. Too young. But goin' to lap up tricks like milk soon. . . . Well, I'd better be gettin' a move. Early show's jus' goin' to begin. Thank you, young sirs."

"I s'pose," said William wistfully, "I s'pose we couldn't *do* anythin' in the show?"

The proprietor scratched his head.

"What c'n you do?" he said.

"I c'n stand on my hands," said William, "an' Ginger can pull funny faces. Jolly funny ones."

The proprietor shook his head.

"Not in our line," he said. "But—tell you what. I *am* short-handed, as it happens. A man jus' come over queer an' gone home. We could do with another hand. Jus' movin' things off an' on between turns. Care to help with that?"

So deep was their emotion that William broke his

boot-lace and Ginger nearly throttled himself with his tie.

"I should—jolly well—think—we would," said William hoarsely.

*　　　*　　　*

The Hubert Laneites sat together in the front row. They'd all been to the circus earlier in the week but they'd come again for this last performance, partly in order to be able to tell the Outlaws that they'd been twice and partly to comfort themselves for the fiasco of their cat show.

"I say," said Hubert Lane to Bertie Franks, "I say, won't old William be mad when we tell him we've been again?"

"Yah," said Bertie Franks, "an' I say, fancy him havin' the cheek to say he knew more about circuses than us an' not even been once. We won't half rag him about it. We——"

His voice died away. He stared down into the ring. For there unmistakably was William setting out the little tubs on which the performing ponies performed. He rubbed his eyes and looked again. He hadn't been mistaken. It was William.

"Golly!" he said faintly.

All the Hubert Laneites were staring at William, paralysed with amazement.

"Golly!" they echoed and drew another deep breath as Ginger appeared carrying the chairs on which the clown pretended to do acrobatic feats. Then the circus began. The Hubert Laneites did not see the circus at all. They were staring fascinated at the opening of the tent into which William and Ginger had vanished. After the first turn they emerged and moved away the little tubs and brought out a lot of letters which they laid on the ground for the talking horse to spell from. After that turn William came out alone and held a hoop for Nellie, the Wonder Dog, to jump through.

Not once did the expressions of stupified amazement fade from the faces of the Hubert Laneites.

THEN WILLIAM CAME OUT ALONE AND HELD A HOOP FOR NELLIE THE WONDER DOG TO JUMP THROUGH.

After the circus they walked home dazedly as if in a dream.

*   *   ·   *

The next day they approached William cautiously, and with something of reverence in their expressions.

"I say, William," Hubert said humbly, "tell us about it, will you?"

"About what?" said William.

"About you helpin' at the circus."

"Oh *that*," said William carelessly. "Oh, I gen'rally help at circuses round about here. I don't always go into the ring like what I did yesterday, but I'm gen'rally in the tent behind helpin' with the animals. Trainin' them for their tricks. Gettin' 'em ready an' such-like. I suppose that one circus tells another about me and that's why they're always askin' me to help. I *said* I knew a jolly sight more about circuses than what you did, you remember."

"Yes," said Hubert Lane still more humbly, "it must be jolly fun, isn't it, William?"

"Oh, it's all right," said William, "it's hard work an' of course it's jolly dangerous. Trainin' the animals an' lockin' 'em up for the night an' such-like." He walked a few yards with an ostentatious limp, and then said, "the elephant trod on my foot yesterday when I was puttin' it in its cage,"—and he touched the scratch that his mother's cat had made. It was certainly quite a showy affair—"the bear gave me this the other night when I was combin' it out ready to go on and do its tricks. It's work not everyone would like to do."

They gazed at him as at a being from another and a higher sphere.

"I say, William," said Bertie Franks, "if—if they

want anyone else to help you—you'll give us a chance won't you?"

"I don't s'pose they will," said William, "'sides this circus has gone now and I don't know when another's comin'. It's dangerous work, you know, but I'm used to it."

And followed by their admiring eyes, he limped elaborately away.

He was limping with the other foot this time, but, of course, no one noticed that.

Chapter 6

William Adopts an Orphan

The Outlaws sat on their usual seat at the back of the school hall and surreptitiously played marbles while the lecturer on the school platform poured forth his spate of eloquence over their unresisting heads. They had not the slightest idea what he was talking about nor did they wish to have the slightest idea what he was talking about. To the Outlaws a lecture was merely a blessed respite from lessons, an oasis in the desert of a school morning, an hour when they could sit, screening themselves from the eye of Authority with an art born of long practice, and indulge in various recreations suitable to the occasion—such as racing the caterpillars they always carried on their persons, playing a game of cricket invented by William, in which a ruler took the place of a bat and a ball of blotting-paper the ball, or marbles. These were not, of course, all the diversions at their command. There was no end to the diversions at the command of the Outlaws during the hour of a school lecture. The idea that a lecturer had anything to say that could possibly be of any interest to anyone would have surprised them. A lecturer was to them simply a man who stood on a platform and talked. It did not matter what he said. You did not listen to him. He was not meant to be listened to.

His sole function was to provide an hour's relaxation in the middle of the morning. Had they been told after a lecture that it had been delivered in the Arabic language they would not have been in the least surprised. It might have been given in any language under the sun for all the Outlaws, deeply engrossed in caterpillar racing, ruler-and-blotting-paper-cricket, marbles and other pursuits, ever knew of it.

A marble dispatched with undue energy by Ginger rolled with a sudden re-echoing noise against the wall. A master rose from the front bench and walked slowly down the room. When he reached the back bench he found the four Outlaws sitting in rigid immobility, their eyes fixed with tense earnestness upon the lecturer. There were no traces of marbles, or caterpillars or anything but a burning interest in the lecturer and his lecture. The master was not for a minute deceived, but there was nothing to go on, so he returned to his seat.

After the short interval dictated by caution, the Outlaws relaxed the rigidity of their pose and the earnestness of their expressions, took out the ruler and balls of blotting-paper and began to play cricket. William bowled, Ginger batted, and Douglas and Henry fielded. The game proceeded uneventfully till an unguarded "swipe" on Ginger's part sent the ball high into the air. It travelled the length of the hall before it descended upon the head of the master who had already visited them. He rose from his chair and once more made his way slowly down to the back of the room. Again he found four boys in attitudes of frozen rigidity, gazing with rapt concentration at the lecturer. Again they appeared to be so deeply absorbed in the lecture as not even to notice his approach. He took up his position, leaning idly against the wall, watching them. The Outlaws, keeping the corners of their eyes upon him, realised with a sinking of their hearts, that he meant to stay there till the end of the lecture. In sheer self-defence they began to listen to what the lecturer was saying.

He was talking about orphans.

He represented an Orphanage to which the school evidently sent an annual contribution. He was pleading for an increase in the contributions. He was urging them to "adopt" an orphan, that is, to pay for its maintenance each year. He had just reached the climax of his speech.

"Those of you who are well fed, well clothed, well looked after,"—William's eye stole round. The master was still watching him. He stiffened to attention again—"owe a duty to those who are less well clothed and fed and looked after. You owe a debt to them. Good things are given to you in order that you may pass them on to others. It's your social duty. Some people, of course, take an orphan into their homes and give it all the blessings of home life. And I may say that prosperity always visits those homes. If every family in England adopted an orphan we could close down our Institutions. That, of course, is impossible, but I hope, dear boys, that you will all give of your best this year so that we may inscribe the name of your school in our book of honour as wholly maintaining an orphan each year."

He sat down amidst deafening applause.

The headmaster, who had been growing more and more restive, because the lecturer had overstepped his time and encroached upon the headmaster's Latin Prose class, arose and, with one eye upon the clock, said how much they all had enjoyed the lecture and how sorry they were that it had come to an end, and that he hoped that the annual Sale of Work would double their subscription, and as time was getting on would the boys go straight to their class rooms, please. Frenzied applause broke out again, prolonged to its utmost limits by the headmaster's Latin Prose class, who had been watching the clock with emotions as deep as the headmaster's, though of a different nature.

The master, who had appointed himself guardian angel of the Outlaws, gave them one last long, meaning glance and went to join his colleagues.

The Outlaws filed out with the others and went to an Algebra class. William could generally be trusted to hold up the Algebra class indefinitely by not understanding. William had a very plausible way of not understanding, and the Mathematical master was so new to teaching that he had not yet seen through it. He was a very conscientious young man and it was a matter of principle with him never to go on to the next step till everyone in the class fully understood the first one. He took William's expression of earnest endeavour at its face value. He thought that William was slow but well meaning and deeply interested in Algebra. And so, provided that William was in good form, no second step in any lesson was ever reached.

But William was distrait this morning. He let slip every opportunity of not understanding and did not even notice the reproachful glances and exhortatory nudges of his classmates. Various others of them tried to take his place but they lacked his skill. The master simply explained their difficulties and passed on. They could not, like William, think of another difficulty while he was explaining the first. The lesson progressed with unwonted speed and the master began to think that he was really making headway with them at last.

The Outlaws streamed out of school at the end of the morning with the others. They scuffled in and out of the ditch as usual on their homeward way, but William scuffled half-heartedly. Obviously his thoughts were still elsewhere.

"I say, we were jolly lucky," Ginger was saying, "I thought old Stinks was going to keep us in."

"Jus' like you," said Douglas disgustedly, "sendin' it right on to his head."

"It was jolly clever," said Ginger proudly, "I bet you couldn't have done it if you'd tried."

"No, neither could you if you'd tried," said Douglas.

William awoke from his reverie.

"Did you hear what he said about it bein' everyone's juty to adopt a norphan?" he asked.

"He *didn't*," said Ginger.

"He did," said William. "I know, 'cause I was listenin'. He said that everyone ought to adopt a norphan. He said that if everyone adopted a norphan all the orphan places would shut up."

"I wish *you'd* shut up."

"All right," encouraged William. "Come on. Shut me up."

Ginger closed with him, and they wrestled till the arrival of a motor car sent them both into the ditch. They found a frog in it, and after another fight that was to decide the ownership of the frog (during which the frog disappeared), climbed out, much invigorated and having completely forgotten what both fights were about.

"What'll we do this afternoon?" said Douglas (it was a half-holiday). "I votes we go to the stream."

"He said," put in William suddenly, "that *everyone* oughter adopt a norphan. He said it brought you luck."

"He didn't," said Ginger again.

"You're thinking of horse shoes," said Douglas, "they bring you luck."

"I'm not," said William doggedly, "I'm thinking of orphans. He said that everyone ought to adopt a norphan. You weren't listening. He said that it brought them luck. He din' say it in jus' those words. He said it in

the sort of langwidge letcherers talk in. But it meant that
it brought them luck."

"He din' say *everyone* ought to adopt one."

"He did. He said it was a sociable juty. He said that
everyone what had clothes ought to adopt a norphan.
You weren't listenin'. I was. Ole Stinks was starin' at me
so's I'd *got* to listen, 'cause with him starin' at me I'd
gotter look somewhere else, so I looked at *him*, an'
when you look at a person you've got to listen to what
they're sayin', even if you don't want to. An' he was
sayin' that it was everyone's sociable juty to adopt a
norphan 'cause it brought 'em good luck. He said all
about them havin' no home an' how we ought to adopt
'em so's to give 'em a home. He said it was a sociable
juty."

"What *is* a sociable juty?" said Ginger.

"Dunno," said William vaguely, "but it's what he
said."

"Well, anyway," said Ginger, "we can't adopt a
norphan, so let's talk about what we're goin' to do this
afternoon. I don' want to go fishin'. I'd rather play Red
Indians."

"We can ask our parents to, can't we?" said William.
"He said *everyone* ought to."

"He didn't. I votes we play Red Indians in Croombe
Woods."

"He did. You weren't listening. I was. I listened all
the time after old Stinks came to stare at us. He said that
if you'd got clothes you ought to take a norphan into
your home to give it blessings. He said it was a sociable
juty, and I'm going to ask my mother to adopt one,
anyway. I'm goin' to tell her what he said."

But there were William's favourite dishes for lunch
—baked potatoes and roast chicken, followed by
trifle—and he completely forgot the morning's lecture

till an aunt, who was lunching with them, fixed her eyes on him grimly and said: "I hope you realise how fortunate you are, William, to have such a good dinner, and I hope that you remember how many little boys there are who haven't got a good home like yours."

This reminded William. He swallowed half a potato and said:

"Mother, may we adopt a norphan!"

"*What!*" gasped his mother.

"I said may we adopt a norphan," repeated William rather impatiently.

"Why?" said his mother.

"A man came round to school this morning and said we'd got to," said William, "he said they brought you luck."

"*What?*"

"That's what he *said*," said William calmly, and with an air of one who disclaims all responsibility.

"*William!* I'm *sure* he never said that."

"He did," William assured her, "you weren't there. I was listening 'cause of old Stinks. He said it in lecturing sort of langwidge, but that was what it meant."

"I never heard such nonsense."

"Aren't you goin' to, then?" said William, disappointed.

"Going to what?" said Mrs. Brown.

"Adopt a norphan?"

"Of *course* not, William."

"Well," said William darkly, "if you don't get good luck now after this, don't blame me. You take a lot of trouble throwin' salt over your shoulder when you spill it and touching wood and that sort of thing, and yet you won't do a little thing like adoptin' a norphan. It isn't as if you'd have to pay anything for one. They *give* them

free. And you needn't buy new clothes for it. It could
wear mine. It could wear my Sunday suit while I was
wearing my weekday one, and my weekday suit while I
was wearing my Sunday suit. And it could sleep with me
and have half my food at meals. It needn't be any trouble
or expense at all, and this man said——"

"William, *will* you get on with your lunch and stop
talking."

"When I was young," said the aunt, "children were
seen and not heard."

William finished his meal in gloomy silence and then
went out to meet the other Outlaws.

"Well, I asked mine," he said disconsolately, "and
she wouldn't. Did you ask yours?"

It appeared that Douglas had mentioned it tentatively, but that his mother had rejected the idea as
summarily as William's.

"Well, then, let's go an' play Red Indians," said
Ginger impatiently.

But once William had formed a project it was never
easy to induce him to abandon it.

"Why shun't *we* adopt one?" he said slowly.

They stared at him open-mouthed with amazement.

"We *couldn't*," gasped Ginger.

"I don't see why not," said William aggressively.
"Why couldn't we as well as anyone else?"

"They wouldn't let us," said Douglas.

"They needn't know," said William. "We could keep
it in the old barn while we were at school an' it could go
about with us after school and we could get food for it
from home. Surely if all of us got a bit at each meal it
would be enough for one orphan. It could sleep with us
in turns. I guess we could easily get him up the stairs
without anyone seeing if we're careful. And he could get
under the bed when they come to call us in the morning

so that no one'd know he'd been sleeping there at all. And we could get him up something to eat for breakfast and then get him down to the barn while we go to school, without anyone knowing. Just keep a look out till no one's about and then jus' get him quickly downstairs. I bet it would be fun. Jus' like hiding a fugitive. I've always wanted to live in the days when they went in for hidin' fugitives. An' he'll be so grateful to us for givin' him a home that he'll do everything we tell him. He'll field balls for us when we play cricket an' make arrows for us an' be the squaw when we're playing Red Indians."

"But—but what about him not going to school?" objected Henry. "There's a lor that everyone's got to go to school. If they find you don't know anythin' when you grow up 'cause of not havin' been to school they put you in prison."

"I wish he could go to school 'stead of me," said William in a heartfelt tone, then suddenly his whole face lit up. "I *say!* I *know* what I'm goin' to do. I'm goin' to try'n' get one that looks like me an' let him go to school 'stead of me an' I'll stay away."

"Yes, an' then when you grow up an' they find you don't know anythin' they'll put you in prison," Henry warned him darkly. "There's a lor about it."

"I shan't care," said William. "I bet it'll 've been worth it. . . . An' he might get on better at school than me, too. He might get me a good report. My father's promised me five shillings if ever I get a good report. If he got me one I'd give him half."

"You'd never get anyone that looked jus' like you, William," said Ginger gazing at William's homely freckled countenance with its scowl of aggressive determination, and shock of wiry hair. "I don't s'pose that there *is* anyone else that looks like you."

"Why not?" challenged William threateningly, scenting a personal insult in the words.

Ginger, who had intended a personal insult, hastily withdrew from his position at William's tone and said:

"Well, I mean that we're all made jus' a bit different. It's a lor of nature. And they know your face so well at school that they'd know at once if anyone came without your face pretendin' to be you. An' then it'd spoil everything."

Despite themselves the Outlaws were becoming interested in the orphan scheme. William could always make the most outrageous schemes sound reasonable.

"How're you goin' to get one?" said Douglas.

"Well, how *do* they get them?" said William.

"I think they advertise," said Henry.

"All right," said William, "we'll advertise."

* * *

The notice was written and pinned up outside the old barn. Though short, it had caused the Outlaws much searching of heart. None of them was widely read, and it so happened that none of them remembered ever having seen the word "orphan" in print.

At first its spelling suggested no difficulties to them, and William wrote:

"Wanted an orfun," with no misgivings at all except for the blots that his crossed nib (William's nibs were always crossed) had deposited on it. It was Douglas who cast the first doubt upon it. Douglas felt it his duty to sustain his reputation as a master of the intricacies of spelling.

"I don't think that's the way you spell it," he said.

"It *must* be," said William firmly, "it couldn't be any other way. It couldn't possibly. How *could* it? Orfun.

Well, you spell or O-R—don't you?—and you spell fun F-U-N. So orphan must be ORFUN."

"Well, what about words like awful," said Douglas, "you spell or A-W then. It might be that sort of an or. It might be AWFUN."

"Well, we'll put it both ways then," said William firmly. "I shun't like one to come along an' not know we want one 'cause of it not being spelt right. We'll put it both ways."

But Douglas was still pondering the problem and the more he pondered it the more beset with difficulties did it appear.

"Then there's the —un," he said, "it might be O-N, not U-N. You know, like lesson. You say it lessun but you write it lesson, O-N."

The subject was becoming too complicated for William.

"Well, let's spell it all the ways it could be spelt, so's if one comes it'll know we want one."

Douglas therefore drew up a fresh notice whose final form was:

	orfun
Wanted an	awfun
	orfon
	awfon

They fixed it on the barn door and gazed at it proudly.

"Well, one's more likely to come along if we aren't here, waiting for it to come," said William. "Things never happen when you're waiting for them to happen. I votes we go out to look for one and then I bet you anything that when we come back we'll find one waiting for us here."

The Outlaws recognised the sound sense of this and

set off. As they were setting off Ginger looked doubtfully back at the notice.

"I bet he won't think much of us not knowin' how to
spell it," he said.

Douglas returned and wrote slowly and carefully at
the foot of the notice:

"we gnow whitch is wright."

*   *   *

Clarence Mapleton stood at the gate of his aunt's
garden and looked gloomily about him. He had been
told not to go into the road and so, in order to assert his
independence, he went into the road and walked up and
down it several times, although the procedure did not
afford him much pleasure, as the garden was far more
interesting in every way. He then returned to the gate
and stood leaning against it in an attitude of dejection.
Though nearly eight years old, he still wore his hair in a
mop of curls and he was still dressed in a tunic suit with
microscopic knickers from which long bare legs emerged
to end in baby socks and strap-over shoes. Despite
appearances, however, there beat within Clarence
Mapleton's breast a manly heart and he felt deeply the
ignominy of his appearance. Nor were the curls and
tunic suit all. Besides the obnoxious name of Clarence
he possessed the name of John, and yet no one called
him by it. They called him Clarence because his aunt
with whom he lived loved the name of Clarence and
disliked the name of John.

He was the apple of his aunt's eye. She worshipped
him from his curly head to his strap-over shoes. She
called him her "little Prince Charming." When he
pleaded for more manly attire, she said: "Oh no, no,
darling. Not yet. You're not old enough for those horrid

boys' suits yet. He's his auntie's darling baby boy. . . ."
And other yet more revolting epithets.

She didn't even let him go to a proper boys' school.
He still had a governess.

"No, sweetheart," she said. "Auntie doesn't want
her darling to go with all those horrid rough boys yet."

Considering the limitations of his circumstances,
however, Clarence had not done badly. He had undertaken his own education to the best of his ability under
the general directorship of the butcher's boy, and the
result was on the whole quite creditable. Despite his
curls and tunic suit he could hold his own in single
combat against the butcher's boy, who was several
inches taller and of a fierce disposition. He could walk
on his hands and he could distort his angelic features
into a mask so horrible that strong men blenched
at it. Moreover, though his devoted aunt should
wash him and change his suit and brush up his golden
curls a dozen times a day,—a dozen times a day he could
conscientiously dishevel himself in order to assert his
manhood.

Lolling against the gate post, his hands in the little
pockets of his saxe blue suit, he was devising various
dramatic means of freeing himself from his ignominious
position. In his imagination strange and wonderful
things were happening.

A band of robbers descended upon the house and
were going to kill his aunt, and he told her that he would
save her if she would let him go to school, give him a
proper boy's suit and call him John. She promised, and
he killed all the robbers. His aunt, despite her many
failings, always kept her promise.

The house was surrounded by Indians who were going
to burn it down. He told his aunt that he would drive
them off if she would promise to let him go to school,

give him a proper boy's suit and call him John. She promised, and he went out and drove off the Indians.

He and his aunt were going through a wood and a pack of wolves surrounded them. They were just going to spring upon his aunt and he told her that he would save her if she would promise to let him go to school, give him a proper suit and call him John. She promised, and he killed the wolves.

Cannibals had captured them and—

He awoke from his dreams with a start.

Four boys were coming down the road—four dirty, untidy boys, in battered tweed school suits, the sort of boys with whom his aunt would not let him play. He watched them in wistful envy. They were talking to each other. They glanced at him as they passed and went on talking to each other. It was that glance that stung Clarence into action. It seemed to say that he was unworthy even of their scorn. He pulled his face at them. They swung round and stared at him with sudden interest. William accepted the challenge and pulled his face back. Clarence, still leaning nonchalantly against the gate, replied by pulling his face again.

"How d'you do it?" said William. Clarence did it once more.

"Mine's a better one," said William, with an inner conviction that it wasn't, for though a masterpiece in its way he realised that it lacked the finish of Clarence's. The butcher boy, who had taught Clarence, was an artist in faces.

Without answering Clarence turned a somersault and then walked across the road on his hands.

William could stand on his hands, but he could never walk on them without overbalancing.

"I c'n do that too," said William, but in a tone of voice that betrayed that he couldn't.

Clarence walked back across the road on his hands, reversed himself lightly and leant nonchalantly against the gate post again. William, feeling that he was not showing up well in this competition of accomplishments, put a finger into each corner of his mouth and emitted a piercing whistle. Immediately Clarence did the same. The horrible echoes died away. William, listening, had an uncomfortable suspicion that Clarence's were the more horrible of the two.

The Outlaws had gathered round Clarence and were looking at him with interest.

"How old are you?" said William at last.

"Eight," said Clarence, mentally adding a month or two on to his age.

"Why does your mother dress you like that?"

"Not got no mother," said Clarence with a swagger.

He had early learnt that his lack of parents conferred distinction upon him.

"Why does your father, then?"

"Not got a father either," said Clarence, with an exaggeration of the swagger.

William stared at him open-mouthed, open-eyed.

"Not got—You're a *norphan?*" he shouted excitedly.

"Yes," said Clarence gratified by the sensation his news had caused. "I'm a norphan."

For a moment William's emotion was too strong for speech. Then he turned to the others, and, pointing to Clarence, said still more excitedly: "D'you hear that? He's a *norphan.*"

They all stared at Clarence.

"Well," said Clarence rather distrustfully, feeling that their surprise was a little overdone, and suspecting ridicule behind it. "Why shun't I be?"

"B-b-but we're *lookin'* for a norphan," said William, still breathless with excitement.

"Why?" said Clarence.

"'Cause we want to adopt one."

"What's that?" said Clarence.

"We want to take one to live with us."

"Take *me* to live with *you?*" said Clarence eagerly.

"Yes," said William.

"An'—an' give me clothes like what you're wearing, an' let me play with you?"

"Yes," said William. "We'd fetch one of our Sunday suits for you, 'an' you could wear one of our weekday suits on Sundays. Will you?"

Clarence looked at them. Four dirty, rough, untidy, scuffling boys—four boys after his own heart. His face was shining.

"I should jus' think I *will*," he said.

"All right," said William. "Come on then."

They escorted him in proud proprietorship down the road.

"What's your name?" said William.

"John," said Clarence happily.

At the bend of the road William plunged suddenly into the grass and brought out a frog.

He glanced affectionately at his orphan.

"I *knew* he'd bring us luck," he said.

*   *   *

They were in the old barn. The afternoon had been a busy one. William had gone home at once to fetch his Sunday suit, and Ginger had gone home to fetch a pair of scissors as the orphan had peremptorily insisted on having his hair cut and being dressed in a school suit before any further proceedings took place. William had done the thing properly, bringing his best boots and stockings, and collar and tie as well as his Sunday suit.

"You can let me have them on Saturday night ready

for Sunday," he explained carelessly, "an' I'll let you have my weekday ones then, so it'll be all right. I bet they won't find out they're gone."

The outfit was far too large for Clarence, and Ginger's cropping of his curls was as unscientific as it was thorough, but words cannot convey the pride that swelled at Clarence's heart, as he swaggered about the barn, passing his hand every now and then with a complacent smile over his unevenly cropped head.

The Outlaws looked at him with some misgivings. He certainly didn't look as they'd meant him to look.

"He's all right, I think," said William doubtfully, "don't you?"

"Yes, I think he looks all right," said Ginger with unconvinced optimism, "anyway, whatever he looks like he looks better than he did in the other things."

"You won't mind stayin' here while we're at school, will you?" said William to Clarence.

"I should jolly well think *not*," said Clarence enthusiastically.

"You see you'll sleep with us in turns an' get under the bed in the morning when they come to call us so's no one'll know, an' then go out when no one's lookin'. An' you can stay here while we're in school an' play games by yourself, an' we'll bring you food an' things, an' you can play with us when we're not in school an' wear our clothes in turn. See?"

He looked at Clarence anxiously, hoping that this *ménage* would meet with his approval. It was evident that it did. It was evident that Clarence accepted the prospect of this strange existence, not only with equanimity, but with exultation.

"Can I *really!*" he said gratefully.

He was certainly an orphan after the Outlaws' own

hearts. But it was after tea-time, and reluctantly they took their leave of him.

"We'll come back soon," William assured him, "and bring you some tea. We'll all get a bit from our homes. You don' mind us goin' just for a bit to get tea, do you?"

"No," his orphan assured him cheerfully, and glancing down at his person, added with pride, "it fits me jolly well, doesn't it?"

When they had gone the orphan amused himself by practising the accomplishments that had won him this proud position. He whistled, pulled his face, and walked round the barn on his hands, and when he was tired of doing that, stroked his unevenly-cropped head and admired his suit, the sleeves of which had to be rolled up almost to their elbows.

The Outlaws returned long before he had exhausted his resources of self-amusement.

They brought with them a large if somewhat varied meal. Ginger had managed to abstract a pot of jam from the larder, Henry had brought a tin of sardines that he had obtained in the same way, Douglas had brought an orange, and William a carton of cream. The orphan hailed the meal with delight and consumed it zestfully.

"It's the nicest tea I've ever had," he announced blissfully as he scraped out the last spoonful of jam and put the last sardine into his mouth.

They watched him with wistful envy. It was certainly a more exciting meal than the ones they'd had at home. And they'd not only brought him the tea. They'd put together what money they had, and been into the village to buy him sweets and toys. They'd bought him a bag of bulls' eyes, a whistle, a pistol and a stick of liquorice. They'd spent their last penny on him. They took their duty as his guardians and protectors very seriously.

"Then there's supper to think of," said William

slowly, as they stood round their orphan watching him consume the remnants of his tea.

There was a shade of anxiety over his face. He realised that their orphan was going to be a drain on their slender resources.

"There's his pocket money, too," he went on still more slowly. "I vote we each give him a penny out of ours every week in turns."

"I don't think he'll *need* pocket money," said Douglas tentatively, but he was over-ruled by the others. When the Outlaws did anything they did it properly.

"Have you ever *heard* of anyone adoptin' a norphan an' not givin' him pocket money?" said William indignantly.

As Douglas had never heard of anyone adopting an orphan at all till that morning he retired from the argument. There was no doubt at all that the orphan appreciated their attentions. He was happily engaged in sucking his stick of liquorice and playing with his pistol. He had handed round his bulls' eyes and lent Ginger his whistle.

He looked up suddenly and said anxiously: "I *am* goin' to stay here with you always, aren't I?"

"Yes," said William firmly.

The way of adopters of orphans might be beset by unexpected difficulties, but William was of the stuff that having adopted an orphan holds him against the world.

"Sure?" said the orphan.

"Yes," said William.

"Golly!" murmured the orphan, ecstatically putting another bulls' eye into his mouth. "Golly . . . Jus' *think* of it."

"Well, he's had his tea," said Ginger restively, "let's go out an' play till bedtime."

So they went out to play. They played Red Indians. The orphan climbed trees and fences, scrambled through hedges and dived into ditches with the best of them. He took falls and knocks without a murmur. William watched him with delight.

"He's a jolly fine orphan, isn't he?" he said to Ginger proudly.

His delight in his protégé was, however, tempered by a slight anxiety about his Sunday suit, that increased as the evening wore on, and the passage of hedges and ditches and the bark of trees left their marks more and more thickly upon it.

To Clarence it was like a wonderful dream—the tweed suit, the stockings, the boots (all many sizes too big for him, but he didn't mind that), the shouting and running and scuffling and scrambling over the countryside with these heroic beings who treated him with such flattering consideration. It seemed far too good to be true. Once or twice indeed he wondered if he'd died and gone to Heaven.

They ended their game at a house that was being built just outside the village. The Outlaws always paid it a visit in the evening when the workmen had gone home. It was, as it were, the Mecca of their day. Its attractions included scaffolding, planks, ladders, half-built walls, perilous chasms and dizzy heights, shavings, sawdust, cement, bricks, and various builders' tools.

An added zest was imparted to the proceedings by the fact that occasionally an irate householder from the neighbourhood, who was to be the inhabitant of the house, would descend upon them in fury to drive them away.

Clarence enjoyed it even more than he'd enjoyed the game of Red Indians. He climbed the scaffolding, walked along the top of half-built walls, slid down planks

and joined in a sawdust battle with a zest and fearless-
ness that made William's heart swell with pride.

"He's a *jolly* fine orphan," he said again to Ginger,
"we couldn't 've got a better one however long we'd
looked for one."

They were standing on the top of a half-built wall.
Opposite it was another half-built wall at a distance of
about two yards. They were of equal height, and the
space between them was spanned by a narrow plank.

"I bet I could walk across there on my hands," said
Clarence, whose orgy of emancipation was going to his
head.

"I bet you couldn't," said William.

"I bet I could," persisted Clarence.

"All right," said William. "Go on. Do it."

Without a moment's hesitation Clarence sprang upon
his hands, and in a breathless silence began to walk the
plank. He got half-way, then overbalanced and fell into
the yawning chasm beneath. The Outlaws peered down
anxiously.

"Hello," called William. "Are you all right?"

A heap of cement at the bottom stirred, convulsed,
and finally gave forth what seemed to be the plaster cast
of a boy miraculously imbued with life.

"Yes," said a muffled voice, "I'm all right. I fell into
the stuff an' din' hurt myself at all. It tastes funny,
though."

The Outlaws scrambled down from the wall to meet
their protégé on the ground. He was completely encased
in cement from head to foot.

William looked anxiously at the point where, according to the rules of anatomy, his Sunday suit must be, then
his unfailing optimism came to his aid.

"I 'spect it'll brush off," he said.

"We can't take him home like that," said Ginger,

"an' it's getting too dark to see. So it must be bedtime."

Again the responsibilities of their position cast a cloud over their spirits. Only Clarence had no misgivings. He gazed at them happily, trustingly, through his covering of cement.

"I got half-way, anyway, din' I?" he said cheerfully. "It was a jolly fine sort of feeling, falling into that stuff."

"We can't take him home like that," said Ginger again.

"Tell you what," said William, "let him go'n' rub himself on the grass on the side of the ditch. I bet that'll take it off."

"A' right," said Clarence, and trotted out in the gathering dusk to the road.

Almost immediately he returned.

"I *say*!" he gasped, "Annie—she's my aunt's maid —was jus' passing. She saw me. I say, let me hide! Quick!"

He leapt into the kitchen floor and disappeared into the bowels of the earth. The Outlaws quickly sought similar hiding places. But after a few minutes it was evident that no one was looking for them and they emerged.

William went cautiously into the road to reconnoitre. He could dimly see a figure fleeing down the road in the distance. Faint moans reached him.

He returned.

"'S all right," he said. "No one's there 'cept some ole luny a long way off. Come on."

They walked home rather thoughtfully. The cement-clad figure was the only really cheerful one. It walked jauntily. It had no thought for the morrow. It trusted its adopters entirely.

"It's your night to have him first, isn't it, William?" said Ginger.

"Yes," said William without enthusiasm.

They had reached William's home.

"Well, good night," said the other Outlaws.

"I say," said William pleadingly, but they were already disappearing.

They felt that after all it was at William's suggestion that they had saddled themselves with this lifelong responsibility, and that it was only fair that he should bear the first brunt of it.

William, left alone with his white-clad protégé in the gathering dusk at his garden gate, gazed about him with a sinking heart.

"Isn't it *fun*?" said Clarence enthusiastically. "What shall we do now?"

"I've gotter get you up to bed now," said William.

This proved easier than William had thought, for Clarence scaled the pear tree by which William always entered his bedroom in emergencies almost as easily as William himself. He stood in William's bedroom, cement dropping all around him, and said placidly: "And now do I go to bed?"

"Yes," said William with a harassed glance at the carpet. "I'd better give that suit a bit of a brush. An' we'll have to try and get it off the carpet somehow, too."

"I say," said his orphan, as if making a sudden discovery. "I'm hungry."

William's expression grew yet more harassed.

"I'll see if I c'n get anything," he said, "you be gettin' undressed. You'll find pyjamas in that drawer. An' get under the bed if you hear anyone coming."

"All right," said the orphan happily. "I'm jolly sleepy. I've had a lovely day. What're we goin' to do to-morrow?"

"Dunno," said William rather shortly, as he descended to the garden by way of the pear tree, and then entered the house noisily by the side door.

Voices from the drawing-room told him that his mother had a visitor. That reassured him, and he went into the dining-room where his supper was laid. Having eaten it, he looked about for something for his orphan. All he could find was a pot of jam in the sideboard cupboard and half a pine-apple that was on the sideboard. He would, of course, be called to account for the disappearance of the pine-apple, but he had no thought just then for anything but his orphan, who must be fed at all costs. He took both upstairs, hoping that his Sunday suit and bedroom carpet weren't really as bad as he'd thought.

He opened the bedroom door to find that they were far, far worse. The situation was in fact beginning to assume the proportions of a nightmare.

The orphan himself was nowhere to be seen, having dived beneath the bed on William's approach, but everything in the room was covered with a thick, white powder. It seemed inconceivable that the human form could accommodate such large quantities of cement.

The orphan emerged when William entered and gazed with gleaming eyes at his supper.

"How *scrummy!*" he said. "It's ever so much nicer than the things I used to have—blancmange and rice pudding and silly things like that."

"Let's hurry up and get into bed," said William anxiously, "someone'll be coming."

The orphan hastily finished his supper, and was in bed in a few minutes—jam and cement and all.

"Your mother doesn't come in to see you in bed like my aunt, does she?" he said anxiously.

"No," said William, "not if we pretend to be asleep.

CLARENCE EMERGED AND GAZED WITH GLEAMING EYES AT HIS
SUPPER. "HOW *SCRUMMY!*" HE SAID.

She'll open the door, and if I don't say anything she'll
think I'm asleep and go away."

But the orphan was asleep already.

William lay awake for a few minutes, trying to grapple
with the problems that confronted him. There was
breakfast to-morrow to think of, there was dinner, tea

and supper. There were four meals to provide every day. There was his Sunday suit. . . . Anyway it was Ginger's turn to have him to-morrow night. . . .

He'd had a very tiring day. He fell asleep. . . .

* * *

Mrs. Brown went to the garden gate to look up and down the road. It was getting dark. Time that boy came home. She hoped that he wasn't in any mischief. . . .

A figure was coming down the road, but it wasn't William. It was the figure of a maid servant, apron and streamers flying in the wind. She was moaning as she ran.

"He's dead . . . he's dead. . . . I've seen his gho-o-o-ost . . . he's de-e-e-ead."

"Who's dead?" said Mrs. Brown.

"Clarence," wailed the maid. "I've seen his ghost. I've seen his gho-o-o-o-ost. Oo-o-o-o. I'm goin' to faint in a minute."

Mrs. Brown led her into the house, installed her in an arm-chair in the drawing-room and gave her some sal volatile.

"Now tell me all about it," said Mrs. Brown.

The maid took a deep breath and, still unsteadily, began her tale.

"Clarence . . ." she sobbed. "He was lorst. We couldn't find him nowhere in the house nor garding. Such a beautiful little chap 'e was, with 'is golden curls," she began to sob again, so Mrs. Brown said:

"Yes, yes. I'm sure he was. Well, and what happened?"

"I keep tellin' you," moaned the maid. "'E got lorst. Disappeared clean. Couldn't be found nowhere. Lured away to 'is death 'e must've been," she showed symptoms of another spasm but collected herself, "an' the mistress sent me out to look for him down this 'ere road while she rang up police stations and," her voice rose again to a wail, "I sor his gho-o-o-ost. He's de-e-e-ead."

"Nonsense!" said Mrs. Brown in a tone that succeeded in quelling an incipient attack of hysterics. "Nonsense! You must have seen a-a tree or a-a shadow or something. There aren't such things as ghosts."

"There are. I seed 'im with my eyes," said the maid solemnly, "not as 'e looked in life. All white an' shinin' 'e was. I seed 'im as plain as I see you now, 'm. 'E didn't look the same as 'e looked in life. 'Is 'ead was different an' 'e wore different clothes. All white an' shinin'. It was 'is ghost. 'E's de-e-e-ead."

The hysterics gathered force again. With relief Mrs. Brown heard her husband's key in the lock.

"Wait a minute," she said. "I'll ask my husband to come to you."

She went out and returned in a few moments with an obviously reluctant Mr. Brown.

"But I say," he murmured, "I can't do anything. I don't——"

"Tell this gentleman what you saw," said Mrs. Brown to the maid.

The maid, who was secretly beginning to enjoy her position as purveyor of news from the spirit world, burst again into her description: . . . "and there I seed 'im . . . there 'e stood all white an' shining. Not the same as he looked in life. 'Is 'ead was different. 'E'd got one of the white things round his 'ead. What d'you call them, 'm?"

"A halo?" suggested Mrs. Brown.

"Yes, a hello round his 'ead an' white robes same as the angels an' there he stood lookin' at me with a wonderful white light coming from him like what you see in pictures of 'em. 'E'd come back to me to give me some message but I was all of a jelly same as you'd have been yourself, sir, an' came runnin' down the road all of a jingle an' this lady'll tell you, sir, that I'd've been dead by now if she hadn't of give me some stuff to drink."

Mrs. Brown looked anxiously at her husband, but it was evident that there was little hope of help from him. He was already looking at his watch and edging towards the door.

"Yes," he said. "Well . . ." he turned to his wife and with a heartless "I'll be back for dinner, dear," vanished.

Mrs. Brown looked helplessly at her visitor.

"Don't you think you'd better go home now?" she said.

"I couldn't," said the visitor earnestly. "I couldn't walk down that road again—what 'is blessed spirit 'aunts—not to save my life, 'm. I never was one for ghosts. I'm still all of a jingle in my inside. I can still hear my ribs knockin' against each other. It's a miracle I'm not dead."

"You came out to look for him and left your mistress at home?" said Mrs. Brown.

"Yes, I came to look for that pore little child what has been lured to his death, an' there when I got to the corner of the road I sor——"

"Yes, yes," said Mrs. Brown hastily. "I'd better ring your mistress up and let her know that you're here, hadn't I?"

"All of the jiggers," said the maid. "I c'n still hear my bones knockin' against each other as plain as plain. There he stood, a white light shinin' from him an' a hello round his head same as in the Bible an'——"

"Yes, yes," said Mrs. Brown again. "I'll ring her up and tell her what's happened."

She was feeling relieved, as she'd heard William come

"I COULDN'T WALK DOWN THAT ROAD AGAIN," SAID THE
MAID. "I NEVER WAS ONE FOR GHOSTS."

in by the side door and go into the dining-room for his
supper. She always felt relieved when William came
home for the night.

She meant to go up to see him as soon as she'd
communicated with Clarence's aunt, but Annie, feeling

that her due position as centre of the stage was not being accorded her, made a bold bid for it by a fainting fit for which a glass of brandy had to be administered. She was only just emerging from it when Clarence's aunt appeared.

Annie, fortified by the brandy, leapt again into her narrative.

"Oh, mum, I was comin' along the road lookin' for him when suddenly 'is spirit appeared to me out of the darkness—all shinin' bright. 'E'd got a little hello round his head same as what they have up there an' long white robes an' beautiful wings. An' he looked at me an' he said:

" 'Give 'er my love,' 'e said, 'an' tell 'er I'm 'appy.' "

At this point Annie was so deeply moved by her narrative that she broke down again. Clarence's aunt broke down too, and they sobbed together.

"Lured to 'is death," sobbed Annie.

"And I loved him so," sobbed Clarence's aunt.

"Shinin' so bright it almost blinded you to look at him."

"The apple of my eye."

" 'Give 'er my love,' 'e said, 'an' tell 'er that I'm 'appy with the hangels.' "

"If only I'd let him have his darling hair cut off."

"Flowin' bright robes an' a narp in his 'and."

As another attack of hysterics seemed to be threatening, Mrs. Brown hastily led Annie across the hall to the kitchen and gave her into the care of her cook and housemaid who enjoyed hysterics and were skilled in the treatment of them.

Then Mrs. Brown returned to Clarence's aunt, composing on the way various little sarcasms with which she would greet her husband on his return.

Clarence's aunt was by now a little calmer.

"Of course I don't really believe that she saw his ghost but it's so *dreadful*," she sobbed. "I'm simply *distracted* by anxiety. I've communicated with all the police stations for miles around. If only I haven't driven him to anything desperate. He wanted to wear those Rugby suits and have his beautiful hair cut off and go to a rough boys' school and be called John and I wouldn't let him. . . . Oh, if only I could get him back safe and sound I'd let him. I *swear* I'd let him. Have you got a little boy?"

"Yes," said William's mother.

"Then you know how they *twine* themselves round your heart?"

"Y-yes," said William's mother rather doubtfully.

"Is your little boy in bed now?"

"Yes," said William's mother, whose listening ear had noted the cessation of bangs and bumps from William's bedroom that meant that he was at rest.

"Will he be asleep now?"

"I expect so."

"Do you go and *gaze* upon him when he's asleep?"

"Not generally."

"I do at Clarence. . . . Do let me go with you and look at your little boy asleep. It will—it will *lull* my anxiety. Let me go and try to imagine my own little Clarence's head upon the pillow, too."

"Very well," said Mrs. Brown rather reluctantly.

They went upstairs. The sound of Annie's voice came from the kitchen. "There 'e stood all bright an' shinin' . . ."

Mrs. Brown opened the door of William's bedroom and they entered on tiptoe.

Upon the pillow lay William's and Clarence's heads side by side. William had not thought of washing his orphan and upon Clarence's cheek a large circle of jam outlined itself vividly against a background of cement. His unevenly cropped hair was quite white. . . .

He smiled happily in his sleep.

Chapter 7

William and the Campers

It was, curiously enough, the Hubert Laneites who invented the game. The Hubert Laneites were not endowed with great inventive powers and it was seldom that they invented any games at all. They generally copied the Outlaws' games, and, even so, played them very inadequately. But there was no doubt at all that Hubert had invented the game of Savvidges, or rather introduced it to the neighbourhood, for it was impossible to believe that he had himself invented so attractive a game. The Savvidges blacked their faces and wore mats or hearthrugs and roamed the countryside in bands, fighting each other and making camp-fires. There were, of course, only two main bands, the Hubert Laneites and the Outlaws. All the boys of the neighbourhood attached themselves to one or the other band. The Hubert Laneites had a good following, but, as usual, they avoided direct combat with the Outlaws and contented themselves with imaginary battles against imaginary foes in which they always came off victorious. And, of course, during the term time opportunity for such exploits had been limited. Now, however, the summer holidays had arrived and all day and every day was at their disposal. But the summer holidays are not like the other holidays. People go away in the summer holidays. It meant that neither band of "savvidges" was ever at its full strength. And the dice of fate was weighted heavily against the Outlaws, for, by a strange chance, it happened that all the members of the Outlaws' band but two went away for the first fortnight of the holidays and the remaining two, as if afraid of what life might now have to offer them, promptly took to their beds with scarlet fever. Even Douglas and Henry were away, and so William and Ginger were left sole survivors of the Outlaw band of "savvidges." And Hubert's band had its full complement. A new courage crept into the breasts of the Hubert Laneites when they realised the situation. A new blood-curdling note crept into their battle-cry, though normally it was a poor sort of affair compared with the Outlaws'. The Hubert Laneites' battle-cry consisted in a long drawn-out "Oo-oo-oo-oo." The Outlaws' was more complicated. It began with a low "Ra-a-a——" growing louder and louder till it ended up with a fierce and sudden "*Hosh!*"

* * *

William and Ginger were holding an emergency meeting in the old barn to discuss the situation. Even William's bold spirit shrank from inviting open conflict with the overwhelming numbers of the foe.

"Well, what'll we do about it?" said Ginger.

"We've gotter not have a battle till after Thursday," said William, "'cause on Thursday a good many of our band'll be back."

He spoke regretfully, however. It was not a policy that appealed to him.

At that moment a Hubert Laneite appeared at the door of the barn. He held a flag of truce in the shape of a

"WE'VE GOTTER NOT HAVE A BATTLE TILL AFTER THURSDAY,"
SAID WILLIAM.

handkerchief tied to a stick and he bore a missive in one hand. He handed the missive to William.

"It's a letter from Hubert," he said, "an' you can't touch me 'cause I've got this handkerchief on a stick. They don't when they've got handkerchiefs on sticks."

AT THAT MOMENT A HUBERT LANEITE APPEARED AT THE DOOR
OF THE BARN. HE HELD A FLAG OF TRUCE, AND BORE A
MISSIVE.

The emissary continued with an air of modesty allied
with omniscience: "In wars they do that when they take
letters. They carry white handkerchiefs on sticks and
then no one can touch 'em."

William regarded the handkerchief dispassionately.

"Call that white?" he said.

"It's white *reelly*," said its owner anxiously, "it only got some ink spilt on it. An' a bit of mud."

"It doesn't count when there's ink spilt on it," said Ginger. "It doesn't count at all. I could tell you of lots of times when they've got ink or mud on the handkerchief and it didn't count. They got shot 'cause it didn't count." The emissary paled and retreated a few steps. "'S'all right," said Ginger scornfully, "we wouldn't bother ourselves shootin' you. Why, I bet that if I *looked* at you hard enough your arms an' legs'd drop off now that you've all that ink an' mud on your handkerchief so's it doesn't count."

The emissary, who had indeed looked upon his white handkerchief as a sort of magic amulet, blinked distractedly, and would have turned to flight if Ginger hadn't barred the way.

"'S'all right," said Ginger reassuringly, "I'm not goin' to look at you. Not long enough to make your arms an' legs drop off, anyway. I couldn't; not with your face."

William was deeply engrossed in the letter. Having read it several times he handed it to Ginger with a scornful laugh. The scornful laugh was for the benefit of the emissary who, however, was engaged in keeping well behind Ginger and watching the back of Ginger's head fearfully. The letter read:

"We the undersined Savvidges challeng the Outlaw Savvidges to a fite on Tuesday afternoon at 3 o'clock on Ringers Hill."

Followed the signature of Hubert Lane and all his band.

The deep cunning of it was all too evident. Hubert Lane knew that by Thursday the Outlaws' band would be reinforced, and he had determined that the fight should take place before that happened. Hubert's band held some good fighters and even William, the optimist, realised that he and Ginger unaided would have little chance against them. But his scornful laugh was very convincing, and so was the tone in which he said to the emissary:

"All right. You tell Hubert that we'll jolly well be there and that he'd jolly well better look out!" There was dark and sinister meaning in his tone. William had never yet let any situation beat him for want of bluff.

The emissary was startled by his tone.

"Why," he said naively, "there's only two of you, isn't there?"

William laughed at this as if highly amused.

"Oh do you think so?" he said, "do you think there's only two of us. Well, you wait and see, that's all that I can say. You wait and see."

"An' now you'd better go an' tell him," said Ginger, "an' I'm goin' to start *lookin'* at you, so be careful of your arms and legs. That handkerchief's no use to keep 'em on."

With a yell of terror the emissary took to his heels, turning round at intervals to see if Ginger was still looking at him, and increasing his pace with redoubled yells when he found that he was. As soon as the emissary had disappeared, William's airy confidence dropped from him.

"Well!" he said dejectedly as he set off homeward with Ginger, "what're we goin' to do *now*?"

"Find some more savvidges to fight for us," said Ginger.

"We *can't*," said William testily, "there *aren't* any. They're all away or in Hubert Lane's army."

"Well——" began Ginger, then stopped short.

They had turned a bend in the road, and there in the field just beyond the hedge were two tents, and down by the stream at the bottom of the field several boys who were strangers to the neighbourhood.

"*Crumbs!*" murmured William.

As if by common consent they crept through the hedge and made their way cautiously down the field past the tents to the stream.

The three boys who were washing mugs there were not reassuring in appearance. They were very clean and tidy, and they were washing the mugs very thoroughly and with an air of conscientious absorption. Not only did they not yield to the temptation to splash water over each other—a temptation that the Outlaws would have found irresistible—but they did not seem even to experience the temptation.

William and Ginger, after watching them in a depressed silence for some time, at last began a tentative conversation.

"You here campin'?" said William.

The biggest boy—a boy with well brushed hair and an almost startlingly clean collar—constituted himself the spokesman of the little group.

"Yes," he said, "we're camping. We came yesterday. Mrs. Griffiths-Griffiths has kindly brought us. She's our Sunday School superintendent."

"Oh," said William, and after a slight pause: "You her Sunday School class?"

"No," said the boy, speaking very earnestly and precisely, "we're taken from all the various Sunday School classes. We're the boys in the Sunday School who've had no bad marks of any kind throughout the year. Never late, never absent, and no mistakes in our collects and no talking marks."

"Oh!" said William faintly.

So overwhelmed was he by this recital of their virtues, that had it not been for the project that was forming in his mind he would have hastened away and given these infant Samuels a wide berth for the rest of their sojourn. Instead, he said insinuatingly:

"What d'you do here all day?"

"We go for walks," said the boy, "we're making a wild flower collection. It's very interesting. We've found quite a lot of new specimens here already. And sometimes we play games."

"What sort of games?" said William.

"Quiet games," said the boy. "Mrs. Griffiths-Griffiths doesn't like rough games."

"I could lend you a cricket bat," said William, still with his ulterior purpose in view.

But the boy shook his head.

"We don't play cricket. It isn't really safe. You often hear of quite nasty accidents in cricket."

"Crumbs!" breathed William, but he still kept his purpose in view.

"I could tell you," he said carelessly, "of a jolly fine fight that you could help in if you want——"

But the boy's face had paled with horror.

"We never fight," he said, "it's wrong to fight. I've known of people who've got very badly hurt fighting. No one who's been in a fight is ever given a Sunday School good conduct medal."

At this William and Ginger turned hastily away.

"No use wastin' any time over *them!*" said Ginger disconsolately.

"N-no," agreed William, but he spoke thoughtfully, and added: "Still—there's a good many of them. They'd made a jolly fine band."

"*Hundreds* of that sort wouldn't make a jolly fine band," said Ginger.

"I dunno," said William. "Of course, we'd have to think out a plan."

"Hundreds of plans wouldn't be no good with *them*," said Ginger bitterly.

But William, who was always less inclined to pessimism than Ginger, said slowly:

"Of course, it would have to be a very *cunnin'* sort of plan."

They were passing the smaller tent now and from it there suddenly issued a tall lady with white shingled hair, wearing a long green smock.

"Good afternoon, boys dear," she said, brightly, "have you come to look at our little encampment? This is what I call our Virtue Rewarded Camp. All these dear boys that you see about have earned this little summer holiday by being clean and tidy and obedient and punctual and industrious every Sunday all through the year. Now that's a record to be proud of, isn't it? And my dear boys are proud of it. Never a minute late for Sunday School and not a single word wrong in the collect. Not a single minute and not a single word. They deserve to be rewarded, don't they? And their reward is this beautiful holiday during which we're going to try to complete our wild flower collection and perhaps begin the study of geology." She looked doubtfully at William and Ginger. "Are you interested in such things, dear boys? If you are we should welcome you as companions on our little expeditions."

"Thanks awfully," said William, non-committally. He still wore his thoughtful expression. After a pause he said:

"Aren't they—aren't they goin' to do anythin' else but get wild flowers an' such-like?"

"Well, dear boy, I think that we are going to have a *great* treat on Tuesday. A missionary lecture is to be given at the Village Hall by a missionary who has just returned from Central Asia, and I think that we shall make an effort to attend even if it means missing an afternoon of our precious flower hunting. Did you know, dear boy, that there are over a hundred different specimens of wild flowers in this neighbourhood?"

William made an indeterminate noise that might have meant that he did or that he didn't, and the lady went on:

"You may join any of our expeditions. You will only derive benefit from associating with these dear boys of mine." She inspected them more closely, and added: "Though I must ask you to make yourselves a *leetle* more clean and tidy before you join us."

"I was all right when I started out," said William hastily. William evidently had reasons of his own for wishing to propitiate the lady. "If I'm untidy now I must have got it since I started out. There's dirt in the air, you know, an' you can't help it blowin' on to you and the wind blows your hair untidy however tidy it is when you start out. I'll get tidy again when I get back home."

"I hope you will," said the lady graciously, "look at my dear boys—how neat and clean they keep themselves. You should take a lesson from them."

"Yes, I'd like to," said William unctuously. "I'll go'n' ask 'em how they do it."

Raising his cap to her with elaborate politeness, he went on to a group of her boys who were sitting round a wooden table outside their tent pasting pressed flowers into albums and tentatively began a conversation with them.

But it was, from William's point of view, quite fruitless. They were interested in their flower collection, they were interested in the prospect of the missionary lecture on Tuesday, they were interested in their own neatness and punctuality and industry and obedience, but they were not interested in anything else. If they had been, of course, they would not have been there. Several times William by circuitous routes brought the subject round to fighting, but blank horror met each reference to it.

"No, we never fight. Mrs. Griffiths-Griffiths wouldn't like it. It's rough and unkind and it spoils your clothes."

"I don't want to fight *anyone*," said a small boy with a piously upturned nose. "I love *everyone*."

"Yes, but when you want to do somethin' *excitin'*——" began William.

The boy with the upturned nose interrupted him.

"When I want somethin' *excitin'* I go out to try to find a fresh flower for my collection."

William went home dejectedly. He knew when he had met with defeat. Never would he or anyone else fire these young paragons with the joy of conflict. And yet he did not wholly abandon hope. Ten boys—ten potential "savvidges" for his band. . . . He didn't see at present how they were going to be enrolled in his band, but he did not wholly abandon hope.

He hung about the camp for the next few days entering into conversation with the campers, but still without success. Any mention of fighting inspired in them the deepest horror and disgust. They pointed out to him that no one who fought ever got a Sunday School Good Conduct Medal, they assured him that they didn't want to fight because they loved everyone, and they showed him with pride the separate badges they had won for cleanness and tidiness and punctuality and quietness. They spent their days going for walks in very orderly formation with Mrs. Griffiths-Griffiths, preparing meals, washing up and being read aloud to by Mrs. Griffiths-Griffiths, who had brought quite a library of edifying books for the purpose. Sometimes they played guessing games and paper games. They all told William how much they were looking forward to the missionary lecture on Tuesday. William, who, as I have said, had not entirely abandoned hope despite the unpromising nature of the situation, exercised great cunning and hid his true nature from them. That does not, of course, mean that he pretended to share their enthusiasm. It means that by exercise of great self-control he listened to their views in silence and refrained from physical assault.

"They wun't be any good," he said despondently to Ginger, "even if anyone *got* them to fight. They're so stupid. That's what I've always thought about all this bein' clean an' tidy," he went on, warming to his theme. "It takes all your strength so that there's none to go to your brain or the fighting part of you. Look at 'em. It proves it, don't it? Look at 'em. It all comes of them usin' up their strength bein' clean an' tidy so that there's none of it left to go to their brains or the fighting part of them. Well, it'll be a lesson to *me*. I want to keep my strength for my brain an' the fighting part of me. I don't want it all used up in keepin' clean an' tidy."

"Yes, but what're we goin' to do about Hubert?" said Ginger anxiously. "It's Tuesday to-morrow an' even if they could fight, they wun't be any good 'cause they're all goin' to this missionary lecture. Haven't you made a plan yet?"

"How can I make a plan?" said William testily, "with nothin' to make a plan from? You can't make plans out of nothin', can you? If they'd been ornery boys I'd've made a plan out of *them*."

"If they'd been ornery boys," said Ginger bitterly, "they wun't've been here at all."

"We'll try'n' think out a plan this afternoon," said William.

"We can't," said Ginger, still more bitterly, "we're goin' to Betty Brewster's birthday party."

Their gloom deepened. Both of them hated birthday parties, and yet both of them were continually being forced by their parents to attend them. It seemed particularly ignominious to have to attend a little girl's party.

"There may be a decent tea, of course," said Ginger, trying to find a bright side to the situation.

"It'd need to be a *jolly* decent tea," said William mournfully, "to make up for Betty Brewster and *that* set. I shun't be surprised if they even have musical chairs an' postman's knock."

He made a sound expressive of deep nausea, then resumed his expression of mournful resignation.

"Anyway, I'll call for you and we'll go together," said Ginger.

"All right," said William, "an' we'll go as slow as we can, an' hope they have postman's knock first so's we miss it. I shun't mind jus' gettin' there for tea and comin' home straight after, though even then they'd serve all the girls first an' they'd eat up all the trifle, an' there'd only be jelly when it comes to us."

* * *

Ginger called for him as he had promised, and together they set off very slowly down the road. The vigorous process of cleaning and tidying, to which they had both been subjected, had increased their melancholy, and they had not even the spirit to walk in the ditch or on the top of the fence that bordered the road.

"Funny," said William gloomily, "that rotten things always seem to happen to you all in a lump. This party an' Hubert Lane's fight. Hundreds of rotten things," he went on bitterly, "all at the same time. Same as that man that swallowed a whale in the Bible."

"You're thinkin' of Job," said Ginger, who was slightly better informed scripturally, "an' the man that swallowed a whale was Jonah. An' he didn't swallow it. It swallowed him."

"I bet it didn't," said William, glad of an excuse for an argument. "I bet he swallowed it. I remember quite well. Rotten things kept happenin' to him. He got a boil an' fell down in some ashes an' then swallowed a whale. An' when he'd swallowed the whale his friends came round to comfort him an' tell him it was his own fault for not being more careful."

They were just passing the Sunday School encampment, and Mrs. Griffiths-Griffiths, still in the apple-green smock, was hovering about the gate. She looked rather worried, and held a letter in her hand. She brightened as her eyes fell upon William and Ginger. They were indeed a sight to brighten any Sunday School superintendent's eyes—neatly dressed, with shining boots and tightly-gartered stockings, with well brushed hair and polished faces, walking slowly and quietly down the road. She had seen very little of them on their previous visits to her camp, as they had carefully avoided her, but she recognised them as the two boys to whom she had spoken on the first day of her holiday.

"Boys dear?" she called over the gate.

They approached reluctantly. The nearer inspection evidently pleased her still more.

"Out for a walk this nice afternoon?" she said. "No exercise like a nice quiet walk. I always tell my dear boys that. Much better than those rough games. And I'm glad to see that you've remembered to make yourselves nice and tidy before starting out. Some boys forget that, but I'm glad that you don't. Where do you live, boys dear?"

William and Ginger indicated their houses. Both could be seen from the road. Further conversation revealed the fact that she had met both William's and Ginger's mother at a tea party at the Vicarage the day before, which she had attended while her charges were putting the afternoon's "bag" of wild flowers into their albums. She gazed at the two of them thoughtfully and in silence for a few moments. Finally she said:

"I suppose that you're going to the missionary meeting to-morrow, dear boys?"

William made a sound that might have meant that he was, and she gazed at them still more thoughtfully, then said:

"Now I'm going to confide in you two dear boys. I'm going to tell you all about my little dilemma."

William, who'd no idea what a dilemma was, but thought it was an internal complaint, made another sound that might have meant anything, and she continued:

"A *very* dear friend of mine who lives over at Melfield has written to ask me to go over to see her to-morrow afternoon. It's the only afternoon that she has free during our little holiday here and so—well, you see the dilemma, don't you, dear boys? I wanted to take my own dear boys to the missionary lecture at the Village Hall and I can't be in two places at once. I want to see my dear old friend and I want to take my dear boys to the missionary lecture. That's my little dilemma."

She ended dramatically and William feeling that some response was demanded made another sound that might have meant anything. She laid a hand on his shoulder.

"Thank you for your sweet sympathy, dear boy. Now I'm coming to the really important part of my little dilemma. No one else can go to see my old friend for me but someone else *could* conduct my dear boys to the

"WILL YOU CALL HERE TO-MORROW, AND CONDUCT MY DEAR
BOYS TO THE VILLAGE HALL?"

Village Hall for me. If I could find two dear boys to play
host, to call for my own dear boys here, to conduct them
to the Village Hall and to bring them safely back, I
should be very grateful to those two dear boys."

Something glowed and flickered in William's eyes but
he spoke in a high-pitched voice of extreme innocence
that to those who knew him was a sign of brewing

mischief. Mrs. Griffiths-Griffiths, unfortunately for herself and fortunately for William, did not know him.

"Me and Ginger will do that for you," he said.

"Dear boys!" murmured Mrs. Griffiths-Griffiths
pressing her hand affectionately upon William's
shoulder, "*dear* boys! How *sweet* of you. When I saw
you coming down the road—such dear clean tidy boys,
walking so quietly and decorously, just as I like my own
dear boys to walk, I thought that perhaps my little
dilemma was solved. *Dear* boys. Will you call here then
to-morrow at 2.30 and conduct my dear boys to the
Village Hall for the lecture and then bring them back
here. I hope to be back from visiting my friend when you
return from the lecture. *Thank* you, dear boys. Now I
mustn't keep you any longer from the enjoyment of your
walk."

They went on quickly to Betty Brewster's. William
was distrait throughout the party. He sat by himself in a
corner, frowning thoughtfully, a far-away look in his
eye. Mrs. Brewster said afterwards that she'd dreaded
having to ask that William Brown to the party but that
he'd seemed enormously improved. At the end he
waited till Ginger was ready to walk home with him.

"Let's go round to the old barn," he said as soon as
Ginger joined him. "I've gotter sort of plan."

*   *   *

The next afternoon William and Ginger, inordinately
clean and tidy, walked neatly and precisely down the
road to the gate where Mrs. Griffiths-Griffiths awaited
them. Her eyes lit up with approval as they approached.

"*Dear* boys," she said, "how nice and clean you look.
My dear boys are quite ready for you. They have spent
this morning polishing up their medals."

The campers emerged from the tents—spick and

span and wearing shining medals on their coats. Mrs. Griffiths-Griffiths ranged them in twos in the road and addressed them.

"Now, dear boys, I want you to walk quietly down to the Village Hall with your dear hosts, who know the way and exactly where your reserved seats are, and at the end of the lecture to walk quietly back home again. Be kind to all dumb animals that you meet on the way and help old people across the road. Goodbye, boys dear. Ready, steady—march!"

The little procession set off. Mrs. Griffiths-Griffiths watched it fondly till it had vanished from sight, and then set off to the station.

William and Ginger marched in silence at the head of the procession. One boy left the ranks to be kind to a dumb animal who responded by biting him in the leg. Another left it to lead an old man across the road. It turned out, however, that the old man had not wanted to cross the road and told him so in terms unbefitting his venerable old age.

Except for those two incidents the journey proceeded uneventfully. But it did not proceed to the Village Hall. It proceeded along the outskirts of the village up through a field and into the old barn.

"Where's this?" said the boy with the turned-up nose inquiringly.

"This is the Village Hall," said Ginger.

They had been brought up to believe what they were told and so they believed him. Sitting accommodation of a more or less adequate nature was ranged about the floor—broken chairs, stools and packing-cases.

"Sit down on these," said Ginger. The campers were accustomed to doing what they were told without question, so they sat down, gazing about them at the walls of the old barn with mild interest but with no suspicion. William had disappeared. Ginger addressed the audience.

"The lekcherer will be here in a minute," he said; "his train's a bit late an' he's got to come all the way up from the station. I'm goin' to tell you a bit about him first. He's—he's a very small man. I'm tellin' you that so's you won't be surprised when you see him. He's the cleverest man in the world an' that's why he's so small. All his strength has gone to his brain leavin' none over to go to makin' him tall. He's quite an old man but he's not much taller than you or me. That's because of him bein' so clever an' all his strength goin' to his brain."

They stared at him open-mouthed with interest and surprise but entirely credulous. It never occurred to them to doubt what Ginger told them. It never occurred to them to doubt what anyone told them. It was not by doubting what people told them that they had won their good conduct medals.

One boy, who had been gazing round the room, said suddenly: "Isn't anybody else coming to this lecture? I thought that lots of people were coming to it."

"Oh no," said Ginger, "this is a lekcher spechul for you. This clever lekcherer what I told you about he's so clever that he's not much bigger than you or me with all his strength goin' to his brain—well, this clever lekcherer heard about you havin' all those medals an' suchlike and so he very kin'ly said he'd come down and give you a lekcher speshul all to yourselves. On Central Asher."

The campers glanced down complacently at their good conduct medals.

"Mrs. Griffiths-Griffiths never told us that," said one of them.

"P'raps she forgot," said Ginger. "I know she was very pleased about it. Pleased at this very clever lekcherer what I told you about, what all his strength has gone to his brain, havin' heard about all your medals an' such like an' wanting to come down an' give you a lekcher speshul. I s'pose with havin' to go off to see her ole friend she forgot to tell you. He'll be here soon, the lekcherer. He's just been givin' a lekcher to the King up in London. That's why he's a bit late."

"Shall I sing our Band of Hope song?" said a small innocent with projecting teeth. "I often do when we have to wait for anything. It helps to fill in the time."

"Yes," said Ginger, without enthusiasm, "you sing what you like, but this lekcherer will be here in a minute."

The small innocent piped up untunefully:

> "My drink is water bright,
> Water bright,
> Water bright,
> My drink is water bright,
> From the crystal stream."

At that moment William entered. No one except his most intimate friends would have recognised him as William. He wore a white beard and wig that belonged by right to his elder brother, but that William frequently "borrowed." He wore an old pair of long trousers, which also had once belonged to Robert, and which William had salved from the Jumble Sale cupboard and cut down to fit him. He wore an overcoat and a muffler. His audience gazed at him with awe and interest as he walked up to the end of the hall. It was clear that they felt not the slightest shadow of doubt. They began to clap enthusiastically as he turned to face them. He bowed slightly, then plunged straight into his lecture without wasting time on preliminaries.

"Ladies an' gentlemen," he began, speaking with some difficulty through his thick beard. "Ladies an' gentlemen, I'm goin' to tell you this afternoon all about a place called Central Asher, where natives an' such-like are heathen, an' what we've gotter do is to convert 'em, same as we converted the people in—in China an' all the other places we learn about in geography, an' make 'em into good people goin' to Sunday School an' belongin' to Band of Hopes an' such-like. We've gotter do that with the people in Central Asher. The people in Central Asher live very wicked an' unhappy lives, jus' worshippin' idols an' bein' eaten alive by crocodiles an' such-like. We've got to convert 'em an' turn 'em into good people, goin' to Sunday School every Sunday, an' then their lives'll be quite different."

He paused for breath, and the campers clapped. They had been told to clap whenever the lecturer paused. Mrs. Griffiths-Griffiths had meant the whole village to be impressed by the keenness of her dear boys. William bowed again, and as soon as the applause had died away continued his lecture.

"Now what people don't know is that there's a lot of Central Asher people livin' quite near here." His audience gasped with amazement, but he continued unperturbed.

"It's a sort of camp of natives that's come over from Central Asher, an' they live on Ringers Hill, jus' a short way from here, carryin' on jus' like what they used to at home, worshippin' idols an' such-like all over the place. Well, what we've gotter do is to convert 'em. We don't need to go right over to Central Asher to convert 'em, 'cause they're jus' here, an' we can get to 'em in a few minutes. Well, now, that's what we've gotter do this afternoon. We've gotter convert 'em."

He paused again for breath. His audience was too

much amazed even to applaud. The innocent with projecting teeth found his voice first.

"B-b-b-but," he objected, "we don't know their language. They don't talk English, do they?"

"No," said William, "they talk Central Ashan. But I know it. It's a very difficult langwidge, an' it took me years to learn, even though I'm jolly quick at learning foreign langwidges. So I can tell you what to say to 'em to convert 'em."

They stared at him helplessly. Even the innocent with projecting teeth was past speech now. But despite their amazement, it didn't occur to one of them even now to question the truth of his words.

"What we've decided to do," continued William, calmly, "is to give a speshul medal in Sunday Schools for convertin' heathen, to wear nex' your good conduct medal. An' I want you to be the first to win this new medal for convertin' the heathen. Wun't you like to win another medal this afternoon, a speshully big one for convertin' the heathen?" Their eyes gleamed. They thirsted for medals as a drug maniac for his drug. They made eager gloating sounds for acquiescence.

"Well, then," went on William, "I'll take you to 'em an' teach you a sermon in Central Ashan that'll convert 'em. I'll teach you the words an' you say 'em to them. Or rather, you'll have to shout 'em. They all shout in Central Asher. They wun't understand you if you jus' speak. The shoutin' is part of the langwidge. The louder you speak the quicker they understand. Now are you all ready to learn the words?"

Eagerly the campers said that they were.

"There are only two ackshual words in the sermon," went on William, unblushingly, "but they're words that mean as much in Central Ashan as pages an' pages in English. Each of these two words what I'm goin' to teach

you is a long sermon convertin' 'em. It's a sermon what
every heathen that hears it gets converted by it, however
long he's been a heathen worshippin' idols an' bein'
eaten by crocodiles an' such-like. Each of these two
words I'm goin' to teach you is a long sermon what
would convert any one what heard it, so of course the
two of them together makes the sort of sermon in
Central Ashan, such as only very important bishops
what have passed the highest exams in bein' bishops
could give in the English langwidge. These two words
mean pages an' pages an' pages of convertin' stuff. Now,
are you ready?"

"Yes," said the campers zestfully.

"Well, one word's 'Ra,' an' the other word's 'Hosh.'
But in the Central Ashan langwidge it isn't only the
words you say, it's the way you say 'em. Now listen very
carefully to me and Ging—an' this other gentleman
here, an' we'll say 'em the way to make 'em mean all
those pages an' pages of sermons, what they mean when
you say 'em the right way. Now listen very carefully.
Come on, Ginger. One, two, three."

Ginger and William drew in their breath and emitted
the battle cry of the Outlaw band of "savvidges." The
campers listened carefully. Then they tried it. It was, of
course, a poor enough attempt. William made them do it
again and again and again, till at last they managed to
instil into it something of the bloodcurdling quality of
William's own rendering. They worked zealously and
conscientiously, occasionally glancing complacently
down at their good conduct medal and picturing the new
medal for converting the heathen beside it.

"Will it hang from a blue ribbon same as the good
conduct medal?" asked the boy with the turned-up
nose. William assured him that it would. When they
were nearly perfect he made another speech.

"Now you've gotter be very careful with these Central Ashans. They've got their speshul ways same as heathens always have. They're fond of killin' people." The campers paled. "It's nothin' to them to kill people. They do it without thinkin'. They don't mean to be unkind or anything. They jus' do it 'cause it's a sort of fashion. They'll stop doin' it, of course, after you've converted 'em. But they've got a very strict rule, an' that is that they never kill people what come to them runnin' an' with their faces blacked. That's a *very* strict rule. When any one comes to them runnin' with their faces blacked they're very polite to them an' listen to what they've got to say. That's a very strict rule with them. An' if the person's wearin' a sort of thing that looks like a mat to us—I've got a few here—they listen to them an' do everything they tell them. Now would any of you like to have your faces blacked, an' one of these little things tied round him before we start convertin' the heathen?"

They crowded round him eagerly.

Ginger appeared with a box full of burnt corks. William dragged forward a pile of odds and ends of carpet. They set to work.

* * *

The Hubert Laneites assembled on Ringers Hill. Gloating is the only word that adequately describes their attitude.

"They won't come, an' if they do, we'll lick 'em."

"They can't get anyone else, 'cause all their people are away."

"If they come we'll lick 'em, an' if they don't come they'll not have taken a dare and be cowardy custards."

"Cowardy, cowardy custards!" sang Hubert, as though he were already jeering at William and Ginger from the usual safe distance.

"Cowardy, cowardy custards!" sang the Hubert Laneites, joyfully.

Then suddenly the words froze on their lips. Their eyes bulged. Their mouths dropped open.

"COWARDY, COWARDY, CUSTARDS!" SANG THE HUBERT
LANEITES JOYFULLY. THEN SUDDENLY THE WORDS DIED ON
THEIR LIPS.

For up the hill came charging William and Ginger at the head of a band of "savvidges." Strange warriors unknown in the neighbourhood, with faces horribly blacked and uttering the Outlaws' war-cry in tones that turned the blood of the Hubert Laneites to water in their veins. The very unfamiliarity of the new warriors made them the more ferocious and terrible in the eyes of the other band. With panic-stricken cries the Hubert Laneites turned to flee.

The Outlaws held the hill.

*   *   *

The campers marched neatly back. They had washed away all traces of the burnt cork, and looked almost as

FOR UP THE HILL WILLIAM AND GINGER CAME CHARGING, AT
THE HEAD OF A BAND OF STRANGE WARRIORS UTTERING THE
OUTLAWS' WAR-CRY.

tidy as when they had set out. They had spent rather a bewildering afternoon, but William had assured them that it was all right, and that the flight of the heathen meant that they were fully converted.

They marched into the tent where Mrs. Griffiths-Griffiths was awaiting them.

William and Ginger, unable to resist the temptation to

hear their charges' account of the afternoon, lay in the field behind the tent, their ears to the flap of the tent.

"Well, boys dear," said Mrs. Griffiths-Griffiths, "now tell me all about the lecture. Was it interesting?"

"Yes very," said the innocent with projecting teeth. "He was a very clever man."

"I'm sure he was, dear. And did he tell you all about Central Asia?"

"Yes, an' he told us about the Central Ashans on Ringers Hill, an' he blacked our faces an' taught us a sermon to convert 'em and——"

"*What?*" screamed Mrs. Griffiths-Griffiths.

William and Ginger crept quietly away.

Chapter 8

The Outlaws and the Cucumber

Mrs. Roundway had always been a friend of the Outlaws. She was a small stout woman with a perpetual smile and a very large heart, who lived in a cottage just outside the village, and made the sort of cookie boys that one would hardly expect to meet this side the grave. Her friendship had begun with William and had gradually extended itself to the others. She seemed to regard boys in a light that was novel and touching to the Outlaws. She talked to them, and liked to hear their views. She made cookie boys for them—beautiful creatures of dough or gingerbread with currants for eyes, nose, mouth and buttons. The Outlaws felt vaguely grateful to her—not so much for the cookie boys as for what the cookie boys stood for, an oasis of grown-up understanding and kindness in a desert world. Most grown-ups of the Outlaws' acquaintance considered boys in the light of a discipline inflicted upon a suffering world by a mysterious Providence. But Mrs. Roundway actually liked them. She didn't seem a grown-up at all.

Mrs. Roundway was a widow with a comfortable income, a comfortable cottage and a comfortable disposition, and one would have thought that she had everything her heart could desire. But she hadn't. Her heart desired to get the first prize at the local flower show for her cucumbers and she couldn't. She could only get the second. Every year she cherished and guarded and tended and fed them as a mother her children, till they assumed balloon-like proportions. She lay awake at night thinking about them. When she fell asleep she dreamed of them. Every year she was sure that she was going to get the first prize. And every year Mrs. Bretherton got it instead. Mrs. Bretherton produced at the last minute an exhibit that put Mrs. Roundway's exhibit entirely to shame, a cucumber so fat and long that it looked as if it had begun by trying to be a pumpkin, and then had decided to be a cucumber, but had a strong sense of proportion.

On the day after the flower show Mrs. Roundway's smile was woe-begone and forlorn, and yet even in the downfall of all her hopes she remembered to make a cookie boy for the Outlaws. She came down to the gate with the smile that was so different from her usual smile, and said:

"Here it is, dears. It's gingerbread. And here's a few extra currants."

William took the cookie boy and Ginger the handful of currants, and they gazed at her sorrowfully, their hearts overflowing with sympathy.

"We're sorry about the cucumber," said William.

"That's kind of you, love," she said. "Yes, I can't pretend I don't feel it. It may be foolish to take it to heart so, but—I can't help it. I was almost sure this time. I know she doesn't take the time and care that I do." She sighed deeply. "I can't think how it is."

"Well, I jolly well think you oughter've had the prize," said William stoutly.

"No, love," sighed Mrs. Roundway. "Her's was

bigger than what mine was. There wasn't no doubt about it."

"Well, I bet you'll get it next year," said William.

"That's very nice of you, love," said Mrs. Roundway and a gleam of hope pierced through the gloom of her good-natured countenance. "Yes, there's always next year to look forward to, isn't there?"

The Outlaws walked thoughtfully down the road, nibbling the cookie boy. Ginger had the arms, Henry the legs, Douglas the head and hat, William the body. Yet so depressed were they by their friend's disappointment that they did not even pretend to be a tribe of cannibals or a herd of wolves. They ate the cookie boy as if he'd been merely an ordinary piece of gingerbread.

"I bet she'll get it all right next year," said Ginger as he carefully divided the handful of currants. "I bet you anythin' she'll get it next year."

"I bet she will, too," said William. "If I'd been judge I'd've give it her this. I say, I votes we keep a look out on Mrs. Bretherton's this year an' see how it goes on. If we know how big it's gettin' then we can tell Mrs. Roundway an' she can sort of fat hers up a bit so's to be jus' bigger. That's what I votes we do, anyway."

The others, swallowing their last mouthfuls of currants, agreed.

* * *

The Outlaws led a full and varied life, and the months slipped quickly by, but they did not forget their plan, and when the cucumber season approached they held a meeting in the old barn to discuss their programme. William took the chair, as usual, metaphorically speaking, for the barn contained no seating accommodation beyond a few precarious boxes.

"Well, I votes that we go round to ole Mrs.

Bretherton's every week an' measure her cucumber an' tell Mrs. Roundway about it so she can fat hers up to be bigger by the day." The proposal was carried by acclamation and the Outlaws, inspired by a pleasant sense of adventure, marched off to inspect Mrs. Bretherton's exhibit. This, however, proved more difficult than they had thought it would. Mrs. Bretherton was not another Mrs. Roundway. Mrs. Bretherton had an irascible temper and a hatred of boys that amounted almost to an obsession. And she was certainly terrifying enough even without her irascible temper, for she was in appearance exactly like the witch of the fairy tales—bent and wizened and malevolent-looking, with a jaw and chin that almost met.

The Outlaws clustered about her gate, uncertain how exactly to begin operations. Then her door opened suddenly, and she came hobbling down the path to them muttering angrily and making threatening gestures with her stick. The Outlaws fled precipitately.

"I thought it was best to run away an' let her think we were frightened," said William nonchalantly when they paused for breath at the end of the road.

Ginger and Henry and Douglas said that that was why they'd run away too.

"It sort of puts them off their guard an'—an' sort of lulls their suspicions," said William who read a good deal of lurid literature.

"Let's go back now," he went on when he had recovered his breath, "and see if she's about."

They crept down the lane. She was still there, glaring malevolently over her gate. As soon as she saw them she picked up a sod and threw it at them. It caught William neatly in the back just as he turned to flee.

They stopped to draw breath again when they'd turned the corner and were out of her sight.

"'We're bein' jolly cunnin',' said William, "we're puttin' her off her guard jolly well."

They agreed that they were but, having put her so successfully off her guard, as William said, wondered what to do next. Direct approach was proved impossible. It would merely necessitate a repetition of that act of deep strategic cunning that was always William's explanation of their flight.

"We'll jus' have to wait till she goes out an' then go round an' look at her frames," said Ginger.

So the next evening they waited concealed in the hedge till the old lady had set off down the road to the village to do her shopping.

They had set out upon the expedition as a desperate adventure. William had said:

"She looks the sort to me who's as like as not to kill you when she got hold of you. Well, that lump of soil she threw at me hurt me jolly hard. I bet if it'd hit my head I'd be dead by now. If I'd not been clever enough to get it in my back 'stead of my head where she meant it to go I'd be dead by now. It's a jolly dangerous sort of adventure an' I think we oughter go armed."

So Ginger had brought his air-gun, Henry his new penknife, Douglas his pistol (it only shot caps but, as Douglas said, it would startle her and then Ginger or Henry could get her with the air-gun and penknife) and William his bow and arrows. Moreover, they had left an envelope at home on William's dressing-table on which was written: "To be opened if we do not return." Inside was a slip bearing the simple legend: "Mises Bretherton has murdered us," and signed by all four Outlaws.

"That's jolly clever," said William complacently. "I read about a man doing that in a book. Then if she kills us they'll hang her an' it'll be jolly well sucks for her."

Not content with these preparations, William and

Ginger had each made a will and left it in their playbox. William's read: "If I di I leeve everythin' to Ginger. Pleese let him have the mouth orgun you tuke of me." And Ginger's read: "If I di I leeve everythin' to William. The ants egs for the golefish are in the toffy tinn."

Henry had not made a will but Douglas, hoping to cause among his relations the panic and chagrin that the will of a rich uncle lately deceased had caused, had made a will that read:

"I leeve everything to charryty."

When finally they set off, thus armed and prepared, creeping with elaborate and ostentatious secrecy along the ditch even in those roads where there was no chance of their meeting Mrs. Bretherton, their spirits were keyed up to a deed of desperate daring. They reached the cottage without meeting with any other adventure than the accidental discharge of Douglas's pistol upon his last cap ("You'll have to look after yourself now," said William grimly, "we can't promise to rescue you if you get in any deadly peril. You shouldn't've kept foolin' about with it.") and a *rencontre* with a frog which delayed them for about ten minutes.

They crouched in the ditch by the cottage and waited till Mrs. Bretherton came down the little path with her shopping basket on her arm. All went well. She passed them without seeing them and disappeared in the direction of the village. Then the Outlaws emerged very cautiously, carrying their weapons, and crept up the garden path headed by William. The elaborate and ostentatious secrecy of their mien would have attracted the attention of anyone upon the road had anyone been upon the road, but fortunately it was empty, so they reached the back of the cottage without question from anyone. And there were Mrs.

Bretherton's cucumbers in her frame. William surveyed them disapprovingly.

"Well, I don't think much of 'em," he said at last. "No, I can't say *I* think much of 'em."

Then he took a tape measure from his pocket (he'd "borrowed" it from his mother's work basket) and measured the dimensions of the biggest.

That done, the Outlaws turned and crept away in the same elaborately secret and sinister fashion in which they had come, pulling their caps over their faces to hide their eyes (Ginger had seen this done on the pictures) and returned home by way of the ditch again, partly because they couldn't bear to relinquish their melo-dramatic rôles and partly because they hoped to meet another frog.

The next day William took the dimensions to Mrs. Roundway and she compared it with hers. The result brought back her old all-embracing smile.

"Mine's bigger," she said. "A fair size bigger . . . though I can't think that it's quite right to——"

But the Outlaws, nibbling the cookie boy she had given them, reassured her.

"There's nothin' wrong with jus' findin' out how big it is. 'Isn't as if we *did* anythin' to make it smaller."

"No," agreed Mrs. Roundway slowly, "an' even if it was bigger I couldn't do nothin' to make mine bigger . . . it's just that one does sort of feel better knowin'."

After that the Outlaws paid a weekly visit to Mrs. Bretherton's back garden while she was doing her Saturday evening shopping and measured her cucumbers. They did not vary the proceedings in any particular from the first occasion. They went armed, they crept in single file through the ditch the whole way, they made wills and left notes informing the world that Mrs. Bretherton had murdered them. Without these preliminaries the expedition would have lacked zest in their eyes. But the great fact was that according to their calculations Mrs. Bretherton's cucumber remained much smaller than Mrs. Roundway's.

"You're *cert'n* to get the prize this year," they assured her earnestly.

The day of the show came and—Mrs. Bretherton won the first prize. Her giant cucumber lay side by side with Mrs. Roundway's making it look a veritable pigmy.

The Outlaws gaped at it helplessly, eyes and mouth wide open.

"B-but it wasn't as big as that last night," said William.

"You must have mis-measured it, love," said Mrs. Roundway trying to hide the bitterness of her disappointment. "It's all right. Don't you worry, love. I didn't ought to've let you go measuring it. It's a judgment on me same as David and the censor."

But the Outlaws were not interested in the moral side of the question. It was the practical side of it that appealed to them. They went off slowly to the old barn, too deep in thought even to eat the cookie boy that Mrs. Roundway had given them. There they sat on the floor and gazed gloomily in front of them.

"After all the trouble we took," said Ginger. "Riskin' our lives every week."

"An' her nearly killin' me with that piece of earth she'd put iron into," said William.

"An' all for nothin'," said Douglas.

"But—it *wasn't* as big as that last night," persisted William.

"You must've mis-measured it same as what she said," said Ginger gloomily.

"Well, I bet I didn't," retorted William with spirit. "I bet I've got enough sense for *that*, anyway. I bet I understand them little strings with numbers on as well as anyone. It *wasn't* as big as that last night."

"Well, what d'you think's happened, then?" said Ginger.

William was silent for some time. Then he said slowly and impressively:

"Tell you what I think's happened. I think she's a witch an' puts a spell on 'em. She goes out the night before the show an' puts a spell on 'em. Well, she *must've* done. It *wasn't* as big as that last night when we saw it. She must've come out afterwards an' put a spell on it. I *know*—'cause I c'n understand them little strings with numbers on as well as anyone. She's a witch. Well, you've only gotter *look* at her to see she's a witch, haven't you?"

The Outlaws, while considering it inconsistent with their dignity to believe in fairies, still believed in the more sinister elements of their fairy tales.

"There *are* witches an' spells an' those things still," went on William earnestly. "Well, how'd her cucumber suddenly get to that size in a night if there isn't? An' look at her face. *Course* she's a witch. It's bein' a witch makes her face like that. Just same as pictures of witches. Well, that's what *I* think anyway," he ended, with an unconvincing note of modesty in his voice. The Outlaws agreed with him and grew still more serious.

"Well, I don't see we c'n *do* much if she's a witch," said Ginger, "we've not got any magic or anythin' like that."

"'Sides," said Douglas, "it's a bit dangerous interferin' with witches. I shouldn't like to turned into a frog or anythin' like that."

"I don't know but that I'd as soon be a frog as a boy," said William thoughtfully. "They don't have to go to school or wear collars or keep brushin' their hair all the time. An' they can play about in puddles an' ponds an' things an' get wet all over without gettin' into rows."

"Yes, but she might change us into worse than frogs," said Douglas, "black beetles or moths or somethin' like that."

"Yes, I shouldn't like to be one of them," said William. "Moths always seem a bit potty to me. Messin' about windows an' flyin' into candles. They don't do int'restin' things like frogs. An' eatin' blankets. They don't seem to have any *sense*."

Seeing that William was about to enter into a lengthy comparison of the habits of the various creatures into which they might be turned by the witch, Ginger hastily drew him back to the point at issue.

"Well, now we know she's a witch," he said, "what're we goin' to *do*?"

"We'll tell the judge," said William firmly, "we'll wait till nearer the show an' see who's the judge an' we'll tell him that she's a witch an' puts a spell on 'em the night before to make 'em big. An' then they won't let it count. They'll give the prize to Mrs. Roundway."

"An' we won't go measurin' it any more?" said Douglas.

"N-no," said William rather regretfully.

William had enjoyed those expeditions in the ditch to Mrs. Bretherton's cottage.

"We'll jus' tell the judge nearer the time about her puttin' spells on 'em."

The affair seemed to have been quite satisfactorily settled and they transferred their attention to the cookie boy, assuming their characters of cannibal chiefs sitting in judgment on the rash white man who had ventured into their territory.

* * *

As the days went on their suspicions that Mrs. Bretherton was a witch grew yet stronger. It was after she met Ginger in the village and looked at him that he lost the new fountain pen that was the joy of his heart. And Douglas, who had secret doubts on the subject, was quite convinced when, on wakening suddenly in the night and feeling sick after partaking of trifle in unwise quantities for supper, he remembered that he had passed her cottage in the afternoon and that she had looked at him out of the window. In fact every misfortune that now visited the Outlaws was laid at Mrs. Bretherton's door. When William was kept in to learn his French verbs again, he felt indignant not against the French master but against Mrs. Bretherton.

"I *knew* somethin' like that'd happen," he said, "I had to pass her house 'stead of goin' the long way round, 'cause I was late an' I din' *see* her lookin' out at me but she *must*'ve, else I wouldn't't've been kept in."

Whenever the Outlaws had to pass Mrs. Bretherton's cottage they passed it with crossed fingers, but even that did not save them from calamity. They invariably lost things or were kept in after passing her cottage. The fact that they lost things, and were kept in just as much when they didn't pass her cottage, had in their eyes no bearing on the case at all.

When it was announced that the judges of the vegetables were to be General Moult and Mr. Buck, the Outlaws held another meeting in the old barn to discuss what steps they should now take.

"We'll all go," said William, "an' we'll *tell* them about her bein' a witch an' puttin' a spell on 'em, then they won't count it."

They approached General Moult first. He received them quite graciously, mistaking them for a deputation from the village boys' cricket club. He was expecting to be asked to be President of the village boys' cricket club. He loved all official positions, and the more things he was President of the better he was pleased. So he ushered them into his little study, smiling an expansive welcome.

"Well, my boys," he said genially. "Very nice to see you. Very nice indeed to see you. I always like a chat with you boys. Well, and how's the world treating you? How's the world treating you, eh?"

William cleared his throat. He'd decided to lead up to the subject gradually. He was aware that the grown-up world in general would receive his news at first with scepticism.

"We wanted to talk to you about somethin'," he said.

"Yes, my boy," smiled the General, "I think you will find me all attention."

"We wanted," said William slowly, "to ask you to do somethin' for us." The General smiled.

"I think I can guess what it is," he said, "and I think I can promise to do it."

The sombreness of William's expression lightened.

"I didn't know you knew about it," he said with interest.

"I think I can guess," said the General, smiling yet more genially. "Little birds carry these things about."

"*Birds!*" said William. "Been turnin' people into *birds*, has she? Crumbs! I din't know that. I thought it was only the cucumber. Not but what I'd sooner be turned into a bird than a moth any day if I couldn't be turned into a frog."

The geniality of General Moult's manner disappeared abruptly. This was evidently not a deputation from the village boys' cricket club asking him to be President.

"What on earth do you mean, my boy?" he said curtly.

William considered that he had led up to his subject sufficiently and might come to plain facts.

"Ole Mrs. Bretherton," he said simply. "She's a witch, an' she puts a spell on her cucumber the night before the show so's she'll get the prize an'——"

The General rose, his face purple.

"What do you mean by coming here with your impudence? What——" He looked closer. He recognised William. The purple of his ferocious countenance deepened. "*You're* the boy who was throwing stones at my walnut tree. You——"

But the Outlaws, feeling that the interview could not now be profitably prolonged, and judging from the General's gestures that he intended to exact summary punishment, had fled through the garden door and down the garden to the road where they met the deputation from the village boys' cricket club just coming in.

"S'no use now," said Ginger gloomily, when they had reached the end of the road and stopped to draw breath. "S'no use even goin' to the other one. He wouldn't b'lieve either, an' if he did ole General Moult wouldn't let him give Mrs. Roundway the prize. They're all mean and stupid like that, grown-ups are."

"What're we goin' to do then?" said Douglas.

They all looked at William. William's face was set in stern thought. In the silence that followed their depression left them. William would surely find a way. And suddenly as they watched, the light of inspiration broke through William's dejection.

"I know," he said. "We'll go'n' hide in her garden the night before when she says her spell over it. An' then after she's gone in we'll say it again backwards an' that'll take it off."

*   *   *

**"WHAT ON EARTH DO YOU MEAN, MY BOY?" SAID THE
GENERAL, CURTLY.**

It was the night before the show. The Outlaws were
inadequately concealed behind the rain tub and the holly
bush in Mrs. Bretherton's back garden. Near them was
the cucumber frame, where she must come to cast her

spell over to-morrow's exhibit. It reposed now in its frame, an insignificant thing, infinitely smaller than Mrs. Roundway's, but the Outlaws had no doubt at all that as soon as she had said the magic words over it it would

"SHE'S A WITCH," SAID WILLIAM, "AN' SHE PUTS A SPELL ON HER CUCUMBER SO'S SHE'LL GET THE PRIZE."

swell to the gigantic proportions of last year and the year before. That expedition had been a truly perilous one. They had not crept into Mrs. Bretherton's back garden while she was in the village as they had done before.

They had braved her, as it were, in her den. They had crept into her garden while she sat in full view of them in her little sitting-room reading the newspaper. William had left a trail of paper leading to the cottage for the benefit of any rescue party that might set out to search for them should they fail to return. Ginger carried a swastika ("borrowed" from his brother), and Henry had brought a police whistle ("borrowed" from his mother). As regards the last William had said scornfully:

"It won't be any good. She'll have turned us into something before they come even if they hear it."

They waited patiently till dusk fell, and still Mrs. Bretherton sat reading in her kitchen, unaware of the four boys watching her intently from the shelter of the rain tub and holly bush.

"P'raps she won't do it till midnight," whispered Ginger.

"We'll stop till she does, anyway," whispered William.

"I'm gettin' *awful* pins and needles," whispered Douglas, pathetically.

"Shut up," hissed William.

Mrs. Bretherton turned sharply as if she had caught the sound of their voices. But after a second or two she turned back to her paper. No sooner had she done so, however, than there came the sharp click of the latch of the gate and steps coming down the garden path. The Outlaws froze again into silent immobility. The steps passed them, and a young man tapped very quietly upon the cottage door. Mrs. Bretherton leapt to her feet, threw down her newspaper and went to the door to admit him. He held a paper parcel under his arm. As he entered the lighted kitchen the watching Outlaws recognised him as a nephew of Mrs. Bretherton's, who lived in a village five miles away, and worked in a large nursery garden there. He opened his paper parcel, revealing a giant cucumber. His words reached the Outlaws through the open window.

"It's the best we've got," he said. "I've raised it special. Will it do?"

Mrs. Bretherton feasted her eyes upon it gloatingly.

"It'll do lovely," she said, and added, "It looks finer even than last year's."

"I'll warrant it is," said the man. He spoke absently. The proceeding evidently weighed rather heavily upon his spirit.

"You're sure no one's got wind of it?" he said. "It's a risky game to play. They caught Ben Seales over at Middleham at it, you know."

Mrs. Bretherton cackled her witch's cackle.

"Yes, but the fool had no frame in his garden. I'm not as daft as that——"

She took out her purse, then looked up with a start.

"What was that?" she said. "I thought I heard somethin' movin' outside."

The nephew listened.

"Cats," he said.

But it wasn't cats. It was the Outlaws creeping out of their hiding places and making their way through her garden to the road.

Once on the road they danced their war dance, then set off marching jauntily to Mr. Buck's.

*   *   *

Mrs. Roundway won the first prize for her cucumber. Mrs. Bretherton and her nephew had been extremely abusive when faced with the accusation, but neither had made any serious attempt to deny it.

Mrs. Roundway was in the seventh heaven. She walked on air. She had to pinch herself to make sure that she was awake. She had fulfilled her life's ambition. She had won the first prize for cucumbers.

The next day when the Outlaws passed her cottage she came running down the walk to them with something in her apron.

"I hope you don't mind, dears," she said, "but I've not made cookie boys, to-day. Just to mark the day, as it were, I've made——"

And she drew from her apron four beautiful gingerbread cucumbers.

Chapter 9

A Little Interlude

So carefully had they kept the secret from him that the whole thing had been arranged and the list of guests drawn up before William discovered that Robert and Ethel were going to give a fancy dress dance. The idea had been originally Ethel's, but Robert received it with intense enthusiasm, and together they each drew up the list of guests. Their original intention was to keep William out of it altogether. Robert had wild hopes of getting William invited to some other party that night, and hiding all the preparations from him so that he might never know that the dance had been given at all.

It was Ethel who pointed out the impracticability of this, and it was Mrs. Brown who said:

"But, of course, William must be here for it, dear. I can't think why you don't want him. He looks quite nice when he's just been washed and his hair brushed. And he can wear his Red Indian suit."

Robert groaned.

"The whole thing's doomed, then," he said. "*Doomed.*"

"But why, dear?" said Mrs. Brown. "It's a nice suit. I've often thought of having his photograph taken in it."

"I mean his being there at all," said Robert.

"But I think he'll enjoy it," said Mrs. Brown.

"Oh, I've no doubt *he'll* enjoy it," said Robert,

bitterly. "Couldn't you send him to an Asylum or an Orphanage or something till it's over?"

"Of course not, dear," said Mrs. Brown. "They wouldn't take him."

"No," said Robert bitterly, "they've got more sense. Well, if he *must* come, don't tell him about it till everything's fixed up. Let's leave him as little time as possible to wreck the thing."

So William was not told till a week before the dance was to take place. He was amazed and hurt by their attitude.

"Well, why didn't you tell me before? *Me? Me* spoil things? Why, I'd've been *helpin'* you all this time if you'd've told me. I bet I c'n think of lots of ways of makin' it go off all right. I don't think we'd better have dancin' all the time. Dancin' always seems a bit dull to me. I vote we have games some of the time. I know a jolly fine game. Half of you go to hide and——"

But he was informed without undue ceremony that he could shut up and keep his ideas to himself, and that he was jolly lucky to be allowed to come at all, and that if he, Robert, had had his way, he wouldn't have been.

"All right," said William with dignity, "if you *want* to have a rotten show that everyone'll say how dull it was the next morning, have it. I know lots of jolly things to do to make a party exciting, but I jolly well shan't tell you any of them now. You'd wish you'd listened to me when everyone's saying how dull it was the next morning. I never see any fun at all in dancin'. I think it'd be more fun without any girls, too. They only spoil things. Oh, all right, if you *want* it to be dull. Have you arranged who you're going to ask?"

"Yes."

"Well, the only ones I want asked are Ginger an' Henry an' Douglas."

"Oh, you do, do you?" said Robert sarcastically. "Well it's not your dance let me tell you, it's *ours*, and if I had my way, you wouldn't be there at all."

"D'you mean to say," said William aghast, "that I can't ask anyone to it?"

Robert assured him that he did mean to say this. William, unable to believe his ears, appealed to his mother, but she too was quite firm.

"Yes, dear," she said. "It's Robert's and Ethel's party. You can come to it, of course, but you mustn't bring any of your friends. You can have a party later."

"But they'd *help*, my friends would," protested William. "They'd *come* to help. They'd help to make it jolly. They know ever so many games an' tricks an' things to make a thing jolly. Seems to me it's goin' to be a jolly dull party—all dancin' an' girls."

"But that's how Robert and Ethel want it, dear."

"Well, I hope they won't blame me afterwards when everyone's sayin' how dull it was the next morning."

"No, dear, I'm sure they won't."

"I once went to a party like that—all dancin' and girls—so I know how dull it is. That party I went to was so dull that if Ginger an' me hadn't started playin' 'Lions an' Tamers' no one would have had any fun at all."

"Well, remember you're not to ask any of your friends, William. It's not your party. You can come to it if you're very good and that's all."

"Can I have a fancy dress?"

"You can wear your Red Indian costume."

"I'd like something new. I'd like a pirate or smuggler or something."

"No, dear, your Red Indian costume will do quite nicely."

William's sense of grievance increased as he recounted the situation to his Outlaws.

"Jus' dancin' an' games an' no fun at all," he said, "an' *they're* choosin' all the people to invite an' they won't let me invite anyone. An' I've gotter wear the ole Red Indian suit, an' I bet *they're* having new things. Pirates and smugglers an' things like that. I asked if I could invite you so's to help make things jolly, an' they said no."

It was Ginger who answered.

"Well, why not us dress up an' come an' be in the summer house, an' you come to us there an' bring us a bit of the supper, an' I bet we'll have a jolly fine party—jollier than theirs."

The Outlaws received the suggestion with cheers, and departed hilariously to consider their costumes.

*   *   *

William had decided from the beginning to have a more exciting fancy dress than his Red Indian suit. He wore his Red Indian suit nearly every day. Everyone knew his Red Indian suit. He tried to evolve a pirate's costume out of an old table-cloth, but the result was so disappointing that even William had to own himself beaten. The day before the day of the dance arrived, and he still hadn't found his costume. But he was not disheartened. He had infinite trust in his star. In the afternoon his mother sent him to the village with a note, and he walked home slowly and thoughtfully, his mind wholly occupied with the problem of his costume. As he went he glanced absently in at the windows of the cottages he passed. Rose Cottage. Ivy Cottage. Honeysuckle Cottage . . . silly names. But he slackened his pace as he passed Honeysuckle Cottage. He took a special interest in Honeysuckle Cottage. It was a very picturesque cottage, but it was not its picturesqueness that appealed to William. It was the fact that it was always let by its owner, and that it had a sort of clientèle in the literary and artistic world, so that it was generally occupied by an author or an artist. William and the Outlaws took a mild interest in the particular "luny" who inhabited Honeysuckle Cottage. They considered most authors and artists "lunies." Its present tenant was a Mr. Sebastian Buttermere, who had not as yet made much of a name in literary circles, but who, like William, had great faith in his star. William had never met him personally, but he knew him by sight, and considered him a good specimen of the "luny" class in general. So the glance that William threw into the window of Honeysuckle Cottage was a longer and slower one than the glance he threw at Rose Cottage or Ivy Cottage. And it was rewarded. He stiffened and stood motionless. For there inside the room was Mr. Sebastian Buttermere pacing to and fro, his hands behind his back, his eyes fixed on the floor, dressed in the flowing costume of a medieval monk. The explanation of this was that Mr. Sebastian Buttermere had a touching faith in his literary predecessors as well as in his star. He had had a writing-desk copied from the one at which Charles Dickens used to write, and (with much perseverance and hair grease) always arranged his hair in the fashion of Thomas Carlyle. He believed that these things had a real effect upon his art. Lately he had read a life of Balzac, in which he had learnt, rather to his surprise, that it was Balzac's custom to wear a monk's habit when he wrote. Mr. Sebastian Buttermere admired the solid success of Balzac's art and immediately ordered a monk's habit. It had arrived the day before, and he was wearing it for the first time. He found it cumbersome and rather hot, and at present it seemed rather to stultify his art than to inspire it, but he had no doubt at all that, when he got used to it, it would be the greatest assistance to him. He had the same unquestioning faith in it that he had in Dickens' writing-table and Carlyle's *coiffeur*. He paced to and fro in the room in it, stumbling over it occasionally because his tailor, who wasn't used to making monk's habits, and had been very much disconcerted by the order, had made it a little too long.

William watched him through the window, openmouthed with amazement. He wasn't quite sure what it was, but he knew that it was a fancy dress of some sort. Then Mr. Sebastian Buttermere raised his eyes to the window, and William walked on thoughtfully, his whole mind bent upon the problem of how to obtain the costume for to-morrow night. The situation was complicated by the fact that William was not on good terms with Honeysuckle Cottage. Though William and Mr. Sebastian Buttermere had never met, Mrs. Tibblets (the housekeeper who "went" with the cottage) was an inveterate enemy of William's. Moreover, though Mr. Sebastian Buttermere had never met William, he had heard of him, and was prepared, when they did meet, to meet on terms of uncompromising hostility. For there were several undischarged accounts between them. At the bottom of Honeysuckle Cottage garden grew a row of hazelnut trees, and upon these Mr. Sebastian Buttermere had set all the hopes that did not centre upon rivalling Dickens and Carlyle and Balzac. He had bought a little book on the culture of the hazelnut tree, and had done all the things that the little book said he ought to do, and he had watched his nuts ripening almost with the pride of the creator. Then one evening William had stripped the trees bare. To do William justice, he did not realise that the nuts were the apples of Mr. Sebastian Buttermere's eye. He thought that they were just nuts. He looked upon them as wild fruits of the woodland that happened to be growing on a tree in a garden, but were still wild and therefore his lawful spoils. He took for granted that Mr. Sebastian Buttermere, with the usual grown-up distorted view of life, did not even know that there were nuts upon his tree, or if he knew that he took no interest in the fact. And on the evening of the very day on which Mr. Sebastian Buttermere, watching over them with tender eye, had decided that his treasures were ripe enough to be gathered to-morrow, William entered the garden by way of a hole in the hedge and stripped the trees. Stripped them bare. Mr. Sebastian Buttermere was so much upset that he made the hero and heroine of the story he was engaged upon commit suicide, though originally he had meant them to get married and live happy ever after. Mr. Sebastian Buttermere, of course, didn't know who had stripped his trees, but Mrs. Tibblets did. She'd seen William departing with his bulging pockets too late to do anything but throw a broom after him. She told Mr. Sebastian Buttermere, and together they sang a hymn of hate for William. Mrs. Tibblets had various small scores of her own against William.

Then there had been the affair of the tulip bed. Again, to do William justice, he did not know that Mr. Sebastian Buttermere was treasuring that tulip bed, that the tulips were special bulbs of a particularly magnificent kind sent to Mr. Sebastian Buttermere by a friend in Holland. William, who in the character of a smuggler was being hotly pursued by Ginger and Douglas in the characters of excise men, took a short cut through the garden of Honeysuckle Cottage (whose hedge had several convenient holes) and leapt across a circular tulip bed that stood in his way. William considered that he had cleared the thing rather neatly and left no footprints on the bed to annoy the owner. He had no idea that he had done any damage till he reached the further hedge and looked back to see the snapped-off blooms lying on the ground.

"Silly having flowers on stalks that high," he had commented sternly. "No one could jump over 'em."

But his meditations on the subject had been cut short by the appearance of Mrs. Tibblets, who had also seen the damage, and had emerged tempestuously from the cottage with a flat iron which she hurled after William's rapidly vanishing form.

And now, as William moved on thoughtfully from the cottage, his mind went back to these two incidents. He realised that they complicated the situation considerably. Useless to approach the cottage openly and request the loan of the costume for a fancy dress dance. Mrs. Tibblets would only throw something at him as soon as she saw him, and she'd got a fairly good aim for a woman. The flat iron had only just missed him. Still, it was a wonderful costume whatever it was meant to be, and William had set his heart upon it.

He hung about the cottage all next morning, dodging into the ditch when Mr. Sebastian Buttermere emerged from the cottage door in his hat and coat, carrying a suit-case, and then coming out to watch Mr. Sebastian Buttermere's retreating figure as it wended its way to the station. Going away for the night. That was all right. It only left Mrs. Tibblets. William glanced at the windows of the cottage and caught sight of Mrs. Tibblets through an upstairs window engaged apparently in dusting a bedroom.

Very cautiously he approached the window of the room where he had seen Mr. Sebastian Buttermere wearing the intriguing garment. There in front of the window was the writing-desk that was a replica of Charles Dickens'. There behind the door hung the monk's habit. William's mind worked quickly. He'd just borrow it for to-night. He'd put it back first thing to-morrow morning. Its owner had obviously gone up to town for the night. No one would know anything about it. The window was open at the bottom, and it seemed almost ungrateful to Fate to miss the chance. He vaulted lightly across the window-sill into the room, took the garment from its hook on the back of the door, bundled it up under his arm, leapt back over the window-sill and set off running down the road. Before he had gone a few yards an upstairs window was thrown up and a boot-tree whizzed past his ear. Mrs. Tibblets had seen him coming out of the garden but, William rightly judged, that was all. She didn't recognise the rolled-up bundle he held under his arm.

He took it home joyfully, and retired at once to the shed at the bottom of the garden to try it on. The result was disappointing. It was too big for him in every way. He couldn't walk in it. It tripped him up at every step. He couldn't get his hands out of the sleeve. The thing that came over his head completely extinguished him. And he didn't know what it was meant to be anyway. He couldn't get up any enthusiasm for it, in spite of the risks he had undergone to secure it. He left it in the shed and, deeply depressed, made his way to the house. As he was going upstairs he glanced into Robert's bedroom. Robert was not there, but upon the bed lay a large cardboard box. William slipped cautiously into the room and opened it. He caught his breath with delight. It contained a pirate's outfit, complete with multi-coloured handkerchief for the head, and an assortment of villainous-looking knives. It was the costume his soul had craved.

Thoughtfully he went downstairs to the kitchen, where his mother was making jellies and trifles.

"Keep out of here, dear," she said, as soon as she saw

him, "we're very busy and you mustn't eat any of it till to-night."

"I don't want to eat any of it," said William, untruthfully, "I came to see if I could help you."

Mrs. Brown was touched.

"No, dear," she said, "I don't think there's anything you can do, but it's very nice of you to offer."

"What's Robert going as?" said William suddenly.

"I've no idea," said Mrs. Brown. "Gordon Franklin is lending him a costume. He says that he has several."

"What's he lending him?" said William.

"I don't know, dear. He said he'd just look something out and send it along. It's just come, but I haven't opened it."

"Has Robert seen it?" said William.

"Not yet, dear. He's out getting some balloons and it's only just come."

William hastily departed, deaf to a sudden discovery of Mrs. Brown's, that he *could* help if he liked by taking a note Ethel wanted taking to Dolly Clavis.

It was the work of a few minutes to fold up the monk's habit, bring it into the house and put it into the cardboard box after abstracting the pirate's costume. Then William retired to the shed and tried on the pirate's costume. It was perfect. With breeches and cuffs rolled up, it fitted him perfectly. He tied the handkerchief tightly about his head and hung the knives around him. There were even golden earrings. It was the costume of his dreams. He could hardly bear to take it off when the lunch bell rang.

He felt slightly anxious at lunch, till his mother said:

"Did you find the costume on your bed, Robert?"

"Yes, thanks," said Robert.

"Have you tried it on?"

"Yes . . . it fits quite well. Going to be rather hot to dance in but quite decent."

William heaved a sigh of relief.

*   *   *

Mr. Sebastian Buttermere did not stay the night in town after all. He had a sudden inspiration for a short story just as he was finishing tea, and returned by the very next train. He'd never had quite such an unmistakable inspiration for a short story before, and he put it all down to the monk's habit. He had a pleasant vision of it hanging behind his study door waiting for him. He really was beginning to feel that he couldn't write a word without it. His heart swelled with pride. So Balzac must have felt. So Balzac must have hurried home to put on his monk's habit and write a story. . . .

He reached the cottage, explained shortly to Mrs. Tibblets that he had decided not to stay in town for the night after all, and went into his study. And there the first shock awaited him. His monk's habit was not hanging behind the door. And the minute he saw that his monk's habit was not hanging behind the door he knew beyond a shadow of doubt that he couldn't write a word without it. He rang the bell furiously for Mrs. Tibblets and pointed at the empty door, speechless with emotion.

"Where is it?" he demanded at last.

She gazed helplessly from him to the bare panels of the door.

"It was there this morning," she said at last.

"Someone's stolen it," he said, stamping up and down the room and running his fingers through his hair. "An enemy. Someone who knows how much I depend on it. Someone who's jealous of my reputation. Who's been here to-day?"

"No one," said Mrs. Tibblets, then her mouth drop-

ped open. "That boy . . . he had something rolled up
under his arm now I come to think, drat him!"

"What? Who?" shouted Mr. Sebastian Buttermere
furiously, feeling the inspiration for the short story
already ebbing from his brain.

"The boy," said Mrs. Tibblets, "the boy who took
the nuts and broke the tulips. He was in the garden, and
he went away with something rolled up under his arm. I
threw a boot-tree at him. I wish I'd wrung his neck."

"Where did he go?" shouted Mr. Sebastian But-
termere, roused as only a mild man can be roused.
"I'll—I'll—I'll teach him a lesson he won't forget.
I—I—I——"

"He went down there," said Mrs. Tibblets. "They're
having a fancy dress dance to-night. That'll be what he
took it for. Wait till the next time I lay my hands on him,
that's all."

But Mr. Sebastian Buttermere was already hastening
down the lane, the idyllic little love story that had
brought him back in such a hurry from London trans-
formed to one of lurid vengeance.

*   *   *

Robert, wearing the monk's habit, was sitting out in
the garden with a girl who had hazel eyes and dark hair,
and whom he had just discovered to be the most
beautiful girl in the world. He simply couldn't think how
he had ever considered anyone else the most beautiful
girl in the world. He now saw all the other girls whom he
had previously considered the most beautiful girls in the
world as creatures devoid of every possible grace and
charm. He felt that his whole life had been wasted till he
met her. He wished, however, that the costume Gordon
had lent him had been a little more romantic. She was
looking at it with dispassionate interest.

"What's it meant to be?" she said. "It looks more like a dressing-gown than anything, doesn't it?"

"It's a monk' thing," he said.

"What sights they must have looked," she said. "Where did you get it?"

Robert began to feel rather cold towards his costume.

"Gordon Franklin lent it to me," he said. "He's got several, you know. I'd hoped he'd send me the pirate's one, but I suppose he's lent that to someone else or is wearing it himself."

"Is he here?" said the girl.

"Not yet," said Robert. "He's coming on later. He ought to be here any time now," then, feeling that it was time the conversation were given a more personal turn, added: "It seems extraordinary to me to think that I've only known you for a few days. I feel as if I'd known you since the beginning of the world."

"Goodness," said the beloved, "I hope I don't look quite as old as that."

"No, I mean that's the sort of *feeling* you give me," said Robert earnestly. "I've felt since I met you as if I wanted to live quite a different sort of life, a higher sort of life. I——" It was at this point that Mr. Sebastian Buttermere appeared, thirsting for vengeance and his monk's costume. He had run the fancy dress dance to earth, and was making a preliminary search among the sitting-out couples in the garden before he entered the house and demanded the return of his property.

He stood before Robert, quivering with fury. This was his costume, and this must be the "boy" who had taken it, the boy who had moreover stolen his nuts and broken down his tulips. He'd somehow expected a younger boy than this, but this was certainly the costume, so this must be the boy. Mr. Sebastian Buttermere, however, had been carefully brought up. He had been taught never to

"I WANT A WORD WITH YOU IN PRIVATE, SIR," SAID MR.
SEBASTIAN BUTTERMERE IN A CHOKING TONE.

make a scene before a lady. He controlled himself
therefore sufficiently to say to Robert, in a choking tone:
    "I want a word with you in private, sir."
    Robert stared, open-mouthed with amazement, at

ROBERT STARED, OPEN-MOUTHED WITH AMAZEMENT. HIS FIRST
IMPULSE WAS TO REFUSE HAUGHTILY, BUT HE REALISED THAT A
SCENE MIGHT BE THE RESULT.

this disturber of his Eden. His first impulse was to refuse
haughtily, but he realised from the purple face and
furious expression of Mr. Sebastian Buttermere that a
scene might be the result, and, though in all imaginary

scenes Robert could conduct himself with haughty ease, he was less sure of himself in real life, and did not want to risk being humiliated by this angry little man before the beloved. He therefore rose with extreme hauteur and dignity, and with an "excuse me" to the beloved, disappeared with Mr. Sebastian Buttermere into the shadow of the trees at the end of the garden. There Mr. Sebastian Buttermere faced him and, quivering with anger, stuttered, "And now, sir, what have you to say for yourself?"

The note of righteous indignation in his voice was very convincing. Robert's conscience went uneasily over the events of the last two days. He'd been out on his motor cycle the day before.

"If it was your chicken," he said, with dignity, "it was right in the middle of the road, and I couldn't possibly have avoided it."

Mr. Sebastian Buttermere choked with rage.

"None of your impudence, sir!" he fumed. He looked at Robert, and the agonising thought of his beloved nuts came to him.

"And the nuts," he shouted, "what have you to say about those nuts?"

Robert's conscience was still centred upon his motor cycle.

"It's not a question of nuts," he said, "the nuts are all in perfect order. I know that the silencer's slightly defective, but——"

"And tulips," screamed the little man furiously, hardly listening to what Robert was saying. "What have you to say about tulips?"

"That," said Robert, still more loftily, "is entirely between the young lady and myself. If I did kiss her it was only with the utmost respect."

The purple on Mr. Sebastian Buttermere's countenance deepened almost to black. Expecting the thief to be a younger boy, he had meant to execute justice on the spot. He wasn't sure whether he'd get the better of this youth in a fight, and thought it perhaps advisable not to risk it. He looked about him. At the bottom of the garden where they stood was an old shed.

"Come into the shed," ordered Mr. Sebastian Buttermere.

His eyes were still gleaming with fury. At once the explanation of the whole incident occurred to Robert. The man who had accosted him so strangely, and who talked so wildly, was a madman. It was the only possible explanation of the incident. He looked about him. They were alone. No one was within call. He must go very carefully. You never argued with or defied a madman, you humoured him. You humoured him and used cunning.

"Er—yes, certainly," said Robert with a mirthless smile, stepping back into the shed. "Er—certainly, with pleasure."

"And now take off that costume," ordered the little man, still choking with rage.

Robert, still wearing the mirthless smile that was meant to humour the madman, slipped off the costume.

The little man snatched it from him, and his rage seemed suddenly to burst its bounds.

"And I'll teach you a lesson, young sir," he shouted. "I'll teach you a lesson you won't forget. You can stay here till someone lets you out, and I hope you stay all night."

Robert sprang forward, but too late. The little man had slammed the door of the shed and turned the key in the rusty lock.

"Let me out," shouted Robert.

There was no answer. The little man had evidently

departed with his costume. Listening, Robert heard his indignant mutterings die away in the distance. In fury Robert flung himself upon the door.

"Let me out!" he yelled. "Let me out."

Then he stopped for a minute and listened again. Footsteps were approaching the shed. He redoubled his efforts, hurling himself at the door and shouting, "Let me out."

A voice answered suddenly from outside.

"What on earth's the matter?"

It was the voice of the beloved.

Breathlessly Robert explained the situation.

"That madman's locked me in here and——"

"What madman?" she interrupted.

"That man who came to us."

"Well, he was quite small. You couldn't have put up much of a fight. I'd be ashamed to say that a little man like that had locked me in a shed if I was your size."

"I tell you he's a madman. They have the strength of ten men. I hadn't a chance. He overpowered me. The key's not in the lock, is it?"

"No."

"Well, how am I going to get out? I can't stay here all night."

"I must say it's all very odd," said the beloved coldly. "I'm not used to people I'm supposed to be dancing with suddenly going off and getting locked in sheds like this."

"I wish you'd do something," said the goaded Robert, "instead of standing there talking."

"What do you expect me to do?" said the beloved still more coldly. "I can't break the door down, can I?"

"No, but you can fetch someone."

"All right. I'll fetch Jameson Jameson. He's sitting out in the tool shed with Peggy Barlow. She's jolly lucky to have a partner who doesn't play the fool like this."

It was at this moment that a horrible truth struck Robert with the force, as novelists say, of a blow between the eyes. Though he was completely clothed from head to foot, it was not a costume in which a gentleman usually appears before his lady acquaintances. He was, in short, attired in his pants and vest, and though the suspenders that secured his evening socks were of chaste and elegant design, still they did not compensate for the general unconventionality of his appearance. He had horrible visions of the beloved returning with Jameson Jameson, of their breaking open the door, and exposing him to view. She'd never speak to him again. Never. No decent girl would.

"I *say*," he yelled wildly through the door.

The beloved had evidently just set out upon her quest for Jameson Jameson, but she returned and said impatiently:

"What is it?"

"Don't fetch Jameson Jameson," he panted through the closed door.

"Why ever not?"

"Well, I-I-I don't want him. I don't want to come out at all. I want to stay here."

"You—*what?*"

"I want to stay in here. I don't want to come out."

"You just asked me to fetch someone to get you out."

"I know. I—I've changed my mind. I don't want to come out."

"Why not?"

"I—I like being in here," said Robert desperately.

"Have you gone mad?"

Robert wondered whether to have gone mad, decided that it might complicate matters still further, and said:

"No. It's only that I—I want to stay here, that's all.

Surely," with a burst of inspiration, "you've heard of
people who like to be alone sometimes."

"If you're tired of me you might say so straight out
instead of going off and pretending to be locked in a shed
like this."

"I'm not tired of you. I think you're the most
beautiful girl I've ever met in all my life."

"Well, I think you've gone mad. First you pretend
that someone's locked you in and you want to get out,
and next you pretend that you've locked yourself in
because you want to be alone. I've read about people
that want to be alone in books, and they always seemed
mad to me. I've never met any in real life. Look here, if
he really did lock you in, I think I could get up to that
little window on the roof and——"

"*No!*" screamed Robert, cowering behind a sack of
artificial manure, which was the only barricade he could
see.

It was clear that the beloved was deeply offended.

"All right," she said icily, "and catch me ever
speaking to you again."

"You don't understand," said Robert from behind
his sack of artificial manure. "You don't understand.
There are circumstances you know nothing about.
I——" He had a wild idea of making her believe that he
was involved in some international plot. But before he
could think of any convincing details, she proceeded:

"Well, if this is the way you think a gentleman
behaves, I'm sorry for you."

It was evidently her Parthian shot. He could hear her
departing through the bushes. He came from behind the
sack of artificial manure, and looked about him. There
was nothing that he could have made a garment from
except the sack that contained the artificial manure, and
even that would have been pitifully inadequate. It was

horrible, horrible. Like the worst sort of nightmare. And the beloved would never speak to him again. The most beautiful girl he'd ever met in all his life. He went to the door and listened carefully. Footsteps were coming through the bushes—firmer footsteps than the beloved's.

"I say," hissed Robert cautiously through the door.

The footsteps stopped, and a surprised voice said, "Hello!" Robert recognised the voice. It was Gordon Franklin, who was coming on late to the dance and was taking the short cut from the side gate.

"It's me," said Robert, in a voice that quavered with relief. "I say, I'm in a most awful hole. You know that costume you sent me?"

"Yes," said the voice anxiously.

"Well, a madman with the strength of ten men came and attacked me, and went off with it and locked me in here. I can't get out and I'm naked. Practically naked that is. I've only got on my underclothes."

But it was evident that Gordon Franklin had little sympathy to spare for Robert.

"Who took it?" he said. "What beastly cheek!"

"I don't know. At least, all I know is that it was a madman with the strength of ten men. He attacked me and overpowered me, and left me in here and went off with the costume. It's lucky I'm not dead. I——"

"Which way did he go?"

"I don't know. I tell you, he overpowered me and locked me in here with only my pants and vest. It's lucky I'm not dead. If I hadn't made a fight for it, I probably should be. I——"

But Gordon still had thought for nothing but his costume.

"I'll go and find the blighter and push his face in for him. I never heard of such beastly cheek! It was almost new, too. I must say that, considering it was lent to you, you might have taken better care of it than that!"

He had turned on his heel and was walking off.

"But I *say!*" called Robert desperately, "you might go to my bedroom first and get me some clothes and let me out. You might———"

But a distant and indignant "almost new . . . beastly cheek" was the only answer, and it was plain that Gordon had departed into the night in search of his costume.

Again Robert looked about him helplessly. The situation was almost worse than before. It would be a long time, thought Robert bitterly, before he borrowed a costume from Gordon Franklin again. All that fuss for a thing that was little more than a dressing-gown—and a rotten dressing-gown at that. He glanced down at his legs, and a cold sweat of horror broke out all over him. He'd given a lot for those suspenders and been rather proud of them, but he'd never be able to take any pride in them again. They'd always be associated in his mind with his horrible night. He'd burn them if ever he got out of this. A sudden nightmare thought occurred to him. Suppose that the beloved relented and returned bringing help. It would be just like her. She was always going off in a huff about something and then relenting. And of course her curiosity would probably give her no peace till she'd solved the mystery of his sudden retirement from the world. She might come back any minute. She'd bring someone with her to break open the door. She might even bring that fop and idiot Jameson Jameson. Robert had a vision of the two of them standing there in the doorway staring at him. He looked about him again desperately. She'd said something about the little window in the roof. Yes, perhaps one might. He swung himself up with a superhuman effort and wrestled with it. It gave. It pushed open. He fell to the ground with the effort of pushing it open but swung himself up again. Freedom! He was out in the night sitting astride the shed. For a moment all his troubles seemed to be at an end. Then he realised that they weren't. He still had to get to the house and up to his bedroom. He slid down from the shed and cautiously approached the house. Both side door and front door were open, and couples were sitting in the porches of each in a blaze of light that came from the hall. He decided to hide among the bushes at a point where he could see the side door where Dolly Clavis sat with Ronald Bell and, the minute the coast was clear, dash into the hall where his mackintosh hung, and then dash up the stairs in it to his bedroom.

He crouched, concealed by a rhododendron bush, watching the door. The music began again. Dolly Clavis and Ronald Bell disappeared into the house. The coast was clear. He rose cautiously, and was just about to creep up to the side door, when he heard someone move in the bushes just near him. He crouched down again frozen to breathless immobility.

*   *   *

Gordon Franklin strode wrathfully away down the garden in search of his costume. The cheek of whoever had taken it! The cheek! The beastly cheek! The best costume he'd got! Well, he'd jolly well find it before the night was out or—— He stopped short. He could see a figure creeping through the bushes dressed—yes, dressed in his costume. It was, of course, William, whose unofficial party in the summer house was being a great success, and whose unofficial guests after an unofficial supper were now engaged in scouting each other in that part of the garden not occupied by the official guests. William was making his way through the bushes to his hiding place, while the others were counting a hundred before they followed to scout him. Engaged in this peaceful occupation, William was amazed and indignant to find himself brutally assaulted by a tall youth who uttered violent threats and imprecations, and then tore his treasured pirate's suit from his person. Having torn it from his person, his assailant strode off with it, still muttering bloodthirsty threats. William stood for a minute, spellbound with amazement. Then his faculties returned, and with them a realisation of the horrible fact that he wasn't wearing any costume at all—or at least any costume that would be recognised in public as such. He must go to his bedroom at once and put on his Red Indian suit. But he couldn't go like this. On the other hand he couldn't go to his friends for help. His proud spirit could not brook the thought of confessing himself the victim of an unrequited attack. No, he'd go round to the side door, wait till all was clear, then dash upstairs. Very cautiously he crept round to the side door. No, it was useless. Dolly Clavis and Ronald Bell sat there. Well, he'd wait till they'd gone. He crouched in the bushes waiting. It seemed to him that he waited for hours. At last the music arose for the next dance and the couple went in. William was just rising when—he heard a sound in the bushes near. He crouched down again and froze to breathless immobility.

*   *   *

Robert and William crouched there, not moving, hardly breathing, till to each it seemed that the coast must be clear, and then at the identical moment they arose and surveyed each other across a giant fern and two rhododendron bushes, both clad in the unconventional attire of vest and pants. They stared at each other in silence, paralysed with amazement, their mouths

ROBERT AND WILLIAM CROUCHED THERE, HARDLY DARING TO
BREATHE, TILL IT SEEMED THAT THE COAST MUST BE CLEAR.
THEN THEY ROSE AND SURVEYED EACH OTHER.

slowly opening wider and wider. The silence was broken
at last by Gordon Franklin, who had caught sight of
Robert and bore down upon him triumphantly. His
successful retrieval of his costume had killed all the
rancour he had felt against Robert for letting it go.

"I say, I've got it back," he said. "Come to the shed
and put it on again."

Robert turned his bewildered gaze from William to
the costume.

"That—that isn't the one," he said faintly.

"Of course it is," said Gordon Franklin impatiently.

"Come on and put it on. We don't want to miss all the dancing."

"B-but——" stuttered Robert weakly.

He looked round for that amazing apparition of William rising from the bushes in his underclothing like Venus from the sea. But it had gone. His brain, he thought, must have been so overwrought by the dreadful events of this night that he had imagined it. Or else it had been some peculiar atmospheric condition that had given the air the properties of a mirror and it had been his own reflection he had seen. A mirage or something like that.

"Do get a move on," said Gordon Franklin. "Or do you want to spend all night admiring that rhododendron in your pants?"

Robert didn't want to spend all night admiring that rhododendron in his pants.

He got a move on.

*　　*　　*

Robert, resplendent in the pirate's costume, was sitting again with the beloved in the garden.

She was gazing at him admiringly.

"I think it was a ripping idea, changing like that into another costume in the middle of the dance," she was saying. "I wish you'd let me into the secret, though. You absolutely had me on toast while you were in the shed changing. I honestly thought that someone had locked you in at first."

"That was only my joke," said Robert.

"I think you look ripping in that pirate's thing," she went on. "I wish I'd brought another costume to change into. It's a ripping idea. I say . . . when did you first begin to feel that we were *real* friends?"

*　　*　　*

Gordon Franklin sat with Peggy Barlow in the conservatory. They were getting on very well together.

"I've been looking out for you all evening," she said.

"I was a bit late," he said, "I couldn't get off before. And then I had to stop to give Robert a hand with his costume. There was a bit of confusion about it. You can bet that I came as quickly as I could. D'you know, I've never met anyone who *understands* as you do."

"That's just the way I feel about you. When did you first——"

* * *

William was in the summer-house with his unofficial guests.

"Well, we took a long time findin' you," said Ginger, "and why've you put your Red Indian suit on?"

"I—I jus' thought I'd change," said William airily, "I got a bit tired of the other. This is easier to muck about in. All right. It's Ginger's turn to hide. Go on, Ginger . . . one, two, three. . . ."

Mr. Sebastian Buttermere, dressed in his monk's habit, sat at the writing-desk, that was a replica of Charles Dickens' writing-desk. His face beamed rapturously. The story was going splendidly. His little adventure of the evening seemed to have stimulated his brain. Quite a Balzacian touch about his characters . . . quite a *soupçon* of Dickens humour. . . .

It was going very well indeed.

* * *

Everything was quite normal again. The little interlude was over.

Chapter 10

The Pennymans
Hand on the Torch

The Outlaws always kept a watchful eye upon the Hall and made the most of its frequent periods of emptiness. They had made an extensive study of the habits of caretakers, knew their (frequent) hours of repose and played undisturbed in the garden and sometimes even in the house itself. But the arrival of new tenants interested them, too, because new tenants, though of course they might prove uninteresting, might also give to life that added zest that the Outlaws always liked life to have. So when they heard that the Hall was let again, their disappointment at being deprived of their unofficial playground was tempered by excitement at the prospect of new neighbours.

They ascertained the time of their arrival in order to be the first to see the new-comers. The Outlaws generally did this when new people were coming to the village. One glance sufficed to tell the Outlaws whether the new-comer was capable of adding any sort of zest to life.

On this occasion the train was rather late and the Outlaws, clustered together on a stile on the road that led from the station to the Hall, grew restive. The Outlaws did not like wasting their time.

"I votes we go away," said Ginger, "we don't want to stay here *all* day, an' it's nearly ten minutes after the time now. We'll never get any decent game if we stay here *all* day."

"You can't call ten minutes all day," challenged William pugnaciously.

"Yes, you can," said Ginger, taking up the challenge with enthusiasm, for the ten minutes' inactivity was telling on his nerves. "*Course* you can. Ten minutes *an'* ten minutes *an'* ten minutes an' it's soon all day. We've had one ten minutes an' soon it'll be another, an' so on, an' that's all day if it goes on long enough, isn't it?"

"Well, you can't say it's all day after only *one* ten minutes," returned William, as pleased as Ginger at finding something to argue about. "It's a *lie* callin' *one* ten minutes a whole day. *Anyone*'d say it was a lie. I bet if you asked *anyone* they'd say it was a lie, callin' one ten minutes a whole day."

Ginger was just going to make a spirited reply when Douglas said, "Here they are," and the station cab trotted slowly into view.

They fell silent and craned forward to look. The cabman, who owed William several, managed to give him one neat flick as he flourished his whip carelessly in passing. William tried to catch hold of the end, failed, and overbalanced into the field behind. He resumed his seat, rubbing the side of his face where the whip had caught it. The incident had stimulated him and turned his mind to pleasant thoughts of vengeance. There were certain perpetual feuds without which William would have found life almost unsupportable, and one of them was the feud with the village cabman. It came next in excitement and general indispensability to the feud with Farmer Jenks.

But the horse was an ancient horse whom nothing

could ever induce to move at more than a walking pace, and so, even with this little interlude, William had plenty of time to inspect the occupants of the cab. There were two—a man and a woman, both very tall, very pale and very thin. Both wore pince-nez and hand-woven tweeds.

The Outlaws gazed at them in silence till they had disappeared from view. Then Ginger said in a resigned tone of voice:

"Well, *they* don't look very int'restin'."

William, however, was not so sure. "You never know," he said, with an air of deep wisdom, "they *might* be. Anyway, I bet it's worth goin' to see 'em to-night."

The Outlaws generally followed up an acquaintance-ship begun in this way by paying an unofficial visit to the new-comer's house after dusk in order to study the household at closer quarters. People seldom drew blinds or curtains, and even if they did there was generally an aperture through which they could be studied.

"Might as well go an' *see*, anyway," repeated William. "We needn't stay if they keep on bein' dull. But you never know. People that look dull often turn out to be excitin'. An' sometimes the other way round."

They waited concealed in the ditch, as was their custom, for the return of the now empty cab, and as soon as it had safely passed them emerged to hang on behind till the cabman saw them and zestfully removed them with his whip.

Then, stimulated by the little diversion, they returned to the game of Red Indians that they had abandoned in order to perform their unofficial welcome of the new-comers.

* * *

Dusk found them creeping in single file through the grounds of the Hall on their way to the house where the new-comers should be spending their first evening in their new home.

A bright light shone from the uncurtained drawing-room window, and this the Outlaws cautiously approached. There was a convenient bush by it that would have screened them from view had it been daylight. They crouched behind it and gazed into the room. And in the room was a marvellous sight. The tall thin lady and the tall thin gentleman had discarded their hand-woven tweeds and were dressed in flowing classical robes with fillets about their heads. The lady was working at a loom on one side of the fire and on the other the gentleman was playing unmelodiously but evidently to his own entire satisfaction upon a flute. The Outlaws stood and watched the scene spell-bound. Then the spell was broken by a housemaid who opened the door and spoke. The window was open and the Outlaws could hear the conversation.

"Please, 'm, the butcher's come to see if there are any orders."

The effect of this remark was instantaneous and terrifying. The woman went pale and the man dropped his flute and both assumed an expression of almost unendurable suffering. For a minute they were silent, and it was clear that they were silent because their mental anguish was too intense for speech. Finally the woman spoke in a faint voice.

"Send him away," she said. "Send him right away. Tell him never to come back again. And—and Mary——" The maid who was preparing to go, turned back. "Never . . . *never* mention the word to us again."

"What word, 'm?" asked Mary innocently.

"The word, the word you said," said the lady.

The housemaid bridled indignantly.

"No langwidge what nobody mightn't hear has never

passed my lips," she said pugnaciously, "not never in all me life."

"The word your mistress meant," said the man in a low pained voice, "was the—the name of the man who spills the blood of our little brothers and sisters."

"*Lor!*" said the maid, her eyes and mouth opening to their fullest extent, "*Lor!* spills the b——. You've bin 'avin' nightmares, 'm. The police 'd get 'im quick if anyone went about doin' anythin' like that."

"No, no," said the man impatiently, "by brothers and sisters your mistress means our little *four-footed* brothers and sisters."

"Oh, *them*," said the maid. "Pigs and such-like. The butcher you mean, 'm, then?"

Again the lady and her husband blanched and exhibited signs of acute suffering.

"Don't. Please, don't. Never mention the word again. Tell him never to come near us again."

"You don't want no meat then, 'm?" inquired the maid innocently.

The word meat seemed to have as devastating an effect as the word butcher.

"Never!" moaned the lady, averting her head, making a gesture with her hand as if waving something aside. "We shall live on vegetables and on vegetables only. And we grow them ourselves. I meant to tell you earlier, but have been too busy. We live the life that nature meant us to live. And macaroni. Macaroni that we make with our own hands and spread out to dry in the sun." The maid departed, and the lady and gentleman continued their weaving and flute playing. Suddenly the gentleman put down his flute and said:

"My dear, we must begin at once to educate these poor benighted souls."

"We must," said the lady, earnestly turning from her

loom, "we must, indeed. We must take them back to the simple life. It is our mission, our service to humanity—our handing on of the torch."

"Yes," said the gentleman, taking up his flute.

Then he began to play again—so untunefully that even the Outlaws couldn't stand it, and had to retreat to the road. There they discussed the results of their expeditions.

"Lunies," said Ginger, contemptuously, "I bet they've escaped from somewhere."

"They're fun to watch anyway," said William. "We can always come an' watch 'em when we've nothing else to do."

Heartened by the thought of this addition to their resources, they went home to bed.

*   *   *

The next morning they arrived early at the Hall, but there was very little to see. The new-comers were not wearing their flowing robes. They were dressed in their hand-woven tweeds, and they breakfasted (watched by their invisible audience) on barley water and macaroni. After the meal the man went out, and the Outlaws, after arranging to meet there again that evening, went to school. Somebody, however, gave Ginger a broken air-gun in the course of the morning, and the burning question of its mending occupied the thoughts of the Outlaws to the exclusion of everything else. They found the air-gun quite unmendable (as Ginger bitterly remarked, "He wouldn't've give it away if it hadn't of been"), but the excitement of taking it to pieces and finding out how it was made almost compensated for this. William, after examining it closely, said that it would be quite easy to make one, and that he meant to set about making one at once. The attempt absorbed all

his energies for the next few days. The result was not
successful as an air-gun, but with a little alteration and
the addition of a mast and William's handkerchief torn
into two pieces for sails, it made quite a good ship of the
easily sinkable sort.

The existence of the new tenants of the Hall was
brought back forcibly to his notice by finding the lady of
the weaving loom in the drawing-room engaged in
returning his mother's call when he returned from
experimenting with the new ship in the pond. The sight
rekindled his interest, and after performing a lengthy
and laborious toilet (in which he attended to his face, his
hands, his knees, his nails, but unfortunately forgot his
hair) he entered the drawing-room and greeted the guest
with the expression of intense ferocity that he always
assumed when he intended to be especially polite. Then
he took his seat in a corner of the room. His mother
glanced at him helplessly. He did not usually accord his
presence to her drawing-room, and when he did she
always suspected that it cloaked some sinister design.
Moreover, his hair looked terrible. It stood up wildly
around the margins of his face whither his washing
operations had driven it. The visitor, introduced as Mrs.
Pennyman, had given him a vague smile and turned at
once to his mother again. Evidently his entrance had
interrupted an impassioned speech.

"It is the ugliness of modern life," she said, "that
shocks Adolphus and me so terribly. The ugliness of the
clothes that we have to wear for one thing is repulsive in
the extreme. In the evenings, when Adolphus and I are
alone at home, we go back to the morning of the world,
and wear the clothes that nature intended us to wear,"
seeing a question in Mrs. Brown's eye, Mrs. Pennyman
explained hastily, "flowing robes completely covering
the human body and combining beauty with grace and

harmony. The world of course is not yet fully educated to them. We have found that we must go slowly and *educate* the world. We tried the experiment of going out in them, but the result was not encouraging. We met with what I can only describe as a hostile reception. We were driven to compromise. In the daytime we wear the ugly garments that convention insists upon, but in the evening, in the seclusion of our own home, we wear the garments that as I said suggest the morning of the world."

"Er—yes," murmured Mrs. Brown, obviously much perplexed by the conversation, "er—yes. Of course."

"And we *weave* everything that we wear," went on Mrs. Pennyman earnestly, "we weave *everything* that we wear with our own *hands*. You see we're going back to the simple life."

"But don't you think," suggested Mrs. Brown tentatively, "that the more modern life's the simpler one? When you don't have to make everything yourself?"

This point of view horrified Mrs. Pennyman.

"Oh *no*," she said. "Oh no. Certainly *not*. Simplicity *consists* in—in making things yourself. You see, Adolphus and I feel that we have a *mission*. We want to begin in this little country village, and once the fire is set alight here it will spread like a—like a *network* throughout England. And we want *your* support, dear Mrs. Brown, in setting it alight."

Mrs. Brown looked about her desperately, as if for escape, but all she could see was William gazing at the visitor, with fascinated eyes drinking in her every word. The circle of upstanding hair round his face gave him a startled and slightly sinister look. The sight did not reassure Mrs. Brown, and she wished that her son had given to this visitor as wide a berth as he usually gave to visitors. She tried to turn the conversation on to the weather, but Mrs. Pennyman repeated earnestly:

"May we *count* on your support, dear Mrs. Brown?"

Mrs. Brown gave a non-committal murmur that evidently satisfied her visitor.

"Thank you *so* much," she said. "Every disciple *helps.* . . ."

Then she discovered that it was time to go to change into her flowing robes to receive Adolphus.

"I always like him to *find* me dressed in them when he returns from his work. It's so much more pleasant for him. It takes him at *once* back into the morning of the world."

When she had gone, Mrs. Brown looked about for William, but William was not there.

The episode had revived all his interest in the newcomers, and he was behind his screen of laurel watching the returned Mrs. Pennyman, dressed in the classical robe again, struggling with strings of dough that ought to have gone into macaroni but hadn't.

* * *

The reformers launched their campaign the next week. They arranged classes in hand-weaving, and they got a lecturer down to speak on "The Reform of Dress," but both were sparsely attended. In fact, the only audience in the latter was a stone deaf old man of Scotch descent, who was only there because he attended on principle every village function to which no entrance fee was charged. Next, Mrs. Pennyman gave a lecture on making macaroni, but as drying in the sun was an essential part of the process, and as there wasn't any sun to dry it in, that, too, was a failure, and the mixture had to be made into a loaf which proved too hard for human consumption.

Nothing daunted, the Pennymans got a speaker to lecture upon vegetarianism. The local butcher was the only male member of the audience at this, and he attended in no hostile spirit, but simply because he was curious to see the Pennymans, of whom he had heard so much. He had never seen them before, because in their passage through the village they always made a quarter of a mile *détour* in order to avoid passing his shop.

William, though his life was too full to allow him to attend the lectures, kept an interested eye upon the proceedings, and still paid frequent unofficial visits to the Hall in order to watch Mr. and Mrs. Pennyman engaged in living the simple life. He did, as a matter of fact, attend one lecture. It was a lecture given by Mr. Pennyman on "The Evils of Modern Life." He discoursed among other things on the modern tendency of having one's entertainments provided for one, and the joy of entertaining oneself. As an example of this, Mr. Pennyman played to them on his flute, explaining quite unnecessarily that he had never had any lessons, but had picked it up entirely himself. All the audience, except William, crept out one by one during the recital.

*   *   *

William was present at his unofficial point of observation when the Pennymans sadly decided that they were not getting on with their self-imposed task of Handing on the Torch as fast as they'd hoped to get on, and that they must compromise again.

"Like all reformers we have tried to go too quickly," said Mrs. Pennyman, who was engaged in weaving on her loom a shade of purple that cried aloud to the heavens, "We must *compromise*. We must meet them half-way. We evidently can't take them *straight* back to the morning of the world. We must find some intermediate position and take them there first."

"I know," said Mr. Pennyman, laying aside his hammer (he was engaged this evening in hand beating hand-beaten copper. The sound was rather more tuneful than that of his flute playing). "Merrie England. Let's take them back first to Merrie England."

And so the Merrie England campaign was launched.

It was launched of course with reservations. There wasn't to be any ale (because the Pennymans had very decided views about the effect of strong drink upon the liver), and there wasn't to be any beef. But there was to be milk and nut cutlets. And, of course, there was to be country dancing, accompanied by Mr. Pennyman on his flute. Mrs. Pennyman made smocks and presented them to all the agricultural labourers in the district. Mr. Pennyman made a shepherd's crook of beaten copper, and presented it to the man who looked after the sheep at Jenks' farm. There was quite a large attendance at the first few country dancing classes, but after that a deputation waited upon Mr. and Mrs. Pennyman suggesting that for the remaining classes of the course they should hire a jazz band from the neighbouring country town, and take lessons in the Charleston and the Blues. Mrs. Pennyman fainted over her loom at the suggestion, and Mr. Pennyman nearly swallowed his flute.

"*Never!*" said Mr. Pennyman dramatically, and Mrs. Pennyman said, still more dramatically, "NEVER!"

So the deputation went away and made arrangements to go into the neighbouring country town once a week to take lessons in ball-room dancing. There were still a fair number left in the country dancing class, however, because there had been rumours of a supper to which all the members were to be invited at the end of the course. They were of that noble kind who had in their childhood doggedly endured the weekly Sunday School for the sake of the annual "treat." But even the Pennymans realised that their campaign lacked "go"; and William, who still could not resist the fascination of the Hall drawing-room, with Mrs. Pennyman weaving and Mr. Pennyman fluting, again formed the unofficial audience when they discussed the situation.

"Things," said Mr. Pennyman, taking the flute from his lips, "aren't progressing as quickly as I'd hoped they would, my dear."

Mrs. Pennyman stooped to disengage her sandal from a clinging mass of soon-to-be hand-woven material. Mrs. Pennyman occasionally got rather tied up in her weaving.

"You are right, Adolphus. We must give them a fillip."

"Have you seen any of the farm labourers wearing the smocks you sent them?"

"I have not, Adolphus. Nor has Jakes once taken out the crook with him as far as I can learn."

"And the country dancing class is smaller than it should be. Everyone in the village should belong to it."

"Have you *told* them so, Adolphus?"

"I have."

"Then tell them again."

"I have told them again."

"It all comes back to the same thing. We must give them a fillip."

"But how, Euphemia?"

For a moment Mrs. Pennyman paced the room in silent thought. In order to assist her meditations Mr. Pennyman raised his flute to his lips and drew from it an unmelodious strain. Mrs. Pennyman silenced him with a gesture.

"I think best in silence, Adolphus," she said. "Music distracts me."

She paced the room in silence several times, watched anxiously by Mr. Pennyman. Then suddenly she stopped and said:

"Of *course!* I *have* it! I *have* it. May Day."

"Yes, my dear," said Mr. Pennyman, looking at her still more anxiously.

"May Day. The first of May. Next month. We must celebrate it. Country dances. A maypole. Morris dancing. A masque. It will give the whole movement a fillip. It will spread from it throughout the whole of England. May Day! The heart and soul of Merrie England!"

Mr. Pennyman rose to his feet reverently and clasped her hand.

"My dear," he said, "you have a wonderful brain."

And so the May Day campaign was launched.

There was to be country dancing, morris dancing, a maypole and a masque. And there were to be free refreshments for the performers. Hearing of the latter the village offered its services in a body. New life and soul entered into the movement. The village green was mown and rolled in preparation for the great day.

William was only vaguely interested in all this. It was the idea of the masque that had gripped his fancy. On hearing it he had had pleasant mental pictures of a gathering of people all wearing comic masks. When he heard that the word meant in this case a play in dumb show his interest waned only to increase to fever point when he heard that it was to represent the fight between St. George and the dragon. He gathered that from a conversation that he overheard between Mr. Pennyman and the Vicar. Mr. Pennyman had caught the Vicar as he was slinking into the Vicarage gates with obvious intent of avoiding him. The Pennymans had been grieved to

find that the Vicar was not quite "sound" on the Merrie
England question. He had refused even to promise to be
present at the May Day celebrations. He always fled in
terror on sight of either of the Pennymans. But this time
Mr. Pennyman caught him very neatly just as he was
entering his gate and stood in his path, giving him no
chance of escape.

"We hope to see you at our May Day celebrations,
Vicar," began Mr. Pennyman very firmly,

The vicar looked about him in a hunted fashion, but,
finding that Mr. Pennyman barred the only possible way
of escape, said:

"Er!—thank you so much, Mr. Pennyman. Delightful, I'm sure. I'm sure it will be delightful. I'm afraid,
though, that I may be unable to attend as I may have to
go to town to—er—to see—to some urgent business that
day. Unfortunate. Most unfortunate. But time and tide,
you know. Well, well, I must be——"

"But we shall *expect* you there, Vicar," said Mr.
Pennyman firmly. "We shall be *most* disappointed if you
fail us. It is to be the beginning of *great* things for the
village."

"I'm sure it will. I'm sure it will," said the Vicar,
vainly trying to edge his way past him. "I'm er— *quite*
sure it will. Maypole dancing, is it not?"

"That's a part of it," said Mr. Pennyman.

"And a May Queen?"

"Yes," said Mr. Pennyman, "my wife will be the May
Queen, of course."

"Er-yes. Delightful," said the Vicar faintly, "simply
delightful. I'm so sorry that I shall unfortunately be
unable to attend."

"Oh, but you *must* be present, Vicar," said Mr.
Pennyman, moving slightly to the left because he saw
that the Vicar was trying to get past him on that side.

"There's going to be a masque as well as the dancing."

"A masque?" said the Vicar, interested despite himself, because he hadn't heard anything about the masque.

"Yes," said Mr. Pennyman, "a medieval masque. A representation of the fight between St. George and the dragon. I am to be St. George, of course. As a matter of fact I have a suit of armour in which I once went to a fancy dress dance in that very character. There will be a certain suitability too in my taking the part of St. George that I think most people will recognise, because I am giving my life to the struggle against the dark forces of modern life and to bringing back the morning to the world."

"Er-yes," murmured the Vicar. "Delightful," and he edged slightly to the right, but Mr. Pennyman edged also to the right, so the Vicar surrendered himself to fate once more, and said:

"And what about the dragon?"

"I can obtain," said Mr. Pennyman, "a very fine dragon. I refer, of course, to a dragon skin such as is used in pantomimes. Some friends of mine once had it for a child's performance of St. George and the dragon. It may be a little small of course, in comparison with my suit of armour, but I think that it will be quite effective."

"And who," said the Vicar, "will be the dragon?"

"There must be two of them, of course," said Mr. Pennyman. "Two boys, as the thing was made for boys. I haven't really thought about it yet. My nephew who is coming to stay with us for the celebration will be one, of course, and I suppose I must get some local boy to be the other."

At this point the Vicar suddenly noticed William, who, enthralled by the conversation, had drawn so near that he was practically standing between them.

"WHAT DO YOU WANT, BOY?" THE VICAR ASKED IRRITABLY.

"What do you want, boy?" he snapped irritably.

"Please can you tell me the time?" said William, with admirable presence of mind.

"No, I can't," snapped the Vicar. The incident had thrown Mr. Pennyman off his guard, and the Vicar slipped past him with a murmured farewell, and sped up the drive into the Vicarage with so patent an air of flight that one almost expected to hear him bolt and bar the Vicarage door as soon as he had closed it behind him.

Mr. Pennyman turned and walked up the road to the Hall in the gathering dusk followed by William. Mr. Pennyman was thinking that it didn't really matter if the Vicar didn't turn up for the May Day celebrations. There was nothing medieval or picturesque or romantic about him. You couldn't, for instance, dress him in a smock or give him a shepherd's crook. No, if the Vicar wanted to go up to town on May Day, he could. They could manage perfectly well without him. Better than with him probably. He walked up the drive of the Hall, unaware that William was still following closely on his heels, entered the front door and closed it behind him. He joined his wife in the drawing-room. She threw him a pained look.

"Adolphus," she said, "do go and change out of those horrible clothes. You don't look like *my* Adolphus in them. . . ."

"I will in a minute, dearest," he said apologetically. "I just wanted to tell you that I saw the Vicar——"

The housemaid entered and said:

"There's a boy wants to see you, sir."

"A boy?" said Mr. Pennyman. "What sort of a boy? What does he want?"

"He says he's come about the dragon, sir."

"The what?" said Mr. Pennyman.

"That's what he said, sir," said the maid dispassionately. "He said he'd come about the dragon."

"What dragon?"

"He didn't say, sir. He just said he'd come about the dragon."

"How mysterious!" said Mrs. Pennyman. "You'd better show him in."

Almost immediately William entered. He wore his most ferocious scowl.

"I've come about the dragon," he began unceremoniously.

"What dragon?" said Mr. Pennyman.

"The dragon you're going to have. I want to be its front legs."

"Oh-er, I see. But who told you about it?"

Mr. Pennyman who was short-sighted did not recognise William as the boy who had asked the Vicar the time.

"Oh, I—I jus' sort of heard," said William.

Mr. and Mrs. Pennyman had drawn nearer to William and were looking at him critically. Then, one on each side of him, they discussed him over his head, William staring in front of him with a completely expressionless face.

"He's—not *quite* the type we want, surely, dear," said Mr. Pennyman anxiously.

"His face won't show," said his wife.

"True," said Mr. Pennyman, "true. Of course his face won't show."

"And of course his motives are very important. If he does it in the right spirit, and—of course, his face won't show. Why do you want to take the part, boy? Is it because you want to help in the task of taking back this village to Merrie England, and thence to the morning of the world."

"Yes," said William.

"It's an excellent motive, of course," said Mr. Penny-man. "It seems a pity not to encourage it. My little nephew Pelleas has offered to take one of the parts of the animal. He may want the front legs. Perhaps you would take the back?"

"I'd rather take the front," said William very firmly, and still with a face expressionless to the verge of imbecility, added: "'Cause of what you said just now about the morning in the world and such-like."

Mrs. Pennyman was touched.

"Clouds of glory!" she said. "How wonderful! Probably in spite of his face he has a beautiful soul. But of course Pelleas too understands and appreciates our message. Pelleas will be with us to-morrow, dear boy. So will you come here then at four o'clock, and we will decide between you."

*   *   *

William arrived at the Hall promptly the next afternoon and was shown into the drawing-room. Pelleas was there with Mrs. Pennyman. Pelleas was about William's age and height, but he was dressed in a Kate Greenaway suit, and his hair was too long. Mrs. Pennyman waved her hand towards William, and said to Pelleas: "This is the boy who's going to be the other half of the dragon, Pelleas."

Pelleas subjected William to a lengthy scrutiny.

"I don't like him," he said at length. "He's ugly."

"But, darling," said Mrs. Pennyman, "his *face* won't show, you know."

"It will to me if we're both inside the dragon."

"It won't, darling, because it'll be dark."

"Well I don't like him, anyway," said Pelleas firmly, "and I don't want to be a dragon with him."

"We'll see what your uncle says," said Mrs. Pennyman vaguely.

Mr. Pennyman entered just then and said that he

PELLEAS SUBJECTED WILLIAM TO A LONG SCRUTINY. "I DON'T
LIKE HIM," HE SAID AT LENGTH. "HE'S UGLY."

would try them both in the skin to see which did the front
legs best.

"But I don't want to be a dragon with him at all,"
expostulated Pelleas. "I don't like him. He's a nasty,
ugly boy. I've been brought up to love beautiful things
about me."

"He can't help his appearance," said Mr. Pennyman,

"and he's a good earnest boy. He's eager to help to bring back the morning of the world."

"I don't care," said Pelleas.

William, anxious to be tried as the dragon's legs, maintained his expressionless expression though there was a gleam in his eye whenever it rested on Pelleas.

Mr. Pennyman took them both upstairs to the attic where the dragon's skin was kept. It was a wonderful dragon's skin, long and green and shiny with glaring eyes and a ferocious open mouth displaying a curving tongue and sharp white teeth. It made William gasp with delight. He knew that unless he were the front legs of this creature life would turn to dust and ashes in his mouth. Mr. Pennyman fetched his sword and they rehearsed the fight. At first they tried Pelleas as the front legs and William as the hind legs, but Pelleas screamed as soon as he caught sight of Mr. Pennyman's sword and said: "Go away. I'll tell my mother. Go away," whenever Mr. Pennyman advanced upon him flourishing it. The engagement between them was unworthy of the name of combat, and so William and Pelleas changed places. William took the front legs and Pelleas the back. And William was superb. Even Mr. Pennyman had to admit that he was superb. He roared and hissed and bellowed. He flung himself upon Mr. Pennyman most realistically, then retired as if beaten back by Mr. Pennyman's gleaming sword. He crouched and sprang and retreated again, and finally, on receiving the death blow, he writhed and struggled with such effect that Mr. Pennyman, who hadn't really wanted him to be the front legs, dropped his sword and cried "bravissimo."

So it was arranged that William was to be the front legs and Pelleas the back ones. Pelleas, on hearing the decision, said:

"I don't care. He'll prob'ly get excited an' stick his

sword right through you an' kill you an' I shan't care if
he does either.''

*   *   *

There was a right merry scene on May Day on the
village green. All the village was assembled, smocks
were much in evidence, and the postman had been
persuaded to carry the shepherd's crook. Great trestle
tables at one end of the green groaned beneath the
weight of flagons of milk and dishes piled high with nut
cutlets and proteid sandwiches. The Vicar had sent a
note regretting that he could not be present, and saying
that important business took him up to town. The
performance opened by the crowning of Mrs. Pennyman
as Queen of the May to the strains of Mr. Pennyman's
flute. Next followed a maypole dance, for which also Mr.
Pennyman played on his flute. This was not an unqualified success. Some ribbons got left out altogether; and
others got finished up before the thing was half-way
through. Moreover, Mrs. Pennyman, who was
enthroned within the circle close to the pole in her
character of Queen of the May, got entangled in the
ribbons and nearly throttled but they managed to get her
out alive, and being a true optimist she said with her first
returning breath that the dance had been a great success.

Then followed the interval during which a dejected-
looking group gathered round the refreshment table,
and tried the milk and nut cutlets, to disperse almost
immediately looking still more dejected.

Then came the masque of St. George and the dragon.
A small hut had been provided as a green room, and
from it now issued Mr. Pennyman clad in bright armour
and followed by his dragon. The spectators formed a
ring, and St. George and the dragon walked round it
twice, the dragon's front legs frisking and curveting in

such an undignified fashion that St. George more than
once had to rebuke it.

Then they faced each other in the ring for the fight.
William was just preparing his roar when Pelleas, in
whose heart the sense of inferiority that appertains to
the hind legs had been rankling ever since the part had
been assigned him, said:

"Best place for you, inside a dragon where people
can't see you."

"Think so?" said William, foolishly staying to bandy
abuse instead of charging his knight.

"Yes I do."

"Well, I'd rather look like what I do than what you
do."

"Oh you would, would you, Monkey Brand?"

"Yes I would, little Lord Fauntleroy."

Neither knew which began it, but suddenly to the
amazement of the onlookers the dragon seemed to be
taken by a sort of internal spasm. It appeared, in fact, to
be writhing in mortal agony. Its front legs and hind legs
were fighting. St. George, awaiting its arranged onset,
was for a moment nonplussed. Then, realising that as it
would not fight him he must fight it, he flung himself
upon it rather more heavily than he meant to because he
slipped and clutched at it to save himself from falling.
William, engaged in a desperate struggle with Pelleas
inside the skin, suddenly found himself attacked in the
rear. Forgetful of everything else he turned in a fury to
repel this fresh attack and the knight found himself
suddenly hurled on to the ground. His armour was so
arranged upon him that once on his knees he could not
rise from them. His enraged dragon, however, seemed
still to be advancing upon him with hostile intent, so he
began to crawl as best he could to a place of safety. The
spectators then beheld the glorious sight of St. George

pursued round the ring on all fours by a ferocious dragon, and finally taking refuge from it in the green room hut. Their depression vanished as if by magic.

A deafening cheer went up. Merrie England seemed at last to have arrived.

*   *   *

The Pennymans left the neighbourhood almost immediately afterwards. They said that it was not worthy of the torch.

Most of the villagers held for the rest of their lives a mistaken conception of the issue of the fight between St. George and the dragon, but they always looked back to the day of the masque with feelings of pleasure.

William's only feeling on the matter was one of regret that he never really finished the fight with Pelleas.